THE
ETCHING

Harold L. Schmidt

ISBN 978-1-63844-458-9 (paperback)
ISBN 978-1-63844-459-6 (digital)

Christian Faith Publishing, Inc.
832 Park Avenue
Meadville, PA 16335
www.christianfaithpublishing.com

Scripture quotations are from The Holy Bible, English Standard Version (ESV), copyright 2001 by Crossway, a publishing ministry of Good News Publishers. Used by permission. All rights reserved.

Printed in the United States of America

For Pastor Jeff Goodman
A true man of God

and

For Courtney Kraus
For leading so many to believe

ACKNOWLEDGMENTS

Thank you to my beta readers for taking the time to read the draft. To my writing partner, A. J. Cirone, your feedback was insightful as were the suggestions made by my friend, Mark Sorenson. Thank you, Julie Ann Kypreos, for permitting me to use jules k. in the book. And to John W. Thompson, "Sanctuary" is an awesome song.

Thank you also to the people at Christian Faith Publishing who helped make the publication of this book possible.

CHAPTER 1

January 11
Thirty-two days until the Olympic skate

Shay's blades flashed across the ice, pivoting and cutting with blinding speed as she executed her footwork sequence to perfection. She finished with a counter turn and then blended into a synchronized arabesque, arms spread like wings, right leg extended high above her head as she glided across the glassine surface. Her music transitioned from melodic violins to drums thundering to a crescendo as Shay performed her final move, the Biellman, spinning on one foot while holding the other over her head, forming a teardrop shape with her body. Twirling into a blur as the last resounding beat of the music reverberated in the arena, Shay swept out of the spin, jammed her pick into the ice, and snapped into her finishing pose.

Remy Madison, Shay's longtime coach, smiled as she stood off ice with her coffee cup in hand. Shay skated to the barrier, and Remy gave her star student a high-five.

"Beautiful," Remy said.

Shay looked to her mother and calibrated her expression. Bethany Dawsey stood in her usual spot on the opposite side of the rink. Her taut look belied her nature. Bethany found a flaw, an imperfection that required correction. Remy tracked Shay's eyes and whispered, "It was great, Shay—practically flawless."

Shay's eyes met Remy's. "Right." Shay looked back at Bethany. "Practically."

Shay skated to Bethany, who handed Shay her water bottle. Shay had just returned from nationals, where she placed first, not only winning the gold but securing a coveted spot on Team USA. To say it stunned the skating world was an understatement. Before this year, Shay had never placed higher than third in a major competition.

"Thanks," Shay said.

Shay had the frame of a dancer, delicate but strong, the nexus of iron and crystal. Her blond hair and liquid blue eyes were captivating. Just three months before her seventeenth birthday, Shay carried herself with the poise of someone much older. She got her looks from her mother, a refined woman, statuesque with her hair always cut in the latest chic style.

"It was fine, honey. I just wish we could get more speed entering the Lutz."

Shay hated the way her mother used the word *we* in all her commentary. It was "we" need to do this or "we" need to correct that, as if her mother was performing on the ice with her.

Remy walked over to Bethany and Shay. "Great extension on the Biellman," Remy said and kept her attention focused on Shay.

In her midthirties, Remy, a former US champion, held her coffee cup like a chalice. She was bundled in a blue ski jacket and matching ski cap. Like most former skaters, she still had the slim physique of a championship-caliber athlete.

"We need more speed going into the Lutz," Bethany said.

The chemistry between coach and student couldn't be better, but Bethany and Remy's interactions were as cold as the air in the rink and getting colder.

"Did you notice the speed going into the Lutz, or did you miss that?" Bethany asked, her eyes pinning Remy's with steely resolve.

"I thought it was fine." Remy posted a tight smile before turning her attention back to Shay. "How's the ankle?"

"Better," Shay replied.

"Fine?" Bethany said, refusing to let Remy's previous comment go unchallenged. "Am I mistaken, because I've never seen *fine* win gold at the Olympics."

Shay's stomach tightened. "Mom, please, just—"

"It's okay, Shay. She just wants the best for you. We all do. See you tomorrow." Remy looked to Bethany and smiled. "Have a nice evening." Remy walked to her office, leaving Shay alone with her mother.

Bethany glowered at Remy's back. "That woman is walking on very thin ice."

Shay wanted to tell her mother to back off, to stop interfering, but Bethany Dawsey was a force to be reckoned with; and the last thing Shay needed was another lecture on who paid for lesson fees, ice time, costumes, and travel expenses. She'd heard it all before. Figure skating was an expensive sport, and Shay knew her mother had worked hard to ensure that Shay had the best of everything.

Bethany glanced down at her watch, a classic Patek Philippe. "I have a client. Be careful on your way home. I didn't buy you a new car to see it wrecked before I make the first payment." Bethany smiled at Shay. "I know I'm hard on you, but look where we are, just four weeks from taking the ice at the Olympics!"

"I know, and I'll be careful with the car."

After a quick hug, Bethany turned and walked out of the arena.

Shay left the ice, covered her blades, and walked to a bench to remove her skates. The arena was empty. Bethany insisted Shay have private ice time for her lessons prior to the Olympics. Shay was an Olympian, one of the few to breathe the rarified air of the best athletes in the world. *I made it*, she thought. *It's real.*

As she removed her skates, she saw him again, the new guy. This was the third night she'd spotted him taking pictures of the ice after she practiced. A few minutes from now, he'd climb onto the Zamboni and resurface the ice for hockey, just as he had before her private ice time began. Why would anybody take pictures of the ice?

Remy walked out of her office and locked the door behind her. This was her fifth-year coaching in Detroit. Before that, she coached for seven years in California, where she trained several promising skaters, gaining a fourth and sixth place at nationals. Having an Olympic team member elevated her stature as a coach. Shay still had her eyes on the new guy when Remy walked up beside her.

"His name's Jack," Remy said. "A little odd."

"A little? He takes pictures of the ice after I practice. I think he's creepy. Always dressed in black. And the earring? Maybe he's one of those Goth people?"

Remy considered this a moment. "Well, he does have a sort of Johnny Depp, Jack Sparrow thing going on."

"*Very* sort of," Shay said, dismissing the resemblance.

"Make sure you ice that ankle tonight."

"I will."

"See you tomorrow."

"I'll be here. And of course, so will my mother."

Remy scoffed. "Skating mothers have been around since the advent of skating. Don't worry. We'll manage it. Promise. Waiting for Curt?"

"He plays at eight. I'll watch the first period and then head home."

Remy turned and made her way toward the arena exit.

The steady hum of the Zamboni's motor echoed in the arena. Jack was about to resurface the ice. Standing atop the machine, Jack gazed out over the steering wheel like a ship's captain navigating uncharted waters. Shay smirked. *Jack Sparrow it is*, she thought and watched as Jack made his first circle of the ice, his head bobbing to the music being pumped through his earbuds.

"Shay!"

Shay turned to see Curt walking toward her, hockey equipment in hand.

"Hey, you!" Shay said.

Curt set his equipment down on a bench. "How's my Olympian?" Curt asked.

"Just waiting to watch the next NHL goalie defend the net."

Curt had a killer smile, and at first look, his blond hair and baby blues would have you guess "surfer dude," but Shay and Curt liked their water frozen and preferred blades over boards. A year older than Shay, Curt was an outstanding hockey player.

As the Zamboni passed the rail in front of them, Jack nodded at Curt and Shay, then turned his attention back to the task at hand.

"Dude's a freak," Curt said.

"You met him?"

"Yeah. The other night. He told the team to have a blessed evening. He drives a crapped-up VW Bug with enough Jesus Fish stuck to it to stock a pond. Keep your distance."

"Thanks. I will." Shay considered telling Curt about Jack taking pictures of the ice after she practiced but decided against it. Curt was protective, and she didn't want a confrontation at the rink.

"Practice go okay?" Curt asked.

"Fine, at least in Remy's estimation. But if you ever lose a needle in a haystack…" Shay let her voice trail off.

"Hire mom?"

"Exactly. If she sees Ray Crock in heaven, she'll tell him he puts way too much ketchup on his burgers."

Curt laughed.

"That smile's beautiful, Golden Boy. Try to keep those teeth."

"Not to worry."

"Really? Because if I were your team's owner, I'd fire the coach and hire someone skilled in cosmetic dentistry."

"It goes with the territory, but my mask protects the pearlies." Curt's eyes were awash in childlike curiosity, a quality Shay adored.

"How's the ankle?" Curt asked.

"Sore but better."

"I need to suit up. You staying?"

"For the first period. Then I need to get home."

"Text me so I know you got home okay."

"Will do."

Shay watched the first period of Curt's hockey game and then headed out to her car. Like a frozen hand, the arctic wind slapped at Shay's face. Bundled in her down jacket, wool cap, and lined leather gloves, she walked to her car at a casual pace.

Shay passed Jack's beat-up VW Bug in the parking lot. You couldn't miss the Jesus Fish planted all over the trunk. She saw a decal of God's hand reaching to Adam's. Shay, having an interest in art, knew it was a part of Michelangelo's iconic painting in the Sistine Chapel. Shay's eyes were drawn to two bumper stickers pasted on the car: *Real Men Love Jesus* and *Jesus Is Coming Back, Look Busy!* She smiled at the second one. At least Goth Guy had a sense of humor, she thought, just as the driver's side door of the Beetle swung open and a dark figure sprang out.

CHAPTER 2

Shay's heart throttled against her rib cage. It was Jack. Their eyes locked. He wore a black ankle-length duster jacket that flapped open in the wind. A silver cross hung around his neck and stood out against his black shirt.

"Can I help you?" he asked.

"No," she stammered, "I was just—"

"Fishing?"

"Reading...actually, your...the stickers, bumper stickers, on your trunk."

"That's the hood. The trunk's in the front."

"Right. Trunk, then. I really have to go," Shay said; and in a hurry to get to her car, she turned too quickly, rolling her bad ankle. The pain was excruciating. Blood rushed from her head, and feeling dizzy, she sat on the pavement and clutched her ankle.

Jack rushed to her. "You all right?"

Shay rocked and waited for the worst of the pain to subside.

"I didn't mean to scare you," he said.

"Well, you did!"

"Should I call someone?"

"No, just leave, okay. Just go!"

"I can't just leave you here."

"I have Mace!" Shay scrambled to unzip the pocket of her ski jacket.

"You're kidding, right?" Jack asked as Shay pulled the palm-sized can of Mace from her jacket pocket and pointed it at Jack's face.

"Whoa, whoa, whoa!" Jack said, raising his hands to signal surrender.

"Back...off...now!"

Jack backed away. "Okay. But I'm going inside to let that guy you were talking to know you're hurt." Jack turned and hurried back toward the arena.

"Wait!" Shay yelled.

Jack stopped and turned back to her.

"You'd be better off letting me Mace you in the face."

"What?"

"Unless you'd prefer a hockey stick across the bridge of your nose, because that's what Curt will hit you with if he finds out you did this to me."

"I didn't do anything to you," Jack said defensively.

"Are you kidding? You scared the crap out of me!"

"I got out of my car."

"In a parking lot with no one else around. Dressed in black."

"I like black. I'm color blind, and it goes with everything."

Shay struggled to her feet. "Stay right there. I'm going to my car."

Jack took a step toward her. Shay raised the Mace. "Don't." Jack froze. Shay fumbled in her jacket pocket and found her keys. She hit the remote, and the door locks opened. "You want me to follow you from a distance, just to be sure you can drive okay?"

Shay's brows shot up. "Follow me? No. Between you and Jack the Ripper, I'd vote for the Ripper. I'm fine. Keep your distance… forever." Shay climbed into her car, closed the door, and engaged the door locks. The pain in her ankle began to subside. She started the engine, flipped the switch to heat the driver's side seat, and waited for the windows to defrost. As the ice melted from the windows, she saw Jack still standing by his car, oblivious to the cold. Shay engaged the driver's side window and opened it halfway. "You're creeping me out."

"Just standing here?"

"You have a gift."

"So I guess you'd have a stroke if your boyfriend stood out here in his hockey mask?"

"Not if I knew it was him, because he's not you. Do you have any idea how strange you are?"

"NOTW," Jack said. "Not of this world."

"No surprise there." Shay closed her window, pulled out of the lot, and drove home.

Shay navigated the circular drive of her home in Forrest Glenn. The gated community prized itself on its beautiful homes. Shay's was a Tudor style with pitched gables, rich decorative timbering, and a stone facade. It was even more spectacular on the inside where a dramatic stone fireplace greeted you as you walked through the door. Shay's parents bought the house fifteen years ago, and after their divorce, Shay's father relinquished the house to Bethany. The moment the divorce was final, Bethany immersed herself in her realty business. She quickly became one of the top-selling brokers in the country. She had always been successful, but after Luke lost his job in pharmaceutical sales and could no longer keep up with his support payments, it forced Bethany to pick up the slack. Within a year, Bethany was making enough money to maintain their standard of living without Luke's help.

Shay keyed in the alarm system code and went inside. Soft hues and dark beams gave the home a cottage in the country feel. It was just after nine, and Shay didn't expect her mother home until after ten. She went to the kitchen to retrieve ice packs from the freezer and then went upstairs to her bedroom to ice her ankle. The room was Shay's sanctuary, the place where she could listen to music and decompress. It was a second master with enough space for her king-sized bed, a walk-in closet, her dresser, nightstands, and a nook with windows overlooking the back garden. The alcove was her special place. It was where her drawing table was set up, a place where she left the competitive world of figure skating and immersed herself in the calming Zen of her art.

Since childhood, her ability to make things come to life in her artwork had already attracted attention. She won several art contests and would apply to the University of Michigan, Ann Arbor, when she finished high school. Currently, Shay was enrolled in an online program that gave her the flexibility she needed to manage both school and her busy skating schedule. She wanted to study Art History, but her mother was pushing her to major in something more practical.

"You can't depend on anyone in this world, Shay. If your loser father taught you anything, it should be that. Major in Sports Psychology, and apply it to a coaching career. Build on what we've created. Art is a hobby, not a job."

Shay grabbed a towel to put under the ice packs. She sat on her bed and looked at her current drawing, a sketch of the famed Russian pairs team, the Protopopovs, performing the move they invented, the forward-outside death spiral, a movement they called the Love Spiral. It reminded Shay that she had promised to send Curt a text when she got home. She grabbed her phone and sent, "Got home. Swak."

Like most guys, Curt wasn't up on the full code of SMS.

"What's Swak?" he asked the first time she sent it.

"Sealed with a kiss," she replied.

After icing her ankle, Shay went to her drawing table and put the finishing touches on the Love Spiral drawing. She set it aside, grabbed her charcoals, and began to sketch Jack's face. Shay could replicate facial images with incredible accuracy. Her best friend, Adley, told Shay she should be a sketch artist for the FBI.

"How rad would that be, Shay? You could help catch killers, kidnappers, terrorists!"

Shay and Adley had been friends since childhood and couldn't be more different. Adley was a drummer in an all-girl rock band and had zero interest in sports. Shay was reserved. Adley was…well, out there. Far. She believed in conspiracy theories and extraterrestrials. She had her own weekly podcast where she discussed finding Bigfoot, encounters with Mothman, and other strange happenings in the universe. Where Shay's fashion sense landed on the latest designer clothes, Adley dressed in what she proudly proclaimed to be "hobo chic." Shay had two American-born parents, and Adley had mixed-race parents. Her mother was Nigerian, her father was American, and Adley ended up with the best of both worlds—her mother's bronze skin and her father's easy smile.

As Shay replicated Jack's face, it occurred to her that Adley might find Jack attractive. Odd was her type, and Jack fit that bill perfectly. Adley was also a true believer. Big Foot and Mothman weren't

Jesus, but both required a willingness to engage in the supernatural. Shay had just finished the drawing when she heard her mother come through the front door.

"Shay?"

"In my bedroom!"

"Come down, please!"

"Can you come up here? I need to stay off my ankle."

"Yes, stay there. I'll be right up."

Shay hid her drawing of Jack. If she didn't, she knew she would have to endure what Adley referred to as "parental waterboarding." Adley's parents were both psychologists, whom Adley lovingly referred to as Frick and Freud. "Instead of water, they drown you with questions," Adley said.

Bethany entered Shay's room, slightly out of breath. "I love this house, but those stairs will be the death of me. How's the ankle?"

"Sore. I iced it, but I'll need to wrap it tomorrow."

"Maybe we should focus on spins tomorrow, give it a little rest?"

"We'll see. How'd it go with your client?"

"Contract's signed. I'm glad I got it out of the way. Ms. Bagley is as high maintenance as they come. If it weren't such a large commission, I would have walked away from it."

"That bad?"

"Not as bad as the work she had done on her face. It's tucked tighter than a trampoline. Now she has a look of perpetual surprise." Bethany mimicked the look.

Shay laughed.

Bethany added, "I asked her who her surgeon was so I could be sure to avoid that catastrophe."

"You don't need that. You look amazing. People should save their money and age gracefully."

"Sure. We'll see what you say in twenty years. Anyway, look at what I got for us." Bethany walked into the hall and reappeared with a custom-made walnut case. She held it up. "For an Olympic medal, we need a world-class showcase."

Shay did her best to react with enthusiasm, but her tentative response confessed her true feelings. "It's…nice, really nice."

"I know what you're thinking, counting our chickens and all that. But I believe in presenting the crown so one can grow into it."

"I guess I'm superstitious," Shay said.

Bethany offered a solution. "How about this? I won't have the case mounted on the wall until we have the medal safe in hand. Deal?"

"Okay."

Bethany took Shay in her arms. "It was a long journey, but we're almost there! And Beijing!"

"I know. It really is exciting. Almost too good to be true."

"You earned it. I know you shocked Kimberly and Gemma. They expected to finish one, two. I've never seen two skaters more put out, especially Kimberly."

Kimberly Jensen and Gemma Leigh were the reigning gold and silver medalists. Expectations were high that they would repeat those placements. Gemma had always been nice to Shay, but Kimberly Jensen had never been a fan and was visibly upset when Shay won the gold. It stunned everyone when Shay finished first.

"Time to get some rest. Every day counts now, every minute. And don't stay up for hours texting Adley."

"I won't. Good night."

Bethany took the walnut case and left the room, closing Shay's door behind her.

Shay went back to her drawing with little fear that her mother would return. The great thing about living in such a spacious house was it afforded privacy.

As Shay put the finishing touches on Jack's face, she thought about seeing him take pictures of the ice after three of her practice sessions. *What was that about?* She realized there was one person who could help her think it through. Shay finished the sketch, took a picture of it with her phone, and promptly sent it to her best friend. True to form, Adley got back to her in less than two minutes.

CHAPTER 3

"You know I love Jack Sparrow," Adley said. "Is it for me?"

Shay lay back on her bed and spoke to Adley through her Bluetooth. "He's the new rink attendant."

"Well, shiver me timbers and put out the plank because I'd walk it for him in a heartbeat."

"Adley—"

"I've always had a thing for pirates. Blackbeard was the bomb."

"I need you to focus."

"Did you know Blackbeard had candle-smoke billowing up from his beard during a particularly fierce battle? Talk about machismo."

"Adley!"

"Okay, okay. Chill."

"I admit he's not bad looking, but believe me, he's like…from another planet."

"Perfect."

"He's a Bible-thumper."

"Not ideal, but we all need something to believe in."

"And he's doing this bizarre thing that's freaking me out."

"What?"

"My lessons are on private time, so the ice is clean before I get on it. After my practice sessions, he takes pictures of the ice. Then he jumps on the Zamboni and resurfaces the ice. Why would he do that?"

"Are you sure that's what he's doing?"

"Positive."

"Two immediate things come to mind. A, he's psychotic and sees something in the ice no one else sees, or B, he's obsessed with you like one of those serial killers, and he's collecting your ice etchings as trophies."

"You're not serious?"

"Look at the bright side. At least he's not sneaking into your house to steal your personals."

"You can't think of a less sick and appalling reason for it?"

"Okay. Try this on. Maybe he thinks you're about to become an Olympic champion and thinks having your etchings would be a cool thing to have? Some people get starstruck."

Shay thought a moment. "I like that one better."

"I could ask Frick and Freud."

"No! Don't say a word, Adley, promise me."

"Fine. Scout's honor."

"You're not a scout."

"I sold Girl Scout cookies once."

"Your sister's, and you took a fifteen percent commission."

"Paid for by the buyers. It was all legit."

"Promise me."

"Fine. Bigfoot Handshake. You can't get a better deal than that."

"I know. I can't wait until I'm the maid of honor at your wedding, and you insist the Bigfoot Handshake be part of the ceremony."

"Duh. Absolutely!"

"I have to get some sleep. Call you tomorrow?"

"You better. And I want frequent updates on Captain Jack. Maybe I'll come to the rink and watch one of your practices."

"Sure. But stay in the background. My mother insists I have zero distractions."

"I can do that."

"Disconnect?"

In unison, Shay and Adley counted down, "Three, two, one," and disconnected. Sure, the Bigfoot Handshake and their disconnect countdown were things they started in their early teens, but it felt good to hold on to their traditions. Shay hoped they'd still be doing both, even after they were old, wrinkled, and craggy.

Shay took a selfie and posted it on Instagram with the caption: "Olympics, here I come!" It amazed her to discover that after her win at nationals, she had gained over forty thousand followers. That meant over fifty thousand people now followed her, and they would expect Shay to keep them updated on her journey to the Olympic Games.

Thirty-one days to the Olympic skate

The next morning, Shay's ankle was throbbing. She had first twisted it at the end of her free skate at nationals when walking toward the bench in the "kiss and cry" area. Talk about klutzy. It didn't seem like anything to worry about; in fact, she almost didn't feel it. She had skated the routine of her life, a flawless performance that caused a cascade of roses to rain down onto the ice. It was a surreal moment; one she had dreamed about since her very first competition. But the ankle continued to bother her that night, and by morning, it had swollen considerably. The team doctor examined her ankle. Conclusion: tendinitis. Skaters refer to it as "lace bite," because it's often caused by the tightness of the laces around the ankle. She would have to wrap and ice it after each practice, take anti-inflammatories, and avoid twisting it again. Unfortunately, stalker Jack—or possibly serial-killer, psychotic Jack—put a fly in that ointment.

Shay headed downstairs to get breakfast, walking gingerly, taking each step as if testing the ankle's stability. The pain wasn't too bad, but she needed to take precautions at practice to avoid irritating it any further. Shay drank her protein drink and started her car from inside the house. It was, aside from the incredible sound system, the feature she loved most about her new BMW. When you live in Michigan and spend half of your life on the ice, you develop a profound appreciation for warmth.

Shay had to get to the rink and spend time moving through her routine off ice. It was part of the discipline she had not mastered before this year, the ability to visualize herself performing her routine perfectly.

"I'm surprised it's so hard for you, considering your ability to visualize art the way you do," Remy had told her.

It was a mystery to Shay as well. She could look at a face and instantly imagine the pencil strokes required to draw a stunningly accurate reproduction. Still, seeing herself perform her jumps had always been a challenge. Footwork and spins were another matter. To Shay, that was like drawing with your feet, and she had no trouble visualizing that. It was as if her mind's eye had the ability to see everything except triple toe loops, flips, and Salchows. Jumps were a blind spot, and it was always a bad takeoff or landing that caused low scores in many previous performances. Working with the psychologist helped her immensely, and it showed in her performance at nationals. Still, the jumps never played in her mind with the clarity of her spins and footwork.

As Shay drove to the arena, she had to pass through one of the blighted areas of Detroit, a reminder that the divide between rich and poor in the city was wide. Shay loved Detroit and hoped the push toward revitalization would help all the once proud and vibrant city's inhabitants have a better life. This was Motor City, the D, the city of Motown—often referred to as Hockeytown and the City of Champions. Shay was proud to be a part of Detroit's winning spirit and hoped her participation in the Olympics would be one more feather in Detroit's cap.

When she pulled into the parking lot, she spotted Jack's VW in the exact spot it had been parked in the night before. Shay parked on the other side of the lot. She wanted to avoid another uncomfortable encounter.

The warm-up room was empty. Shay put her earbuds in, positioned herself in her opening pose, and pressed Play. *Swan Lake* flowed into her ears. It was the theme of her choreography, both music, and its interpretation. As Shay moved through her routine—poses, spins, footwork, and jumps—she played it like a movie in her mind, focused on the perfection of each element. She did her best to avoid putting too much pressure on her ankle. She recalled her mother's comment about speed going into the Lutz. It took Shay out of the moment, interrupted the mental flow. Now she was out of the routine and into a phantom argument with her mother. *Faster, Shay! Mom, please, just—just what?* Shay did her best to get back into the mental groove, but it was too late. She stopped her rehearsal and yelled, "Just butt out, okay!" She put her hands on her hips and turned to see Jack standing in the doorway.

"Just you and the little people in your head, huh?" Jack said.

"God, are you stalking me!"

Jack shrugged. "He might be, but I wouldn't call it stalking. More like nudging. Sometimes, I get the impression he's directing me like those guys directing planes at the airport—the way they flag you in." Jack started an exaggerated improv, waving this way and that as if directing a plane to the gate.

"I meant you."

"Me? No. I'm not stalking you. I'm emptying the garbage." Jack pointed to the can, picked it up, and dumped the contents into the barrel in the hall. "How's the ankle?"

"Not your business."

"Are you always this pleasant, or have I caught you on a good day?"

"May I be frank?"

"I'm having trouble picturing it, but sure, Frank, go ahead."

"I could have you fired, okay? I could say you're stalking me and doing weird things and have you fired. I don't want to do that, but I will. Do we have an understanding?"

"Yes, we do."

"Good."

Jack turned and left the room. Shay listened as the wheels of the garbage barrel clattered down the hall. The sound stopped. A moment later, Jack was back at the door.

"Just one last thing. God loves you, Frank. Don't forget that." Jack smiled and walked back into the hall.

A moment later, Shay's phone vibrated. It was her mother. She took the call.

"Hey, Mom. What's up?"

"I need you to come to my office right away."

Shay could hear the stress in her mother's voice. Something was wrong. "Why? What happened?"

"It's Luke. He's done it again, to both of us. Just get here. People are waiting." Bethany disconnected.

Shay gathered her things and rushed to her car.

CHAPTER 4

Bethany's real estate office was ten minutes from the rink. Shay slammed her foot down on the gas pedal and roared out of the lot. Shay made it in six. When she ran inside, her mother was sitting in the office behind her desk. A man and woman, both dressed in business attire, were also there.

"What's going on?" Shay asked breathlessly.

"This is my daughter," Bethany said.

The woman, dressed in a tailored gray pants suit, stood and extended her hand. "It's good to meet you, Shay. I'm Maya Lopez, and this is Ray Pond," she said, indicating the man who now stood. "We're from the State Department." Mr. Pond nodded, posted a businesslike smile, and sat back down.

"The State Department?" Shay asked.

"Something's come up with your father we'd like to talk to you about," Ms. Lopez explained.

"This is so Luke," Bethany muttered.

"Can you just tell me?" Shay pleaded, her mind swirling with possibilities.

"Your father's been arrested," Ms. Lopez said.

Shay's first thought was Luke had fallen off the wagon again. The last time she saw him was when he was arrested on their front lawn. She was ten years old. He showed up high on drugs and begged Bethany for forgiveness so they could be a family again. He slurred his words, screamed, and begged until her mother called the police. His addiction led to his being barred from seeing Shay. When she was fourteen, her mother gave her the details regarding Luke's fall from grace, and it wasn't pretty.

"His job was to sell prescription drugs, but he took them instead. He had a good job, a family, and threw it all away to get high. He could have seen you, provided for you, but drugs were more important to him than you were. I wish I had a better story to tell you, but the truth is the truth."

Shay cried for days, and then her heartbreak turned to anger. How could he be so weak? How could he abandon her and her mother just to get high? Shay immersed herself in her skating and her art. She buried her feelings and banished Luke from her mind. As far as she was concerned, Luke Gerrard never existed.

"Okay. They have arrested him. But you're the State Department?"

"In China," Ms. Lopez said. "Why don't you have a seat, and we'll explain everything."

As Lopez and Pond laid out the circumstances of Luke's arrest, Shay did her best to absorb the information.

"He was arrested for attending an illegal house church in Chengdu, Sichuan," Ms. Lopez said.

"China? Are you sure it's Luke?" Shay asked.

"Yes, we're sure," Pond said. "He went as a tourist. It appears he broke from the group one evening to attend a house church, one that's unregistered and, therefore, illegal. And this particular underground church is one the Chinese government has decided to make an example of. Because you're his daughter, we thought it important you be informed."

Shay looked to her mother and then back to Lopez and Pond. "But my father…he—we, I mean—we're not even religious."

Ms. Lopez spoke in an empathetic tone. "Your father became a very active member of the church in the past year. We've spoken to his pastor."

"Found God, is that it?" Bethany said, her voice dripping with sarcasm. "Everybody has to find God. He's always lost, and they spend all their time finding him. One big ring around the rosary if you ask me."

Ms. Lopez's eyes flashed to Bethany, a momentary break in her focus and concentration.

Shay noticed the tiny silver cross on Ms. Lopez's necklace.

Ms. Lopez turned her attention back to Shay.

"I'm sure this is confusing, but—"

"Confusing?" Bethany said, once again interrupting Ms. Lopez. "This is what Luke does. Ruins things, especially where Shay and I are concerned. But passionate about faith? That's a new one. In college, his nickname was Lukewarm because he never got excited about anything. Oh, wait, he did suddenly get passionate about becoming a drug addict, so maybe it's a trend?"

"Mom," Shay said, her eyes pleading with her mother to stop interrupting.

Mr. Pond continued, "We want you to know we're doing everything we can to have him released, and we're committed to keeping you both informed as events unfold."

"You'll do no such thing," Bethany said. "The bed he made he needs to sleep in. I agreed to let Shay hear this from you, but as you can see, he is no longer of concern to us. The only thing important now is to keep this in strict confidence, as we discussed."

Mr. Pond turned his attention to Bethany. "You need to understand, Ms. Dawsey, there are forces at work here we have very little control over."

"Forces you can't control? You're the United States government. Don't give me that crap!"

"Mom!"

Bethany glared at Shay. "Let me handle this. You do not understand the harm this could cause."

Mr. Pond continued, "There are private organizations whose mission it is to let the world know when people are being persecuted for their beliefs. We don't control those organizations, so we can't promise this will not be spread through other channels."

Bethany stood up and began pacing. "This has to be contained."

"Why?" Shay asked.

Bethany stopped and turned to her. "Beijing, Shay. Think! If it gets out an American Olympian's father has been imprisoned by the host country..." Bethany's words trailed off. Now Shay understood. At the Games, human interest stories were like gold, and this story had it all.

Bethany turned to Ms. Lopez and Mr. Pond. "The best thing you can do is get him quietly released before the Games begin. That means no victory laps for a man stupid enough to get himself caught and selfish enough to do this to his daughter."

"We'll do our best," Lopez said. She turned to Shay. "And good luck at the Games. We'll be rooting for you." Lopez reached into her pocket and retrieved two business cards. She handed one to Bethany and the other to Shay. "If you ever want to get in touch with me."

After they left, Bethany went ballistic. "What have I told you all these years! Promise me you won't let his foolishness be a distraction."

"Fine, Mom. Calm down."

"Don't be condescending." Bethany began pacing again. "If this leaks out, you need to be prepared. You'll tell them you haven't spoken to your father in years, that you wish him well, but he's no longer a part of your life. Understood?"

"Yes."

"He did this on purpose." The door chime rang. Bethany checked her watch. "Now, of all times." Bethany breathed in and let the air out in a measured breath. She smiled at Shay. Shay had seen it before, her mother's ability to rein in her rage and refocus instantly. "We're strong, right? We won't be distracted. We go on as if nothing happened. Get to practice. I'll be there when I'm finished."

Shay hugged her mother. "It'll be okay, Mom. Promise."

A woman's voice called out from the main office. "Ms. Dawsey?"

"Coming!" Bethany said.

A few minutes later, Shay was in her car, driving back to the rink. When she pulled into the parking lot, she realized she had driven there on autopilot. She was numb. She tried to arrange the things she had learned into a cohesive whole. *Luke. Church? China? Arrested?* Like working a Rubik's cube, Shay got some squares aligned, but others refused to fall into place. Luke stepping foot in a church? Shay remembered how, as a little girl, her parents refused to let her attend Sunday school with a friend who had invited her to Easter Service. "People are entitled to believe in foolish things. That's their right," Luke told her. "But we don't."

The knock on the passenger-side window startled Shay. She turned and saw Adley. Shay disengaged the door locks. Adley opened the door and leaped inside. "Brrr, freezing out there!"

"Why aren't you in school?"

"I'm sick." Adley faked a cough and smiled. "See?"

"I don't get it. You could be the valedictorian, but you miss half your classes, never study, and show such little interest in education?"

"*Au contraire*, mademoiselle. I love education. It's school I can't stand." Adley quickly pivoted. "I can't believe your mother bought you a BMW. How I despise the conspicuous consumption of the nouveau riche."

"Sure, you do. That's why you drive a despicable Mercedes."

"Used."

"Bought by your parents until you got your license."

Adley shrugged her shoulders. "Fine. You got me. Can we talk about Captain Jack now? Can I assume his car is the Love Bug with all the Jesus Fish on it?"

"That would be the one."

"So I was thinking last night about the whole taking pictures of your etchings in the ice thing."

"And?" Shay asked expectantly.

"Frick and Freud were having their usual passive-aggressive debate at the dinner table last night when I had a revelation." Adley let the comment hang there for a moment.

"Adley," Shay said in an admonishing tone.

"If it's what I'm thinking, Jack may be creepier than you think."

Shay sighed. "Wonderful. What?"

"Rorschach Test. Maybe he really is psycho—albeit cute for a guy sporting some serious Charlie Manson androgyny—and he's using your etchings as his own personal Rorschach Test?"

Shay's brows tugged together. "The inkblot thing?"

"Precisely."

"Okay, so I'm totally creeped out now."

"It connects him to you in the psycho-stratosphere of twisted thoughts and strange obsessions. Are you going to introduce me?"

Shay glared at Adley. "You think he might be a lunatic, and you want a formal introduction?"

Adley leaned back and put her knees on the dash. "I like to keep a wide circle of friends."

"Believe me, you don't want him in your circle regardless of how wide it is."

"He's good-looking and mysterious. Just my type."

Shay pinched the bridge of her nose between thumb and forefinger. "My head's spinning. How can you tell if you have a migraine?"

"Your head hurts," Adley said.

"Gee, Adley, thanks, that's so very helpful. You should go to medical school. I mean, actually attend," Shay said in a snippy tone.

Adley pulled back as if Shay had something contagious. "What's with you?"

"What's with me? How about the Olympics? How about a sore ankle, a creep watching me, and my mother and coach at each other's throats?"

"You need to chill. Seriously."

"Just forget it."

Adley peered at Shay with knowing eyes. "Spill."

"Things are crazy right now, okay? Just…back off."

Adley whistled. "Wow. Know what? I think I'll do just that." Adley opened the car door. "Adley, wait," Shay pleaded; but Adley ignored her, slammed the car door, and stormed off.

"Great," Shay whispered and lowered her head until it rested on the steering wheel. She ignored the incoming call on her phone, got out of her car, and slammed the door.

CHAPTER 5

S hay stepped on the ice and began her warm-up. The first part of her session wasn't private. With nationals just ending and Shay being the only skater to qualify for the Olympics, there were only a few skaters in the rink. Today, some newbies were taking lessons. Other than that, the ice was hers. Her ankle was still tender, so she wrapped it and tied her boot extra tight. She performed her footwork sequences, and it seemed to be holding up. Her spins were okay. The outer-back camel was the only one that felt unstable but jumping was out of the question—at least for today.

Remy came out of her office and watched Shay work through her routine, scrutinizing every move as her Olympian reacted to the music being pumped through her earbuds. Remy could tell Shay was babying her right ankle. Sprains were notoriously unpredictable, and Shay could ill-afford to lose practice time this close to the Games. But there was something else. Shay's pacing was off. Her flow from one musical sequence to the next didn't reflect the emotional impact of each transition. It was a subtle but critical aspect of Shay's choreography. When Shay finished, she grabbed her water bottle off the boards and skated to Remy.

"Ankle stiffened up?" Remy asked.

"A little." Shay took a sip of her water.

A moment passed where nothing was said. It was awkward, a rare occurrence between student and coach.

"Are you okay?" Remy asked.

"Yeah. Fine."

"Okay," Remy said skeptically. "Your mom still harping about the Lutz?"

"She thinks it's worth the risk," Shay said.

"It's not. And with your ankle as it is, we can't risk working it. You'll nail the triple-triple combination, the triple Axel, spin like a top, and skate clean. We play to your strength. That's our strategy."

Shay thought a moment, wondering if she should tell Remy about Luke but decided against it, fearing Remy would make a bigger deal out of it than it was.

The open session ended. Now Shay would have the ice to herself. A moment later, Jack appeared atop the Zamboni, ready to clean the ice. Shay turned to Remy. "I don't want him to clean it."

"What?"

"It's unnecessary. It's hardly used. Just the little kids."

"We have five minutes before the ice is ours. Let him do his job."

Jack stood atop the Zamboni like he was captaining his own ship. He looked to Remy and Shay and waved.

"I don't want it cleaned!" Shay said and skated out to the Zamboni, leaving Remy stunned.

Jack had the Zamboni on the ice when Shay skated to him. "Hey!" she yelled, but Jack had his earbuds in and didn't hear her. Frustrated, Shay skated in front of the Zamboni, turned, and planted herself directly in the machine's path. Jack saw her and stopped. He stood up and looked at her, then grabbed his phone and positioned it to take a picture.

"Don't move!" Jack said. "Just stay like that." He took a picture.

Once again, Jack had done the unexpected, leaving Shay at a loss.

"This is fantastic! Stay there! Just one more!"

Jack shut off the Zamboni, climbed down, and stood off to the side to take another picture.

"What are you doing?" Shay shouted.

"Pose again! Total defiance!" Jack said, his voice filled with excitement.

"I don't want the ice resurfaced!"

Jack snapped several pictures and shuffled over to Shay to show them to her. "We just recreated one of the most iconic pictures ever taken!"

Shay threw her hands up. "Are you listening to me?"

"We just had a moment."

"Are you on something?"

Jack looked down. "Ice. Same thing you're on." Jack held the phone up and showed Shay the picture. "Tiananmen Square. Nineteen eighty-nine. Student-led demonstrations in Beijing. Thousands arrested. Some were killed. One student stands in defiance."

Remy, watching the exchange, called out, "Shay?"

Jack continued, "One image can change the world. You need to remember that."

Shay looked at Remy, then back at Jack. "Leave the ice the way it is, Jack." She began to skate away. "You're on my time."

Jack grinned. Saluted her. "Aye, aye, Captain."

Despite Shay's best effort to stay focused, practice wasn't going well. Her footwork was sloppy. She had trouble centering her layback spin and worked too hard to move from one element to the next.

"We might want to consider taking a few days off to give the ankle a chance to heal," Remy suggested.

Shay looked across the rink at her mother. "That's not going to happen."

"It may have to. If you damage it any further, you'll have to withdraw."

"Let's give it another couple of days, okay?"

Remy considered this a moment. "Okay. Are you staying off it when you're not at practice?"

"For the most part."

"Oh, I almost forgot. A commentator wants to meet with you on Thursday to get your backstory for the *Up Close and Personal* TV spot."

"What time?" Shay asked.

"Ten in the morning. They'll meet us here. They tried to contact you earlier. I think they left a message."

Shay remembered receiving a call after she and Adley had their altercation in the car. She had forgotten about it.

"Don't say anything about your ankle. I don't want to take the pressure off your competition. I want the conversation focused on the power of your artistry, not an injury," Remy said.

"Okay."

"We've got five minutes." Remy glanced at Bethany and then back at Shay. "We can work on speed into the Lutz. See if we can put your mom at ease. Just the entry. You game?"

"Sure," Shay said in a flat, less-than-enthusiastic tone.

"Are you okay?" Remy asked, sensing there was something Shay wasn't telling her.

Shay averted her eyes from Remy. "Yeah, I'm fine."

Shay worked her speed into the Lutz, doing her best to make it appear effortless, one of the elements considered in the component score. She looked at her mother and saw her smile. Shay loved her mother, but when Luke lost his job and walked out of their lives, Bethany's dormant trait of needing to be in control took center stage. Shay understood why it happened, but that didn't translate into the patience required to deal with Bethany's need to dictate every aspect of Shay's life. Working her speed into the Lutz would make her mother feel like she was in control, at least for the moment.

After practice, Shay checked her phone and saw two missed calls, one from Curt and one from an unknown number. Her mother walked up as Shay unlaced her skates.

"Nice speed going into the Lutz," Bethany said. "We're going to need that quad. How's the ankle?"

"Still hurts a little, but I'm hoping to jump again tomorrow. A TV crew's coming to do the *Up Close and Personal* interview on Thursday morning at ten."

Bethany's eyes widened. "I have a client. You just found this out?"

"I missed the call earlier, so they contacted Remy."

Bethany snorted. "You'd think they'd do a better job of planning these things. Well, we have no choice, so we'll make it work. Let's hope we don't get any more surprises. Remember what I said about Luke. I'll deal with his drama. Lord knows I have a lot of practice at it. I need to get going, and you need to get home to ice that ankle."

33

"Okay."

"Did you talk to Remy about the quad Lutz?" Bethany asked as she rummaged for her keys in her purse.

Shay's stomach tightened. "She said it would be a good idea if I could work it, but with the ankle the way it is, it's way too risky at this point."

Bethany knew Remy was never in favor of trying the quadruple Lutz. She would be bullheaded about it regardless of Shay's injury.

"You protect her. Loyalty can be a good trait, but it can also distort your judgment." Bethany found her keys, kissed Shay on the cheek, and smiled. "We're fine. Just obstacles to maneuver around. Nothing to worry about. See you later."

"Okay."

Shay sat on the bench and texted Curt, "Still at Rink."

A moment later, Curt texted back, "BRO."

Shay smiled. Curt made up his own abbreviations. Instead of the conventional BRT (be right there), his meant "be right over."

Shay heard the Zamboni's motor and looked up. Jack was back at it, resurfacing the ice. She thought about their encounter earlier. How he took that picture, then told her about people being arrested in Beijing hours after she was told Luke was arrested there. *So weird*, she thought. But then again, Jack was the definition of weird. Despite this, there was something about him that had a...what was it? A pull?

The thought made Shay think of Adley, who would say it was the universe trying to tell Shay something. That's what Shay loved about Adley; she could make the strangest things sound plausible. Shay regretted the way she reacted in the car with her friend. Their years together made it impossible to hide it when either of them had something on their mind, and Shay rarely reacted so aggressively with her friend. The reality was she could trust Adley with anything, so why hadn't she shared the information about Luke? It might be useful to have someone besides her mother to help her sort it all out. Shay decided to text Adley and make amends, "BFHS?"

This was their personal text message for a Bigfoot handshake. A moment later, Adley returned with a text of her own: "2nite TTL XOXO."

Shay relaxed. Adley was her rock, the one she could count on no matter what. Sure, Shay was dating Curt, but it had only been two months, and she wasn't sure she could bare her soul to him. Their relationship was still in the "let's see where this goes" stage. What she needed to do now was go home and relax, maybe sketch a new drawing? Her art calmed her. Then when Adley came over, she would do what she had promised her mother she wouldn't do—she'd tell Adley everything.

CHAPTER 6

Shay sat at her drawing table, staring at her sketch pad. She intended to draw a skater performing an arabesque, but an image of Luke bled through the page, first his restless green eyes and then an outline of his sculpted face until a picture of her ruggedly handsome father became manifest. It was as if her mind had discovered the opening frames of an old movie. A minute later, she was drawing.

When the doorbell chimed, Shay tore the sketch from her pad and hid it in her closet. She went to the intercom in her bedroom and pressed the button. "Who is it?"

"Adley."

"It's open. Come on up."

A moment later, Shay and Adley performed the Bigfoot handshake, by standing as far away from one another as they could before reaching forward and shaking hands. Then they embraced.

"Love you," Adley said.

"Love you back," Shay replied.

Adley leaped on Shay's bed, sprawled out, and began making a snow angel. "I love your bed. I've got memory foam, and I hate it. It's like sleeping on an old marshmallow. And believe me, I remember that."

Adley was dressed in patched jeans, a tattered flannel shirt, and brown lace-up boots. She made her own clothes. She bought secondhand at thrift stores and then customized the clothes to her liking.

"Okay," Adley said, "time for true confessions. You want me to go first, or do you want to start?"

Shay plopped down on her bed next to Adley. "I'm not sure where to start."

"Be random. Then we'll patch it together."

"All right. But this has to be supersecret, okay? I promised my mother I wouldn't speak a word of it."

"Cross my heart and hope to die…on my memory foam mattress…dreaming of Jack."

"Adley," Shay admonished.

"My lips are sealed…with a kiss from—"

"If you don't stop, I'm clamming."

Adley mimed zipping her lip.

Shay sighed and began. "First, some people from the State Department showed up today and told us Luke's been arrested in Beijing."

Adley's eyes nearly popped out of the sockets. "Shut…up!"

"Second, I tried to stop Jack from resurfacing the ice, and he took a picture of me and started talking about some revolt that happened in Beijing."

"That's odd," Adley said.

"I'll say. And third, I started thinking about him again. Not Jack, my dad."

Adley sat up. "Geez, Shay, I'm not sure what to say. What was he arrested for?"

"For attending an illegal house church. The people from the State Department said the government is cracking down on the preacher they found my father with. Bethany's livid. She thinks Luke did it on purpose, got himself arrested in Beijing right when I'm going to the Games. Now we have to hope the media doesn't pick up on the story and make a big deal out of it. That's why you can't say anything to anybody."

"Wowza, what a mess," Adley said.

"Tell me about it. I'm four weeks away from leaving for Beijing, and my father's in jail. In Beijing!"

"And the Captain Jack thing, what was that again?"

Shay explained the encounter with Jack and told her about the picture and Jack's reference to Tiananmen Square.

"I remember reading about that. I saw the picture, too, of a guy standing in front of a line of tanks. It was epic. No weapon. Just one guy with a satchel in his hand standing in defiance. Wait a second. I'll show it to you." Adley tapped some keys on her phone and showed the iconic picture to Shay.

"That's incredible," Shay said.

"Talk about risking everything. I couldn't do it."

"I don't think most people would do it. It's courage or crazy or somewhere in between."

Adley read the caption beneath the picture. "It was a democracy movement. The guy became known as Tank Man, and the footage of him defying the tanks was an image seen around the world. It says they estimate that thousands were killed or arrested."

"When Jack showed me the picture, he said an image could change the world." Shay walked to her bedroom window and gazed out at the night sky as she spoke. "I keep wondering if there was any way Jack could know about Luke because the whole Beijing thing seems random on one hand, yet what are the odds, right? Luke in Beijing and Jack bringing up Beijing? But even if he knew, I'm the one who randomly walked out onto the ice, so there's no way he could've expected that."

"That is a weird coincidence," Adley said. "But I don't believe in random."

Shay knew Adley would latch onto a cosmic explanation. Her weekly podcast was about strange happenings, and although Shay wasn't one of the "out there" crowd, it still felt good to talk to Adley about her situation. The basement in Adley's house was set up as a studio complete with soundproofing, high-end mics, and high-tech equipment. Frick and Freud thought podcasting was good for Adley's self-esteem. "No. You believe in Sasquatch, Slender Man, and Shapeshifters."

"To name a few." Adley leaped off the bed and plopped down next to Shay. "It's the universe, don't you see! It's talking to you!"

"Yeah? Well, I don't speak the language."

"Don't doubt me on this. It's the only thing that makes sense."

"I don't have time to listen to the universe or anything else right now. It's hard enough to compete at the Olympics without having your mind pulled in seven different directions."

"No problem. You stay focused on your training, and I'll keep my cosmic ear to the ground for you. There's something going on here. Maybe Captain Jack is a conduit plugged into your energy?"

"He's plugged into something, but I'd vote for the crazy socket long before considering my energy."

"That's because you don't believe in anything you can't see."

"Not true. I believe in plenty of things I can't see."

"Name them."

Shay thought for a moment. "Atoms. Gravity. That dinosaurs once roamed the earth."

"That's my point. You believe in the scientific stuff, but you discount the paranormal when, in fact, much of science was once considered paranormal before it wasn't."

"Such as?"

"Frankenstein. Now we exchange body parts like underwear. In a few years, much of the paranormal will be proven true, leaving your myopic thinking in the dustbin of history."

"Myopic? There's the queen of perfect SAT scores we all know and love," Shay said.

"Right. And to the chagrin of my beloved teachers who despise me for not conforming to their idea of what an intelligent person should think or believe. It slays them. All they do is regurgitate the party line which includes such oxymorons as 'academic freedom,' which is code for 'you better think what we think, or else.'"

Shay just stared at Adley and smiled.

"What?"

"I love your rants."

"Hey, if you want to be a rebel, you've got to have a cause. Speaking of which, I need to get going so I can prepare for tomorrow night's podcast on the 'Phantom Tollbooth from Hell.'"

"What's that?" Shay asked.

"Nope. You need to tune in like everybody else."

They hugged, and then Adley added, "You know, maybe it's not such a bad thing if Luke got some religion. I mean, if it's the twelve-step thing, maybe it'll be good for him, right?"

"Maybe. But my mother said Luke would need a lot more steps."

"He's your dad. You can take him out of the picture, but he's still a part of your world."

"Says the daughter of Frick and Freud."

"For shrinks, they're pretty good parents."

"Agreed. They raised you. A brilliant, well-adjusted, and only mildly insane daughter who believes in poltergeists, zombies, and wizards…just to name a few."

"They accept the fact I'm paranormal, just like my interests." Adley grinned.

After Adley left, Shay opened her closet door and looked at her sketch of Luke and then rolled it into a ball and tossed it into the wastebasket. Adley might be right about Luke still being in her world, but Shay was determined to keep him out of the picture. She flopped down on her bed, took another selfie, and posted it on Instagram with hashtags and "Good night, all!" written inside a heart. *Need to feed the beast*, she thought and then sent a text to Curt letting him know she was going to sleep. He'd text her back after the game and let her know how he did. They were both absorbed in trying to make something big happen—Shay at the Olympics and Curt for his upcoming tryout for the Detroit Red Wings farm team. Between practice sessions, lessons, and Curt's games, they had little time to spend with one another; but they knew that when the Olympics and Curt's upcoming tryout were over, that would change.

Shay closed her eyes and tried to clear her mind, even chanting to herself in an attempt to control her breathing. It was something she could do in yoga class, meditate until her thoughts became passersby, never staying long enough to materialize. But the image of Luke's face superimposed on Tank Man refused all attempts to suppress it. *Some people get pink elephants. I get Luke as Tank Man*, she thought. This is how she saw Luke when she was a little girl, not as Tank Man, but a superhero—*her* superhero. She glanced back at the wastebasket and retrieved the balled-up sketch. She held the crumpled paper in her fist, held it the way she might hold her estranged father's hand, and drifted off the sleep.

CHAPTER 7

Thirty days until the Olympic skate

Shay pulled into the parking lot and saw Jack's car. She intended to get to the arena earlier, but the snowfall and swirling winds foiled that plan. The last thing she needed was to get in an accident with her new car, so she crept the entire way. Now she had arrived just as the general practice session ended, and that meant Jack would be on the Zamboni about to resurface the ice. Shay grabbed her skates and ran into the arena. She was too late. Jack had already made several circles around the rink.

"Darn it!" she muttered, put her skates down, and glared at him with palms up in the universal pose of "what gives?" She marched onto the ice and into the Zamboni's path.

Jack stopped, turned off the motor, and removed the earbuds from his ears.

"I told you not to resurface the ice, did I not?" Shay said.

"That sentence is a little confusing, but I'll say yes."

"Yet here you are, again, resurfacing the ice, are you not?"

Jack looked at the Zamboni and then out at the ice as if he needed to check before answering. "I will say yes, but the did-I-nots and are-you-nots have me off-kilter. Why don't you be Frank again? I had a much easier time understanding him."

Shay slapped her hands on her hips. "I don't want the ice resurfaced before my *private* ice time. My time, my ice. Are we clear?"

Jack looked over to Remy, who stood by the boards with a steaming cup of coffee in hand. "Talk to your coach. She told me to resurface it. She said, and I quote, 'Resurface the ice, Jack.' And I said, and I quote, 'Shay told me not to.' And she said, and I quote—"

"Just forget it!" Shay said and shuffled off the ice toward Remy.

"May I carry on?" Jack asked while Shay's back was to him.

Shay ignored him. Jack looked to Remy, who smiled and nodded. Jack started the Zamboni's motor and continued to resurface the ice.

"Why did you tell him to resurface the ice?" Shay asked the moment she got to Remy.

"Why wouldn't I? That's what he gets paid to do, resurface the ice between practices."

"I don't want it resurfaced. Odds are I won't be skating on clean ice at the Olympics. Situational strategy."

"At the Olympics, there won't be any divots. This morning, there were several. You have a bad ankle, and I'm not taking a chance that you'll irritate that injury because of said divots, so I told Jack to resurface the ice. And we both know this isn't about strategy, so exactly what is it about?"

Shay set her skate bag down and crossed her arms over her chest. "Fine. He's strange. He's creepy. In fact, I'd like him not to be here when I'm here. Can you arrange that?"

Remy glanced over at Jack, who was bouncing to his music as he completed his last circle of the ice. "Maybe, but he'll probably lose his job, so I'll need specifics."

Shay plopped down on the bench. "Just forget it. But I don't want him resurfacing the ice before I practice. Can I get at least that?"

"Did he do anything to you? Threaten you? Is he stalking you or something?" Remy asked.

"No, he just—he does odd things. You saw what he did yesterday. Just jumps off the Zamboni and starts taking pictures of me."

"Did it occur to you he just might... I don't know...like you? After all, you're not terrible looking. Except for your neck, which might be considered abnormally long outside of the swan family. And the way your nostrils flare when you're mad, that's a little—"

"Okay, okay—just stop," Shay said, working to contain a smile.

"He's studying photography," Remy said. "He wants to be a photojournalist, take pictures that matter."

Shay continued lacing her second skate. "You seem to know an awful lot about him. He's a Bible-thumper, did you know that?"

"Young Christians today don't carry Bibles. They have them on their phones, so they don't thump them. Finish lacing up. We have a lot to do and very little time in which to do it. How's the ankle feeling?"

"Better."

"Great. I'd like to work on jumps. You all right with that?"

"Yeah. I'm good with it."

Shay flashed across the ice, pulling crosscuts with the power and artistry that made her one of the best figure skaters in the world. She cut a hard outer edge, planted her toe pick, and leaped into the air. She landed the triple Lutz slightly short of full rotation.

"Lower the free leg, and engage the hips," Remy instructed. "One more."

Shay did as Remy instructed and landed the next triple Lutz in perfect form.

Bethany clapped, having entered the rink moments before Shay began working the Lutz. "Better! Excellent speed in and out! Now the quad!"

Shay smiled and waved to her mother before rejoining Remy by the rail.

"A compliment without a string attached," Remy said.

"Only because we worked speed into the Lutz."

"You know what they say about gift horses, right?"

"Never look one in the mouth."

"Exactly."

The rest of the practice session went well. Shay's ankle felt better, and she regained her focus. *Control what you can control*, she told herself. As Adley often said, it was time for Shay to pull up her big girl britches and take charge of the situation. Bethany was so happy with the practice session she even complimented Remy.

"I love the way everything flows," Bethany said.

Shay's long program was a retelling of Odette, the swan princess in the ballet, Swan Lake. The story was a favorite of Shay's, and she loved the way Remy had synthesized the music and choreography into a powerful competitive rendition of the classic ballet.

"Great advice on the Lutz. I also thought it had a lot to do with our free leg," Bethany added.

There it is again, Shay thought. It was "our" free leg as if Shay and Bethany shared the appendage.

Shay spotted Jack. He was climbing the steps toward the nose-bleed section of the arena.

"Be back in a minute," Shay said. She was determined to find out what Jack was up to. When she found him, he was taking pictures of the ice. "What are you doing?"

"Taking pictures." He snapped several more shots of the ice.

"I can see that. The question is, why?"

"Because it interests me, does it not?"

"Hilarious."

"Have you ever heard of accidental art?" Jack asked.

"Let me guess. Art done by accident. But that isn't really art. Art requires intention."

"It does?"

"Yes."

"So if I accidentally knock over a paint can and it mixes with other colors of other paint that accidentally got knocked over, it's not art?"

"Not literally, no."

"Even if my accident replicates a Jackson Pollock, and I hang it on a wall?"

Shay rolled her eyes. "If you see it as art, then maybe. Can we get back to why—"

"What if two people, one knowing and one unknowing, take part in creating a painting or, in our case, an etching? Art or not art?"

"Our case? There is no 'our case,' Jack, and this is precisely what's creeping me out, you thinking that you and I in any way, shape, or—"

"I resurface the ice with intention before you etch an accidental image into it with your blades. So am I just the guy who shakes the Etch-a-Sketch while it's you that creates the art? But I'm the one who intended it. So, based on your definition, am I the artist and are you my instrument, or are you the artist even though you intended nothing?"

Shay, frustrated, was once again astounded by Jack. Every encounter with him was something so unexpected she found herself consistently playing defense. "I didn't come up here to get in a philosophical argument. I came up here to find out why you're taking pictures of the ice after I've skated on it. Can I have an answer, please?"

"For my philosophy class."

The revelation stopped Shay cold. "Your philosophy class?"

"Yes. And I admit to using you as an unintended coconspirator in my argument."

"Which is?"

"I'm not sure, actually. I keep changing my mind."

Shay stared at Jack as if he were one of Adley's shapeshifters. He kept turning her expectations upside down. Still, she was less afraid now that she realized there was an academic explanation for his taking the pictures.

A voice came from behind Shay and startled her. "Hey."

Shay turned and saw Curt.

"Oh, hey," Shay said, startled to see him there. "I thought you were at the gym this morning?"

"Pipes froze, so I came over to see you." Curt glanced at Jack, then back at Shay. "And here you are. Everything okay?"

"Yeah, yes, fine," Shay said.

"Why are you way up here?" Curt asked, looking around at all the empty seats to emphasize the point.

Shay looked around for a moment, as if it startled her to be where she was. "Oh. Well, Jack is a photographer."

"Really."

"Yes. And I asked him to take a picture of the ice after I skated on it, something I could capture and frame. Just a different way of seeing my skating." Shay eyed Jack hard. "Right, Jack?"

"We were discussing what makes art," Jack said. "Yeah, I took a picture of the ice. It's her etching. I could give you a copy if you'd like?"

It was clear from Curt's expression he wasn't buying what Shay and Jack were selling. Curt's attitude annoyed Shay. She didn't enjoy being judged or watched over. She got enough of that from her mother and Remy. "Jack's also using the pictures for a philosophy class he's taking, the question being, is there such a thing as accidental art? Jack's position would be that there is. Am I representing that correctly, Jack?"

"It's a bit of a mind-bender, depending on your point of view."

Curt was taken off stride by the matter-of-fact tone in Shay's voice. His eyes flashed from Shay to Jack, and then he smiled. It was forced. "I'm not big on philosophy, but I think, therefore, I am famished." He looked to Shay. "Let's go. We'll get some breakfast."

Shay didn't appreciate Curt's directive tone.

"I can't," Shay said, determined to make it clear to Curt she wasn't about to blindly follow his direction. "I've got to stretch and ice my ankle."

"Yeah. Okay," Curt said. "Walk you down, then?"

Shay turned to Jack. "Can you send me the picture?"

"Where to?"

"I'll give you my number. You can text it to me."

Shay gave Jack the number, and he entered it into his phone. "It'll be there in a minute," Jack said.

"And I won't be needing more," Shay said, giving Jack the not-so-subtle message that she didn't want him taking any more pictures that involved her "accidental art."

"Right," Jack said and stayed where he was as Curt and Shay turned and walked away.

"I thought I told you to keep your distance from that guy," Curt said as he and Shay walked down the stairs toward ice level.

Shay stopped and waited until Curt realized she wasn't walking down behind him. He turned and saw that she had stayed on one of the landings. "What are you doing?"

"You told me? I'm not liking this sudden thing you have where you think you can tell me what to do. I'm a person, not a puppet, and I don't need a boyfriend who thinks I should 'take direction' from him." Shay used air quotes to make her point.

"What's with you all of a sudden?"

"Nothing. It's just that I have plenty of people telling me what I should or shouldn't do every minute of my life, so if you'd avoid joining that chorus, I'd appreciate it."

Curt rubbed the back of his neck and thought a moment. He looked up at her. "Yeah, I guess I have been that way a little. I was just surprised to see you up there with the Jesus Fish guy."

"His name is Jack, and I've confirmed he's harmless, as long as you can get used to his unique ability to surprise you at every turn."

Shay's cell phone rang. It was Bethany. "Hey, Mom, I'm with Curt, and we're almost—" Shay paused abruptly. "What?"

Curt couldn't hear the words, but he saw the expression of concern on Shay's face.

Shay disconnected.

"What is it?" Curt asked.

"Things are about to blow up. Come on, we need to go. I'll explain on our way down."

CHAPTER 8

Shay met her mother in Remy's office with Curt by her side. Bethany paced. News of Luke's arrest had made the local news.

"It will be everywhere before the end of the day," Bethany said. "There's no way to stop it, but there is a way to contain it." Bethany looked at Shay and gave the marching orders. "Remember what I said. You haven't seen or spoken to your father in years. You wish him well, but he's no longer a part of your life. You tell them under the advisement of the State Department you will not answer questions regarding your father. Understood?"

Shay nodded. Curt squeezed her hand. She appreciated having him with her. She needed the moral support.

"What about social media platforms?" Curt said. "If she composes a response, she could refer reporters to her statement on Instagram, Facebook, and Twitter, then state she has no further comment as per the State Department."

Bethany's eyes darted to Shay. "Yes, we do that this minute!"

Shay pulled out her phone, created the message, and sent it out on her social media platforms. "Done. What now?"

"We stay focused," Bethany said. "You can't let this distract you any more than it already has."

A moment later, Remy looked up and, through her office window, saw a woman attempting to flag down Jack while he resurfaced the ice. "It begins. That's Jasmine Thomas from KVOZ TV."

If it weren't such a serious moment, watching Ms. Thomas try to chase down Jack would be comical. She wore heels and almost stepped out onto the ice, a move that would have resulted in a fall. Her saving grace was the cameraman who grabbed her shoulder before her heel moved off solid ground. Not to be deterred, Ms.

Thomas looked around the arena in search of someone to speak with. Finding no one, she ran around the rink in a vain attempt to flag Jack down.

"We wait until her back is to us, then we leave." Bethany said. "If she spots us—"

"I'll run interference," Remy said.

A moment later, Bethany, Shay, and Curt exited Remy's office and made a beeline toward the exit. It would've worked perfectly if the cameraman hadn't spotted them.

"Jasmine!" he yelled and pointed at Bethany, Curt, and Shay.

Remy attempted to step between Jasmine and the exit, but the reporter pushed herself past Remy and starting yelling, "Shay! Shay, just a minute of your time!"

"Get home," Bethany said. "I'll deal with Ms. Thomas. Go!"

Curt and Shay ran for the exit. Bethany turned and glared at Jasmine, who continued her mad dash toward the door.

Jasmine, seeing Bethany was there to obstruct her, tried the other doors but discovered what Bethany already knew. They locked those doors. The arena only opened all the doors for hockey and public sessions. Frustrated, Jasmine tried to push her way past Bethany, but Bethany stood her ground.

"You need to move!" Jasmine growled.

"Actually, I don't, at least not until my daughter is out of your crosshairs."

Livid, Jasmine turned and yelled to the cameraman, "Film this! I'm being unlawfully detained!"

The cameraman lifted his camera and pointed it at Bethany.

"Wait, let me freshen my lipstick first," Bethany said and remained steadfast while she casually retrieved a lipstick from her purse and opened it.

Remy watched this unfold and admired Bethany's ability to control a situation. You'd think she was a movie star getting ready for a close-up. As Bethany applied her lipstick, Jasmine stood open-mouthed as she watched Shay and Curt drive away. Bethany put her lipstick away and looked at Jasmine. "The only statement Shay will be making has been made on social media." Bethany looked into the camera. "I've instructed my daughter not to speak to the press about her estranged father, and believe me, my daughter follows my instructions. Our focus must be on preparing for the Games. Shay has not spoken to her father in years. She wishes him no ill will and hopes he will be released, but they do not have nor have they had any father-daughter relationship for many years. That is all we have to say on the matter, and any attempt by the press to engage in further questions regarding this issue will be futile."

Jasmine, sensing an opening, changed her tactics. "What about you, Ms. Dawsey? How do you feel about your ex-husband's plight?"

Jasmine saw something new in Bethany's eyes, a cold, primal gaze; but then, just as Jack had cleared Shay's etchings from the ice, it was gone, replaced by an unreadable expression. "Nice try," Bethany said and then turned and walked to her car.

Back at the house, the reaction to her statement on social media stunned Shay. There were over ten thousand responses on Instagram alone, and most made some reference to prayer. Shay kept glancing at her phone, shocked by the outpouring: "Praying for you," "You're in my prayers," "Stay strong. God is with you and your father." It hadn't occurred to Shay that Luke had done something worthy of praise. Didn't these people realize what a distraction this was? Didn't they see how selfish? Now she had to fend off reporters and deal with feelings she hadn't felt in decades while attempting to skate her best at the Olympics. Shay's face reddened as the responses continued to pour in, most having to do with Luke's willingness to risk everything for his faith. She threw her phone down on the bed just as Curt came into the room with a cup of hot chocolate. He could see the tension in her face.

"You okay?" he asked.

"You want to see Bible-thumpers? Look at my Instagram account. God this, God that, 'Praying for you, Shay,'" she said, in a mocking tone. "And Luke's suddenly a martyr to be admired. Bethany's right. He did this on purpose." Shay plopped down on the bed and put her head in her hands. "What a mess!"

Curt put the cup of hot chocolate in her hands. He sat next to her and pulled her to him. "Ignore them. People believe in all kinds of crazy things, right? Look at Adley. She thinks Bigfoot's roaming your backyard."

Curt was right—people believed in nutty things, but now she was forced to deal with it at the worst possible time. So much was happening, and she was having trouble focusing on anything. She heard the ringtone from *The Twilight Zone* coming from her phone. It was Adley. She answered.

"Hey, Adley."

"Turn on channel five right now!" Adley said.

"Why? What's going—"

"Your mother's all over local television, and she's epic!"

Shay grabbed the remote for the TV in her room, turned on channel five, and went pale.

"Is that your mother?" Curt asked.

"Shish!" Shay said, holding a finger up to Curt as she watched the tail end of her mother's exchange with Jasmine Thomas. When Jasmine asked Bethany how she felt about her ex-husband's plight, Shay stiffened. She had seen that reptilian gaze in her mother's eyes before, usually preceding a relentless verbal tirade. But this time, Bethany had held back to avoid the trap Jasmine had set.

A moment later, Jasmine was on air standing in front of a pawnshop on the outskirts of Detroit. "Luke Gerrard has an apartment above this store where he's lived for the past eighteen months. I spoke to several neighbors who said Mr. Gerrard would often help others who lived nearby, bringing the elderly residents' food and driving them to the store. I also spoke to the store's owner and landlord of the apartment who stated that Mr. Gerrard was a God-fearing, good man. All said they will pray for his safe return. The timing couldn't be worse for Shay Gerrard, Detroit's very own Olympic hopeful. For those of you who would like to read Shay's statement, we have posted it on our website. Back to you, Todd."

Shay shut off the TV and, for a moment, just stared at the blank screen. Shay was emotionally frozen. "He lived right here… in Detroit."

Curt put his hands on Shay's shoulders. She seemed diminutive now, childlike.

"Maybe he was trying to get his life together, right? Maybe he was going to try to see you?"

Shay, at war with herself, felt a rush of tears fill her eyes. She turned to Curt. "You should go. I appreciate your being here, but I need some alone time."

"Sure, absolutely," Curt said and kissed her on the cheek. "Call me if you need me. Morning, noon, or middle of the night. I mean it."

"Thanks," Shay said. "I will, promise."

After Curt left, Shay went to her nightstand, retrieved the balled-up sketch of Luke, held it in her hand, and squeezed.

CHAPTER 9

S hay, trapped between sleep and wakefulness, meditated to allow the tsunami of thoughts that had broken through the levee of her mind to flow through unimpeded. Despite this, the events of the day refused to subside. Shay glanced at the clock on her nightstand. It was just after two in the morning. It was futile to try and sleep. She got up, went to her drawing table, and stared at her drawing pad. She opened it, and her mind's eye reached back to her childhood and retrieved images of Luke. Whenever an image formed in her mind, it moved to her artist's hand, rendering it on the page exactly as she envisioned it. To some extent, all great artists have this gift, but with Shay, the effortless ability to draw the image was unique. Now thoughts of her father, memories of their times together before their world came crashing down, were at the forefront of her mind. The first was an image of her dad with open arms as she ran to him as a child. Then another of her father's magnetic smile, and a third of the two of them building a snowman in their front yard. How had this happened? How could it be that her dad was in jail in a foreign country for his faith? *My father*, Shay thought. "My dad," she said, trying on the words in the same way she might try on a new outfit or a pair of shoes.

Luke found religious people to be intellectually stunted. When Shay thought about people devout in their faith, organ music grinding out old hymns and elderly hands clinging to tattered Bibles were what came to mind. Before she passed away, Shay's grandmother had taken Shay to church during her summer visits. Luke didn't like it, but there was little he could do about it.

Shay steeled her resolve. She promised her mother not to let Luke's situation be a distraction, and she intended to honor that

53

promise. Her mom was the one who had to pick up the pieces after Luke decided popping pills was more important than his wife and daughter. Sure, she and her mother had their disagreements, but Shay understood how hard her mother had worked to keep Shay's life intact after Luke's betrayal.

Shay lifted a page of her sketchbook and saw the drawing of Jack she sent to Adley. She thought about the conversation she and Jack had earlier that day, how everything Jack said was so unexpected. And that whole philosophy thing? *I clean the ice with intention just before you etch an image into it with your blades. So am I just the guy who shakes the Etch-a-Sketch while it's you that creates the art?* Who would have ever expected that?

And that was the point about Jack. Everything about him was wildly unpredictable. Shay continued to draw Jack's form, placing the chain around his neck and adding the silver crucifix that stood out against his dark tee shirt. His black jeans and silver belt buckle were next, and she completed the sketch by adding his military-style boots. When finished, she felt her eyes being drawn back to the crucifix and thought of the bumper stickers on Jack's car. *Real Men Love Jesus* and *Jesus Is Coming Back. Look Busy!* "You are one weird guy, Captain Jack," she whispered. She checked her social media platforms. She had gained an additional four thousand followers since news of Luke's arrest. The fact that over fifty thousand people followed her was hard to comprehend. Thoughts and prayers flowed in, and Shay was reminded of how many people were fooled into believing what Luke often referred to as the biggest fairy tale of all, that a man came back from the dead. But Shay knew her ability to gain followers could be valuable in the future, so she took a selfie with the note: "Thanks for all your well-wishes. Much appreciated. Shay." Her time at her drawing table did the trick. She yawned, lay down on her bed, and fell asleep.

Twenty-nine days until Olympic skate

Bethany made coffee and peered out of the kitchen window. Snowflakes the size of goose feathers drifted down from the sky, swinging like miniature hammocks. She couldn't recall ever seeing flakes so large, and Bethany had lived in Michigan all her life. She also saw the news trucks lined up in the street. The story of Luke's arrest and that his daughter, Shay Gerrard, was an Olympian had gone viral. The Olympics were in Beijing, and an American figure skater would compete in front of the world while her estranged father was being held in prison by the host country. This would be a media circus the likes of which the Olympics hadn't witnessed since 1994 when Nancy Kerrigan was attacked. *In Detroit. What are the odds?* Bethany thought.

"Hey, Mom," Shay said as she walked into the kitchen and opened the door to the refrigerator. "Thought you'd be at the office by now?"

"Not with the vampires lined up in the street."

Shay went to the window and saw the news trucks. "This is crazy."

"And it will only get worse. I don't want you watching the news or reading stories about this. No good can come of it."

"How did they get past the gate?"

"I've already got a call out to the homeowner's president to discuss it. Maybe they paid off a guard, who knows? But we'll get it corrected. What good is a gated community if they let everyone in?"

Shay turned to her mother. "Luke was living in Detroit. Did you know that?"

Bethany blanched. "Of course not. I have no interest in Luke, but nothing he does would surprise me, especially when it comes to self-interest. Does it shock me he suddenly arrives in Detroit just as his estranged daughter is about to make it on the world stage? I should've predicted it. Luke does what's good for Luke, and let the rest of the world be damned. Grab your protein shake, and let's go."

"I can drive myself," Shay said.

"Not in this weather with a bunch of reporters trying to chase you down. That's what happened to Princess Di. They care about the story, not safety. We ignore their questions and drive to the rink."

Bethany was right. Once outside, the reporters hit them with a barrage of questions. One walked onto the driveway to block Bethany and Shay from leaving. Bethany stepped into the car and held up her cell phone. "I'm recording you trespassing! If you don't move, I'm calling the police!"

The reporters began calling out questions to Shay. "How do you feel about your father's arrest?" "Will you call out the Chinese government at the Games?" "Shay, what is your relationship with your father?"

"Get in!" Bethany yelled.

Shay got in the car and shut the door. The last question hit Shay hard. Suddenly, her relationship with her father, one even she didn't really understand, was being questioned by complete strangers. What business was it of theirs? Why would they even ask?

Bethany glanced at Shay. "You okay?"

Shay turned to her mother and forced a smile. "It isn't going to stop, is it?"

"I'd like to say it will die down, but it won't."

"It's none of their business, right?" Shay said, her voice pleading for affirmation.

"No, it isn't. But that won't stop them. This is a turning point for us. We can let it distract us or use it to strengthen our resolve."

Shay knew her mother was right. This *was* a turning point. If she let the situation knock her off her game, any chance of winning the Olympics would be gone.

They pulled up to the arena and spotted more reporters by the entrance. Shay never imagined there were this many of them in all of Detroit. As soon as Shay got out of the car, the onslaught continued. Bethany fended them off. "No comment. You're wasting your time," she said, shielding Shay. Once inside, Shay walked into the arena and saw a camera crew had set up outside Remy's office. That's when she remembered the *Up Close and Personal* interview was scheduled for this morning. How was she going to deal with that now? Remy saw Bethany and Shay and waved them into her office.

"This is a nightmare," Bethany said. "I hope you told them Shay will not be addressing questions regarding Luke. If they ask anything about it, she'll walk out."

"That may not be wise," Remy said.

Bethany's eyes flared. "Not wise? Shay's relationship with her father—or lack thereof—is nobody's business but ours."

"I understand," Remy said. "But the more she ignores the pink elephant in the room, the bigger it will get. Part of being an Olympian is a willingness to share personal stories. Like it or not, this isn't going away."

"What should I do?" Shay asked.

"Speak honestly. That's the best advice I can give," Remy said.

"I disagree. The more she tells, the more they'll ask. If you don't direct the press to avoid asking questions about Luke, then I'll do it," Bethany said.

Shay thought for a moment and then turned and looked at Bethany. "I think I should. I'll tell them the truth, that I don't have a relationship with him but wish him well and hope for his release."

Remy looked to Bethany. "They'll want to interview you as well."

Bethany took a moment to consider it and then looked to Shay. "Direct them to the statement you made on social media. I'll do the same. That's how we contain it."

Shay looked out of Remy's office window at the makeshift backdrop for NBC News. This was so unlike anything she imagined the day she made Team USA, and it would continue right until the moment she took to the ice in Beijing.

CHAPTER 10

Shay's stomach grumbled as a technician worked to get her lapel mic in place. Reflexively, she looked to the arena's exit. She wanted to run. But where? Right into another hornet's nest of reporters? No, she needed to remain calm and on point.

"Shay?"

The voice came from behind her, but she didn't turn until the technician completed her work. "Yes?"

The tech smiled. "You're good," she said and walked back toward the cameraman.

Shay turned and saw a woman with piercing green eyes smiling at her. She extended her hand. "Haley Edwards, NBC News."

Shay rubbed her palm on her thigh and shook Haley's hand. "Hi. Sorry, I'm just—"

"Nervous a bit?" Haley asked.

"A little."

"It's been a crazy thirty-six hours for you. You're fine. We're just two girls having a conversation. Follow me." Haley indicated one of two chairs positioned in front of a backdrop with the Olympic Rings and the NBC logo on it.

Shay walked onto the makeshift set. The heat of the television lights felt good, and when she sat and looked into the camera, the shift in her breathing and pulse surprised her. A sense of calm washed over her. Shay glanced at her mother, who stood off to the side and gave Shay a thumbs-up. She was ready.

Haley took her seat and introduced the audience to Shay. The first several questions were about making Team USA. "You shocked everyone with your stellar performance at nationals. How are you feeling about your chances at the Games?"

Shay shifted in her seat. "Good. I mean, the competition is really strong, and I'm just honored to be able to represent my country and the city of Detroit."

"It seems Ling Yue of China will be a real hurdle. She is the first female skater to successfully perform a quadruple jump in competition."

"Yes. She's an amazing athlete, very strong when it comes to her jumps. She's a formidable presence on the ice, and I'm looking forward to competing against her at the Games."

"Will you include a quad?"

Shay's eyes flicked to Remy and then settled back on Haley. "I'd like to keep them guessing on that one."

Remy smiled and gave Shay a thumbs-up.

"Fair enough."

Haley shifted gears. "Would it be okay to ask about your father?"

Shay's throat went dry. She reached for the bottle of water on the table between them, smiled awkwardly, and took a sip. Every muscle in her body tensed.

"There's not much I can say…that I'm allowed to say. We weren't close. I wish him well." Shay took another sip of water. Her hands trembled. Beads of sweat gathered on her forehead.

"You're aware of the Chinese crackdown on Christians. Of the persecution?"

Shay's heart throttled in her chest.

"This must be hard for you," Haley said, "to have your father jailed in the county you're about to skate in."

Shay's lips quivered. "He was just attending a church," she whispered.

"Stop rolling that camera!" Bethany screamed and marched onto the set. "This isn't about Luke Gerrard. This is about us! This is our journey, and if Luke wanted any part of it, he had years to make that known!"

"Ms. Dawsey, please step away," Haley Edwards said.

"I'll do no such thing!" Bethany screamed.

The cameras never stopped rolling. This was the high-drama news organizations dreamed of. The interview stopped, but the damage was done. By seven that night, the segment was all over television and social media, painting Shay as a confused young woman and Bethany as an unhinged stage mother.

Bethany waited until they were in Remy's office before unleashing a tirade. "This is your fault, Remy! Your idea! I hold you accountable!" she raged, pointing a finger just inches from Remy's face.

"Mom!" Shay yelled.

"I'm seriously considering dropping you for another coach, and it would be more than a consideration if we weren't this close to the Olympics!"

Remy's eyes burned with indignation. "You wouldn't need to. If it weren't for Shay, I'd volunteer to get as far away from you as I could, and after your performance just now, you wouldn't get a reputable coach to have anything to do with you. I have news, Bethany. This isn't about you, and if you care about Shay and her chances in the Games, you'll back off. Now, if you'll excuse me, I'm about to be interviewed."

Before the night was over, the interview with Shay and Bethany's wild outburst on the set was national news. Most expressed a level of sympathy for Shay's detached response when asked about her father's imprisonment, but Bethany was portrayed as the worst kind of stage mother. It hurt Shay. Her mother could be demanding, but Shay knew Bethany loved her and wanted only the best for her. Why couldn't people see that? Why were they all being so cruel? The commentators said nothing of her mother's hard work and sacrifice, not a word about being a single mother raising her daughter to become a member of Team USA. When Luke shattered their lives with his addiction, it was her mother who was left to pick up the pieces. Now she was being vilified, and Shay felt powerless to stop it.

The next morning, Bethany fumed as she tossed the remaining coffee in her cup into the sink. "He almost ruined me once, and he's at it again." Bethany gathered her keys and pocketbook.

"It'll be all right, Mom, you'll see."

"Seven years, and now he pushes himself back into our lives. Not another word to the press, agreed?"

"Agreed," Shay said.

Bethany walked toward the door. "We need to get going."

"There was a time..." Shay hesitated. "You loved him once. Right?"

Bethany paused but kept her back to Shay as she considered her answer and then turned. "I didn't give up on Luke, Shay. He gave up on me and, shamefully, on you. I held no grudge. I moved on. And he repays us with a selfish need to be the center of attention. We leave for Beijing in twenty-nine days. We need to power through this and stay laser-focused on skating our best at the Olympics. We owe it to each other and to the country."

They left together, ignoring the reporters who waited for them on the street. Despite Shay's protests, Bethany insisted on driving Shay to the rink. As Shay listened to the music pumping through her earbuds, the encounter she had with Jack flashed in her mind.

God, are you stalking me? she had asked.

He might be, Jack had responded, *but I wouldn't call it stalking. More like nudging. Tapping you on the shoulder. Just remember, God loves you, Frank. Don't forget that.*

Then there was Adley's proclamation: "It's the universe, don't you see! It's talking to you!"

"Ridiculous," Shay muttered.

"What?" Bethany asked.

"Nothing," Shay said.

But she knew at that moment, she wanted to talk to Jack. She needed answers.

CHAPTER 11

Most Olympic-level skaters used designers to make their costumes, and Shay was no exception. Jules, of jules k., had agreed to design her Olympic outfit; and today was Shay's first opportunity to try it on while performing her routine. Jules insisted on several practice runs to ensure the comfort and utility of the dress. Shay and Bethany were both thrilled with the jules k. concept. The dress was midnight blue mesh over Lycra with over a thousand crystals sewn in. When Shay appeared from the locker room in her outfit, Remy could not hold back her excitement.

"Wow, that's stunning!"

Bethany, who owned every jules k. handbag ever made, had the same response. "That will dazzle on the ice. Simple and sophisticated. It's beautiful! How does it feel?"

Shay moved around, stretching into various poses before commenting. "It feels awesome."

"Let's get on the ice and run your program," Remy said.

Shay was about to sit down and put her skates on when she heard Adley's voice.

"Aye, aye, matey!" Adley said and waved to Shay from atop the Zamboni.

Adley was standing next to Jack as he steered the Zamboni beside the rail and stopped.

"That outfit's an eyepopper!" Adley said.

Shay was still trying to process the fact that Adley was with Jack.

Adley waved to Shay. "Talk to you right after practice, okay. Carry on, Captain!" Adley said, pointing the way forward as if she and Jack were about to embark on a long journey.

"Yes, ma'am," Jack replied, making a last pass with the Zamboni before exiting the ice.

Bethany looked to Shay. "What's Adley doing here?"

"Moral support," Shay said and finished lacing her skates.

Shay began her warm-up, a process as choreographed as her competitive routine. Having a plan ensured no time was wasted and no critical element was missed. Opening pose, hit spins and spirals, and then jumps. The ice was fast, the kind hockey and speed skaters love and figure skaters despise. Figure skaters do best on warm, supple ice; and Shay sensed she would have to be more precise in her footing. The ice was hard. Great for speed, not great for cutting edges and holding landings. On the positive side, her ankle felt better than it had in days. The trick was to ensure it stayed that way. Before going on the ice, Remy gave Shay last-minute instructions on her triple-triple combination, one of the most difficult, the Lutz-loop. Because of the edging, there was no room for error.

"What's our mantra?" she asked.

"A little difference makes a lot of difference."

"Especially with that combination. A degree tighter in the arms will give you the spin rate you need. Less than that will cause you to short it, a major deduction."

The mantra "A little difference makes a lot of difference" applied to all aspects of Shay's skating. Remy was firm in the belief that the gap between first and eighth place at the Olympic level of skating was minuscule. Details mattered. Slight variations in thought or technique separated the skater's sitting in the stands from those standing on the podium. A little more effort, a little more concentration, a little more focus—that was the ticket to world and Olympic-level success.

The dress felt terrific. Shay moved across the ice with the lightness, power, and speed judges looked for. She successfully completed most of her elements. Only the triple-triple remained. As she approached the takeoff, she reminded herself to draw her arms in tight. She landed the combination solidly with superb flow exiting the loop. Adley whooped it up as Shay headed off the ice.

"Yes, Shay Gerrard, next Olympic Champion!" Adley yelled.

Jack and Adley sat together in stands watching Shay practice. Shay wasn't surprised at how quickly Adley had befriended Jack. Connecting with people was Adley's strong point. Shay never met someone so comfortable in their own skin, a trait that resulted in other people feeling comfortable around Adley. As Shay often told her friend, "You could get the queen's guard to let their guard down."

Everything felt good. Shay was ready. Now she waited. For most skaters, this was the most stressful part of the competition. Managing it was critical. Remy insisted on replicating various wait times depending on Shay's order of skating. Today she would have to wait for thirty minutes before taking the ice to run through her long program. Depending on the draw, Shay had various strategies to execute between her warm-up and skate time. She would listen to her music through her headphones and visualize a flawless performance and then stretch and keep herself limber, still listening to her pre-skate playlist. When the last skater was two minutes into their routine, Remy would let her know it was time to skate and provide her with last-minute instructions.

In past years, she would run her programs back to back this close to a major competition, but the tendinitis in her ankle made that a risky strategy. If it flared up again, it could cause her to withdraw from the Games, and no one was in favor of taking that risk.

"It's time," Remy said. "You've got this. Let's try all the elements but focus on flow. How's the ankle?"

Shay flexed her foot and moved her ankle in a circular motion. "It's good."

Shay skated to center ice and stilled herself in her opening pose. She waited as Remy worked to replicate the variations that might occur during a real competition. She would sometimes start the music the moment Shay hit her pose and, at other times, waited five to ten seconds before engaging her music. Having a coach that paid meticulous attention to detail gave Shay confidence she was well-prepared to skate.

When the music began, Shay moved into several intricate turns and then powered into her opening jump, a triple Salchow. The take-off was faulty. The fast ice required more adjustments. Shay pulled off the landing, but her free leg swung wide, causing the jump to edge out and lose speed. When the ice was this hard, she had to battle to cut secure edges. The rest of the routine was less than stellar. No major falls, but aside from the triple toe loop and double Axel—the easiest in her program—her jumps were off. Frustrated by her performance, she skated to Remy with her head down and hands on her hips.

"Well, that's good. We needed to get that one out of the way," Remy said, doing her best to lighten the moment.

"The ice is fast," Shay said.

Remy could read her skaters. It was another one of her talents as a coach, the ability to sense when something was wrong. "You're dealing with a lot right now. Give yourself space. We'll figure it out, okay?"

"Do you believe in coincidences?" Shay asked abruptly.

"There's an out-of-the-blue question."

"Do you?"

Remy waited a moment before answering. "Yes, sure, there are things that happen randomly. But overall, I think people and circumstances are in our lives for a reason."

"Because God put them there," Shay said.

"Oh," Remy said, "this is about that."

"Adley doesn't believe in coincidences, and Jack thinks God is whispering in my ear."

"And what do you believe?"

"That's my problem. This is all so crazy. I'm not sure what to believe. Sometimes, things feel random, and other times, they don't."

"I wish I could give you the answer, but there are things you have to discover for yourself. I'd love to tell you being on the world stage at the same moment they arrested your father is no coincidence, but it doesn't matter what I believe, only what you believe."

"And if I don't know what I believe?" Shay asked.

"Then let your heart be open, and your answer will come. Now, back to the matter at hand. The costume looked amazing on the ice. How did it feel?"

"It's great. I don't think I've ever had anything fit this well or looked this good."

"Jules k. was a great choice. We stay the course, right?"

"Yes," Shay replied. Her eyes darted to Jack and Adley. "Can I go? I think I should rest my ankle until this afternoon's session."

"Yes, that sounds like a good idea. This afternoon, we'll focus on the short program. Warm up and run, just like we did with the long."

"Okay."

"And ice that ankle."

Shay removed her skates and walked straight to Jack and Adley.

"We met," Adley said, pointing to Jack.

"I see that." Shay looked at Jack, boring her eyes into his. "I need to talk to you."

Jack, Shay, and Adley went to Sacred Grounds, a coffee shop in town. Shay had to fend off some photographers on her way to Jack's car. The reporters realized that a sharp "no comment" was all they would get from Shay or her mother.

The coffee shop had a warm, inviting ambiance. When you walked inside, it felt like you were stepping into a cabin in the woods. The interior was all logs and beams, but it was the stone fireplace that made the shop a favorite of the locals. The crackle of the fire, the spicy aroma of burning wood, and the plank wood floor gave the shop a rustic feel. Adley's band played there every couple of months, so Adley did her best to patronize the business as often as she could. The trio ordered hot chocolates and scored a table near the window. Jack's hot chocolate had extra whipped cream, and after he sipped it, a white mustache settled on his upper lip. Shay waited for him to wipe it with a napkin, but Jack just left it there, adding to it as he sipped.

"So what do we need to talk about?" Jack asked.

"I need your word this will be a private conversation. No talking to the press about what I say. Agreed?"

"Sure," Adley said.

"Yeah, no problem," Jack replied.

Shay fixed her gaze on Jack. "So it appears my father went pedal-to-the-metal Jesus Freak, and I'm trying to understand how that happens to a person. I thought you might be able to help."

Jack grabbed a napkin and swept the whipped cream from his lip.

Adley's brows lifted. "Well, that was direct."

Jack smiled. "He's bugging you, isn't he?"

Shay rolled her eyes. "Know what? This is exactly why people get annoyed with 'the faithful.'" Shay used air quotes to emphasize her point. "I'm just trying to understand my father. If you can't help me without beating me over the head with God, then forget it." Shay pulled her eyes from his and sipped her hot chocolate.

Adley turned to Jack. "It's tough being America's Sweetheart twenty-four seven."

Shay glared at Adley.

"People come to believe in a million different ways. I can't tell you what drew him to God," Jack said.

"Fine. What drew you, then?" Shay asked.

"More like what drew me back. I grew up in church, but when I was fifteen, I started questioning everything, the whole notion of there being a God at all. I started experimenting with drugs. Nothing heavy but enough to get me in trouble."

"But then?" Adley asked.

"I realized I wasn't rebelling. I was conforming, falling in lockstep, and I'm not very good at that. My friends were following so-called rebels who really weren't rebels at all. Just a bunch of pretenders who risked nothing to take a so-called stand against their parents. That's why I turned back to my faith, to follow the one who truly risked it all and paid the price for it. Jesus. He turned the world upside down. Even now, to be a Christian in our world is to be a rebel, to live outside the culture."

"NOTW," Shay said.

"That's right. In this world but not of this world. Aliens. Strangers in a strange land," Jack said.

"I just don't understand why Luke, of all people, would risk everything like that," Shay said. "There's drinking the Kool-Aid. Then there's *really* drinking the Kool-Aid."

Adley turned to Jack. "Don't you just hate the way she beats around the bush?"

"A very sucky trait," Jack said.

"Maybe I don't have time for that," Shay said.

"If you want to know what inspired his faith, you need to find out more about his walk," Jack said.

"His walk?"

"His journey, what he went through in the past year to get him where he is," Jack said.

Shay thought of the business card the lady from the State Department gave her. Where had she put it? She pulled out her phone, reached behind the case, and retrieved it. "I have to make a call," she said and tapped the number into her phone.

CHAPTER 12

Twenty minutes later, Shay, Adley, and Jack were on their way to Hill Park, a suburb fifteen miles outside of Detroit. Shay got Luke's address from Maya Lopez, the State Department lady. They had gone to the coffee shop in Jack's car, and he volunteered to drive Shay to Luke's apartment. Shay saw the loose candy wrappers and empty soda cans strewn about inside the car and felt a need to comment. She lifted a Tootsie Roll wrapper and held it between her fingertips. "I thought cleanliness was next to Godliness?"

"Nowhere in the Bible," Jack said.

Shay let the wrapper fall from her fingers. "Or evidenced in your car."

"It gets away from me sometimes," Jack said, keeping his eyes riveted on the road ahead.

"It's trash, Jack, not your pet dog or bird or whatever," Shay said.

"I have a snake," Jack replied.

"Get…out!" Adley said, slapping Jack on the shoulder. "What's his name?"

"Floyd. Next, I'm in the market for a miniature donkey."

"Jack, Floyd, and Jackass. I can see it," Shay said.

Jack ignored Shay and glanced in the rearview mirror at Adley. "The snake in the garden of Eden and Balaam's donkey are the only two animals in the Bible who could speak."

"That's cool," Adley said, nodding like a bobblehead doll.

"It's ridiculous," Shay said.

Adley bristled. "No, it isn't."

Jack beamed. "See? It isn't."

"Adley also believes in Slender Man, Bigfoot, and the Tollbooth from Hell," Shay said.

"Really?"

"Truly."

Jack smiled. "A tollbooth makes perfect sense."

Shay tossed her head back against the headrest. "I'm in the company of crazy."

"For the wages of sin is death," Jack said. "Pay up."

Shay's eyes widened. "There!" she said, pointing to the apartment above the pawnshop she recognized from the TV spot. A sign on the window said, "Bebchuk's Pawn & Trade."

Jack parked the car. When Adley got out, she looked down and saw how far Jack had parked from the curb. "It's okay. We'll call Uber and get a lift to the curb."

Jack craned his neck toward the open passenger-side door. "That bad?"

"Not if you're okay parking in the middle of the street," Adley said.

Shay smirked. "Maybe you should let Jesus take the wheel."

"Funny," Jack said. "Give me a minute. I'll get closer."

Shay got out of the car and joined Adley on the sidewalk.

"We'll wait," Adley said and watched as Jack, after three attempts, managed to get within a foot of the curb.

Jack cut the engine and joined Shay and Adley on the sidewalk. "I'm a touch dyslexic," he said as if that explained everything.

"Color blind, dyslexic. Any other disabilities we should know about?" Shay asked.

"I'm a sinner," Jack said.

Adley laughed.

"Don't encourage him," Shay said.

They walked to the back of the pawnshop and found the stairs that led up to the second-floor apartment. "This isn't the best neighborhood, so I doubt the door's gonna be open," Adley said.

The wooden stairs were steep. A pair of battered garbage cans, a discarded mattress, and a rusted bicycle rested against the back of the building. The walls were littered with graffiti.

Shay led the way up. When they got to the landing, Shay tried the door but found it locked with a deadbolt.

"What now?" Adley asked.

"The pawnshop," Shay said. "The owner must be the landlord."

Just as she said it, they heard the sound of boots crunching in the snow and saw a burly giant of a man standing at the bottom of the stairs.

"Did we climb stairs or a beanstalk?" Adley whispered.

"You kids need to get down from stairs...right now," the man said. He had a heavy Russian accent and a raspy voice. His coat was too small to button, and the knit cap on his massive head was stretched to the brink.

"I was looking for my father," Shay said.

"Say?" the giant replied, not quite hearing her.

"I'm Shay Gerrard." Shay pointed at the apartment door. "Luke's daughter."

"It's her dad," Adley added as if he might need additional confirmation.

"Shay?" he asked.

"Yessir."

"Come in store," the man said. "I will give key...maybe. We will see." He turned himself, lifting each foot with effort, maneuvering like a battleship shifting at sea.

The store was small, and the giant was a megaton of a man that reminded Jack of the wrestler Andre the Giant. The store's low ceilings and tight isles enhanced the man's size.

"So you're daughter, eh? Is right? I need proof. Maybe you are newspaper, yes?"

"No," Shay said. She reached into her wallet and withdrew her driver's license. She handed it to him.

He studied the picture and then looked up at her. He did this several times as if he wasn't sure of the resemblance. Then he smiled. "You have his eyes, yes?"

"Yes," Shay said.

"I am Iosif Bebchuk," he said. "Your father and I, we are good friends. Very good. Like brothers. What tragedy this. I pray for him to be let go."

"Thanks," Shay said.

"The reporters come…every day. They try to get information. I refuse. No words from Iosif. They are like Pravda." Iosif emphasized "every day" and "no words" in a declarative cadence that broke his speech pattern.

Shay saw a large silver cross with intricate ornamentation hanging on the wall and felt an undertow of distaste. The idea that such a symbol would hang in a pawnshop tapped at her cynicism. She pulled her eyes from the cross and returned to Iosif. "Can we go in?"

Iosif reached beneath the counter and produced a keyring attached to a wooden plank. He set it on the counter. "Lock door when you leave. Check to be sure. Tight as drum. You are not the first to try and get in, yes?"

"Yes," Shay said, "we'll be sure to lock it and return the key."

"He talks about you. He has pride here," Iosif said, tapping his fist to his chest. "You see? For you. He'd say, 'My daughter is best skater in world. You will see this, Iosif."

Shay produced a faint smile. "Thanks for letting me know." Shay took the key, and the trio headed out into the cold.

The lock was frozen, and it took several tries before Shay was able to turn the key. Even then, the door fought back against being opened. Shay bumped it once with her shoulder, but the doorjamb refused to budge.

"Hey, America's hopeful, be careful with that shoulder," Adley said and rammed her own shoulder into the door. It creaked but didn't open. She turned to Jack.

"Your turn," she said.

Jack kicked the door with his boot. It flew open, slamming against the wall.

Shay stepped into the small apartment and scanned the space. It was a studio, functional but sparse, with a musty smell. The apartment felt like the inside of a freezer. Shay wrapped her arms around herself. It was clean and livable but a far cry from the upscale home Shay grew up in, a stark reminder of just how far Luke had fallen.

"Not exactly the Ritz," Adley said.

The tiny kitchen had a stove, a sink, and a microwave resting on a yellow Formica countertop. The cabinets were walnut colored with porcelain knobs; and the linoleum floor in front of the sink, an institutional green, was worn down to bare wood. The wallpaper, a faded vintage floral design, did little to temper the apartment's bleak vibe. It had a distinct retro feel, as if time had stopped, a thought reinforced by the clock on the kitchen wall. Shay's hands were cold, but the clock's hands were frozen. A musty odor pervaded the space.

"Why is that creepy?" Adley asked, pointing at the timeworn blue fabric recliner resting in the middle of the room, its footrest extended as if the chair itself was in repose.

"No television," Jack said. He walked to the tray table beside the chair and picked up the framed photograph of a little girl atop her father's shoulders, both caught in the midst of laughter. Jack's gaze lifted. His eyes met Shay's. He extended the picture to her. She paused. Adley took the picture from Jack and handed it to Shay.

"He kept you near him," Adley said.

Shay hesitated and then took the picture from Adley. Her other hand went reflexively to her heart when she saw herself at age five, laughing as she sat atop Luke's shoulders. She fought to control the wave of emotion washing over her. On a tiny piece of paper stuck in the bottom of the frame, Luke had written, "My baby girl." Shay's lips pursed. She handed the picture back to Adley. "It was a long time ago."

Jack picked up the only other item on the tray table, a small book—the leather cover worn and its pages dog-eared, evidence of frequent use.

"Is that a journal?" Shay asked.

"A devotional. Daily readings about scripture."

"Oh," Shay replied, disappointed. She hated to admit it, even to herself, but she wanted to know more about her dad, and finding a journal would have been a goldmine.

Shay went right for the kitchen cabinets, searching for evidence of her own. She expected to find bottles of alcohol but found nothing but canned goods and other nonperishable items. She checked the refrigerator. No alcohol. Just condiments, a jar of pickles, and a half-empty bottle of Diet Dr. Pepper.

Adley peered over her shoulder. "I'll have a swig of that," she said, pointing at the soda bottle.

"It's flat," Shay said.

"Just how I like it." Adley took the bottle from the fridge, uncapped it, and drank. Shay looked to Jack with a "Can you believe it?" expression and walked toward the bedroom.

Shay paused a moment, pushed the door open, and gasped.

CHAPTER 13

J ack and Adley rushed to Shay's side and saw the disembodied image radiating in the darkness.

"Whoa," Adley whispered.

"What is it?" Shay asked, her voice tight.

"The *Shroud of Turin*," Jack said. "It's under a black light. Your dad must have missed turning it off or left it on purposely to scare intruders." Jack flipped the bedroom light on, and the poster-sized image hanging on the wall above Luke's bed ceased to glow.

Shay was entranced.

"It's a reproduction of what many believe to be the burial shroud of Christ. It's one of the most viewed images in the world," Jack said.

Adley stepped closer to examine it. "Supercool," she whispered.

"It's a photographic negative," Jack said, "historically accurate to the methods of crucifixion at that time."

Shay walked to the light switch, never moving her eyes from the poster, and turned it off again. Beneath the black light, the facial characteristics of the image became more distinct. Shay felt herself being drawn toward it, or was the image moving toward her? There was something unmistakably captivating about the image.

Jack stepped up alongside Adley. "After Jesus was crucified, the Gospels state that Jesus was wrapped in a piece of linen cloth before being placed in the tomb."

"Do you believe it? That it's really the one they buried him in?" Shay asked.

"This is so out there. I need to talk about this on my podcast," Adley said.

"There's conflicting evidence, but I think it's real," Jack said. "There are over a hundred whip marks on every portion of the body.

Jesus was whipped before he was crucified. And bloodstains form a circle around the man's head. This would account for the crown of thorns pressed down on Jesus's head. It's the most analyzed artifact in the world."

"But you only *think* it's real," Shay said. "Not exactly a ten on the believer meter, Jack."

"I'm talking about the authenticity of the Shroud."

"Real or not, it's giving me the best creeps I've had in months," Adley said. "It's... I don't know how to explain it... weirdly captivating."

"Many believe it's evidence of Jesus being resurrected from the dead."

"Like a zombie," Adley said with a measure of awe in her voice.

Jack scoffed. "I'm not an expert on zombies, but Jesus came back as he was *before* they crucified him. Fully alive."

Jack's comment had the effect of disarming the Shroud's hold on Shay. "Right up there with pigs that fly," she said and flipped on the light. "And snakes and donkeys that talk. I need to get back. If I'm not at practice in thirty minutes, my mother will go into panic mode."

Jack and Adley got in the car. Shay went into the store to return the key to Iosif. She found him laughing as he watched a twelve-inch TV on the glass counter of the shop.

"Thanks," she said and set the key on the counter. "We locked up."

Iosif pointed at the TV. "*I Love Lucy*. Who doesn't love Lucy, yes?"

"Yes, well, thanks again. I need to go."

"Your father, he loves you. You should know this," Iosif said.

"Yeah, well, he's had an odd way of showing it."

"Sometimes, people lose their way. Pressure of life can be heavy... for some, too much. We are broken people in fallen world, yes?"

Shay wanted to agree with Iosif for no other reason than she sensed he was kind.

"I guess," was the best she could muster.

On the ride back to the arena, Shay couldn't get the Shroud out of her mind. It wasn't unusual for visual images that intrigued her to linger; but this felt different, like an x-ray plate embedded in the soft tissue of her brain, dark, bright, and strangely radioactive.

"You okay?" Adley asked.

"Yeah, fine," Shay said. But her mind drifted back to the image and then to Luke. *You were just twenty minutes away*, she thought.

"That was a great picture of you and your dad," Jack said as if he could read her thoughts.

Shay tucked a strand of hair behind her ear. "We were in the backyard. He would put me on his shoulders and say, 'Reach for the stars, baby girl. Always reach for the stars.'" For a moment, Shay felt like she was five again. She could hear the echo of her laughter and feel her arms as they stretched toward the sky. "It was fun back then, when he could be my dad."

As Jack pulled the VW into the arena parking lot, Shay spotted her mother's Lexus. "If my mother asks, we were at Sacred Grounds the whole time."

Jack parked. Adley stepped out of the car and looked down. "Right between the stripes on one try. Nice work, Captain."

Shay headed into the arena with Jack and Adley. Bethany was standing in the lobby, waiting. "Where were you?" she asked as soon as Shay walked through the door.

"At Sacred Grounds with Adley and Jack."

Bethany ushered Shay away from her friends. "It's not in our best interest for you to be socializing with Adley and the Zamboni boy. Lord knows what could come out of Adley's mouth, and he looks like one of those Gothic weirdos."

Shay was about to mount a protest but thought better of it. Private ice time was expensive, and she had six minutes until the ice was hers. She would bring it up later. She wasn't about to ignore her friends, especially Adley, who was like a sister to her. And there was something about Jack that intrigued her. Like Adley, he was so comfortable with who he was and what he believed, and she needed him to help her understand Luke.

"You should see how they're portraying me on the news," Bethany said. "Suddenly, your father's Saint Luke and I'm Cruella

DeVille. Thank goodness I drive a Lexus, or they'd be calling me Cruella DeVille in her Coup De Ville."

Shay suppressed a laugh; and even Bethany, who wasn't one to find humor in things, smiled.

"It has a ring to it," Shay said, teasing her mother.

Bethany pulled her shoulders back. "I'll embrace it. No sense in trying to prove them wrong."

"I'm here because of you. You're the reason I have this chance."

Bethany pulled Shay close. "Be careful, or you'll tarnish Cruella's image."

"Oh, right. Just between us then," Shay whispered.

Shay was determined to focus on the day's practice, to ignore the emotional cyclone swirling around her, and to prove she had the psychological grit to conquer the distractions. The key was her ability to replace negative thoughts with positive visualization. She wanted to manage her stress, not eliminate it. Too much pressure caused her muscles to tense up, and too little left her muscles passive, slowing her reaction time. She clenched and released her fists, regulated her breathing, and visualized a successful run of her short program. She stood up and felt a slight ache in her ankle. Between her time at Sacred Grounds and then at Luke's apartment, she hadn't had time to ice it.

Remy came out of her office and joined Shay by the rail. "Not wearing the competition costume for the short?"

The encounter at Luke's apartment had caused Shay to forget about testing her competition outfit during both competition programs.

"It's in my office. You ran out of the arena and left both costumes behind."

"Do I have time to change?"

"Yes. This afternoon is stretch, warm up, and run the short. We need to test the costume because…"

"A little difference makes a lot of difference," Shay said, completing their mantra.

"Exactly."

Remy's obsession with details could be annoying. Still, Shay had ignored Remy's advice by not icing her ankle between sessions and thought it would be bad karma to ignore her again. *Bad karma*, she thought. *Listen to yourself, Shay. You're as Twilight Zone as Adley.* Shay changed outfits and was back on the ice in less than ten minutes. She thought about Luke again and the enigmatic image that hung above his bed. *I need a Zamboni for my mind to erase this madness.* Losing focus also let her know her process was fragile and how easily she could be knocked off her game.

Focus. Visualize. See it happening.

Shay moved through her choreographed warm-up, completing all the elements, and then joined Remy by the rail for last-minute instructions. Today, she would skate as if she had drawn the first position. For the short program, she preferred first since stamina wasn't an issue, and her nerves had little time to unsettle her.

"You're ready. It's time to enjoy the moment. Tuck tight on the Lutz. You've got this," Remy said and sent Shay to center ice.

Shay struck her opening pose and waited for her music to begin. This time, Remy waited a full ten seconds before pressing play, a skater's eternity, but Shay held her position, moving fluidly when the music began. The ice felt better, more secure. Shay edged into her footwork and felt the steel blades bite into the ice. She felt "very Ginger Rogers," a comment Remy made whenever she witnessed perfect flow in the brackets, counters, and rockers that comprised Shay's opening footwork sequence. Shay had no idea who Ginger Rogers was at first, but Remy made her rising star watch films of Ginger Rogers dancing with Fred Astaire. "Like there's nothing beneath their feet. That's flow. That's perfection."

"Bend your knees!" Remy said. "Settle in!"

Shay's blades ripped at the ice as she accelerated across the surface, each backward crosscut increasing her speed. In a single fluid motion, she swiveled her torso and stepped into her forward spiral, extending her leg high above her head, spreading her arms like wings, and tipping her body even farther forward until her free leg was directly above her. Cold air swept over her face. She made the move appear effortless. That was the goal, to put the synthesis of athleticism and artistry on full display. Shay flowed from one move to the next with seamless skill. Her next element was the double Axel. Shay stepped into the takeoff, but her free leg was late in relation to her timing, and she stepped out of the jump, something that rarely happened on the double Axel. Shay continued to perform her camel-sit-camel and then her layback spin before entering the most difficult element, the triple Lutz, triple loop. She picked up speed and focused on the entry, a deep left back-outer edge, before catapulting herself into the air by hitting her right toe pick. The takeoff felt right, but she failed to maintain a tight, low free leg, a position that slowed the speed of rotation and caused her to short the Lutz. It was futile to attempt the triple loop from this position, so the combination was a loss. She continued through the rest of the program, hitting the triple flip, but once again, the landing was less than stellar. Her performances in both the long and short program had been a disaster.

Shay glided back to Remy.

"It's okay," Remy said. "We'll work through it. You're a little off today."

Bethany, who had been in her usual spot on the other side of the rink, was beside them in a heartbeat.

"What was that, Shay? A double Axel?"

Remy glared at Bethany. "She'll be fine. Her concentration—"

"Don't patronize me, Remy! She has never missed that many required elements before, not in any program ever! She is backsliding, and I hold you responsible!"

Remy's eyes bored into Bethany's. "This is not the time for this, do you understand me?"

Bethany stiffened. "This is it for you. After the Games, you're finished. We should have moved on to a proven world-level coach years ago. I warned Shay about the price of misplaced loyalty. Now I realize I should have heeded my own words!"

"Mom, stop it. It's not her fault!"

Remy looked down at Bethany's spiked heels. "Just in case you're confused, those are pumps your feet are jammed into, not boots, and they have spikes, not blades. I don't tell you how to sell real estate, and you will not tell me how to coach my skaters. Find a new coach whenever you like, but until that time, butt out!" That said, Remy turned her back to Bethany and walked back to her office.

CHAPTER 14

S hay felt like an eggshell on the verge of cracking, a feeling so alien to her she wasn't sure how to process it. She had a talent for remaining calm before competitions, an inherent gift that allowed her to steer clear of the emotional tempests that rattled other skaters. But this typhoon had unnerved her to the core. It wasn't enough she was about to skate in the Olympics—add her father's arrest, the blowup between her mother and her coach, and the onslaught of the press regarding her relationship with her father—and it was a wonder she could skate at all. The ride home didn't help. The tug-of-war between Remy and her mother had reached a point where both were pulling as hard as they could, and Shay was the rope between them taut and ready to snap.

"The gall of that woman!" Bethany said. She clutched the steering wheel like it was a neck she was choking the life out of. "The moment the Olympics are over, she's done!"

Shay didn't respond. When Bethany's temper was at a fever pitch, the best strategy was to let it burn itself out. Shay kept her eyes closed and bobbed her head to the beat of her playlist to enhance being in her own world.

When they got to the house, Shay got the ice pack and went to her bedroom. Feeling unmoored, she lay on her bed and put the ice pack across her ankle. She had exchanged texts with Curt earlier in the day. Like her, he was immersed in training, working out in the gym, and practicing on the ice. Shay imagined herself in that goalie cage getting hammered with a hundred pucks flying at her from all directions. Amidst the chaos of her thoughts, a single image bled through—the enigmatic picture of the man's face in the burial cloth known as the Shroud of Turin. It was amorphous, yet there was something compelling about the image. Shay went to her computer and entered "Shroud of Turin" into her search engine. A moment later, she had thousands of hits and selected several articles with information about the Shroud. It was clear there was passionate disagreement about the Shroud's authenticity. There were powers on both sides of the argument with a vested interest in validating or discrediting it. Was it a medieval fake or a relic of Jesus Christ? Radiocarbon dating in the 1980s suggested the Shroud dated between AD 1260 and AD 1390. Still, critics contend the researchers used patched-up parts of the cloth to date the samples, and each would have been much younger than the rest of the garment. A prominent priest also stated the Gospel of Matthew clarified that "the earth shook, the rocks split, and the tombs broke open after Jesus was crucified, so even geologists admit an earthquake at Jesus' death could have released a neutron blast that would throw off radiocarbon dating and could have led to the darkened imprint on the Shroud." Nonbelievers, including many notable scientists, stood by the carbon dating results and proclaimed the cloth to be a forgery.

"They make that claim, but the image in the cloth is not a stain, nor is it painted on the Shroud. The image is seared into the cloth with a technology not yet explained," a priest argued. "How could it have been forged with medieval technologies when modern technologies won't do?"

It was clear it would remain an ongoing controversy. What was incontrovertible was Luke's belief in the Shroud's veracity. It wasn't logical to believe he would hang the image above his bed if he didn't think it was real. Was the Shroud the thing that sent him over the edge? She remembered what Jack told her—*One image can change the world.*

If one image could change the world, it had the power to influence one man, especially if he was weak and in need of something to believe in. Isn't that what happened with most people who "found God"? *How many get religion when their circumstances are dire? When they need something, anything, to hold on to?*

Shay found it hard to believe the Shroud was real, but the image was etched in her mind, and she knew there was only one way to erase it. She headed to her drawing table and got a text from Adley reminding Shay that Adley's podcast *Paranormal Happenings for Paranormal People* was about to begin. Adley had rigged her phone so people could call in. Shay grabbed her phone, put in her earbuds, and found the link. A moment later, she was drawing as she listened to Adley's podcast.

"This is Adley Atkinson coming to you *alive* from her top-secret bunker in an undisclosed location in the suburbs of Detroit."

Shay smiled. Adley's "top-secret bunker" was located in her basement, but Adley had a talent for creating suspense by varying the tone of her voice.

"Tonight, loyal listeners, we're inviting calls from the franchised, the disenfranchised, and most importantly, true believers in the para-normal. Speaking of which, yours truly had an encounter in the last twenty-four hours with an eerie, disembodied image that blew the needle off my heebie-jeebies meter, but that's a story for another show. Tonight, we're exploring the infamous Tollbooth from Hell, the phantom tollbooth that appears late at night on Route 66. Join me for a mind-bending evening of the otherworldly on *Paranormal Happenings for Paranormal People.*"

Shay thought all the callers were as crazy as Adley, but she enjoyed listening to Adley's program, and especially to the callers, many of whom Shay thought unhinged. The younger ones were entertaining. The older ones, callers Adley referred to as the X-Filers, were downright creepy. How anyone beyond the age of thirty could believe in Sasquatch and still get a driver's license was a mystery to Shay.

As she listened to the podcast, Shay sketched the amorphous face of the ancient man embedded in the Shroud. Much as it had beneath the glow of the black light earlier that day, the image floated untethered in her mind's eye. Shay's hand moved with precision as she translated the picture onto the page.

The first call-in to Adley's podcast was definitely an X-Filer.

"It happened to me, just after midnight on old Route 66," the caller said. The man had the gravelly voice of a chain-smoker. "I headed out past Winslow. Got myself on Old 66, just cruising along jammin' to some oldies when it come out of nowhere, just appeared before me like it had been there all along. But the thing is, missy… it wasn't!"

"Wow, that's radical," Adley said. "So, what happened?"

"I slammed them brakes o' mine down so hard I practically pushed my boot through the floorboard! Then I turned and burned. I wasn't about to pay my way into hell, no-sir-e-Bobbsey twins!"

Shay worked the drawing as several more callers made outlandish claims about spotting the tollbooth when a young male voice got on the line.

"Hello there," Adley said. "Who do I have the pleasure of speaking with?"

"Jack," the caller said.

Shay stopped drawing. The voice sounded like Jack's. Why would a Christian be listening to a paranormal podcast? Wasn't that blasphemy or something?

"Welcome to the program, Jack. Are you calling about an experience you had with the Phantom Tollbooth from Hell?"

"No. I've never been on Route 66."

"But you'd like to comment on it?"

"I don't think it exists, if that's what you're asking."

"So you don't believe in the supernatural?"

"Oh, I definitely believe in the supernatural."

Shay grabbed her phone and sent a text to Adley, "It's CAPTAIN JACK!"

Adley continued, "I see. But not the tollbooth?"

"No," Jack said. "But I do believe in the authenticity of the disembodied image you spoke of earlier."

Shay texted Adley, "TOLD YOU!"

Adley spoke to her audience: "Full disclosure to my audience, the caller on the line, me, and a close friend of mine were together earlier today when we saw what appeared to be the disembodied image of a man under a black light."

"Not just any man," Jack said. "Many people believe it to be the burial shroud of the risen Christ."

Adley liked Jack but knew the last thing her audience wanted to hear was a Jesus Freak, a fact confirmed by the rash of negative comments now flashing on her social media platforms, begging her to disconnect him.

"He's a Bible-thumper. Cut him off!"

"Christian interloper!"

"I feel like I'm going through the tollbooth right now! Hang up!"

"You're a good guy, Jack, but this is a paranormal podcast and—"

"And I'm talking about a man who was raised from the dead. Is that, or is that not, supernatural?"

"If you believe it, but this isn't a religious podcast."

"I'm not talking about religion. I'm talking about a dead man who came back to life. I guess I'm confused by people who believe in Phantom Tollbooths, Slender Man, and Sasquatch but have no interest in a man who actually walked the earth, was crucified, and came back to—"

Adley disconnected. Her social media platforms were blowing up. "Oh, wow, it looks like I lost the connection with that caller."

Shay texted Adley, "SMART MOVE!"

Shay's eyes were drawn back to her sketch pad. The image was complete, yet she barely recalled drawing it. Stunned by the accuracy of her reproduction, she found herself drawn into the cryptic impression embedded in the cloth. Why was this image so compelling? Immersed in the drawing, she failed to hear the bedroom door open behind her. It was Bethany, and her mother's eyes locked on Shay's sketch of the Shroud.

CHAPTER 15

"What is that?" Bethany asked, her eyes fixated on Shay's sketch.

Shay flipped the page of her sketchbook to a blank sheet. "Just doodling. Callers into Adley's podcast started talking about strange relics and brought up that one."

"And what strange relic is it?"

Shay lifted her arms and wiggled her fingers. "The Shroud," she said in a melodramatic voice. "Adley's podcast is about the paranormal. Sasquatch. Bigfoot. UFOs."

"Life seems paranormal at this point," Bethany said. "I got a call this evening from Ms. Lopez. She informed me the State Department was in negotiations to have your father released, and they feel progress is being made."

"Oh, well, that's good, right?"

"But there's a sticking point. See if you can guess what the sticking point might be."

Shay shrugged. "I have no idea. They want money? Some trade thing we're not willing to budge on?"

Bethany laughed. "If only."

"Then what?"

"Try your father. Saint Luke has decided to play the martyr to the hilt."

"I don't understand?"

"Welcome to the club. I have no idea what makes religious zealots do what they do. But your father, the Saint of Detroit—that's actually what the TV anchor on NBC News called him tonight—is refusing to be released unless his pastor friend is released at the same time. And now, thanks to your father, this has become an international story."

Shay picked up her phone and noticed the onslaught of hits to her social media accounts.

Bethany walked to the mirror and examined her face. "Ghastly. All this stress." She turned to Shay. "They have asked us to meet with the Olympic Committee spokesperson to discuss a strategy for handling the press. It appears the Saint of Detroit is hell-bent on turning this into a grand spectacle. Imagine that." Bethany forced a smile. "It's nothing we can't handle, right? This is about us, our journey and our future. You stay focused on skating, and I'll stay focused on running interference with the media. Deal?"

"Deal," Shay said.

Bethany kissed Shay's cheek. "Get some sleep."

"I will."

"And stop listening to Adley's podcast. People are losing their minds."

Shay waited for Bethany to leave the room before reading some of the thousands of posts hitting her social media accounts. A few disparaged Luke, expressing their displeasure that his antics were bringing politics into the Games. But most responded with promises of prayer, and the Christian community was supportive of Luke's refusal to be released without the release of Pastor Jin Chen, the de facto leader of those who opposed the Chinese government's crackdown on Christians. Shay got on the Internet and began to read about Pastor Chen. One article declared,

> A secret Chinese court has sentenced Pastor Chen to ten years in prison for "subversion of state power." Pastor Chen has been an outspoken voice of some of China's past atrocities, including the massacre in Tiananmen Square in 1989, and forced abortions that went on for many years. Pastor Chen fears that recent crackdowns on churches are a harbinger of evil things to come, and his fears have not gone unfounded.

Shay recoiled. *Forced abortions? Did that truly happen?* It seemed inconceivable to her, but there it was in black and white. The mere thought of it seemed like something out of a horror film. She kept reading. The Chinese government was arresting pastors, bulldozing churches, and even going so far as to "rewrite the Bible" to align with government thinking. It all seemed so unreal to her. Now? In this day and age? How could this even be possible?

Shay lifted the blank sheet of paper from her sketch pad and gazed at her sketch of the Shroud. It seemed the more she tried to avoid looking at it, the more power it had over her. *My pink elephant*, she thought. She posted several comments in response to statements being made on her accounts. "Thanks for all the prayers and good wishes. My goal is to stay focused on my skating while remaining hopeful my father and Pastor Chen will be released soon." As she read about Pastor Chen's passion for his faith, she thought about Luke. Had the man known in college as Lukewarm suddenly found something to be passionate about besides selling and becoming addicted to prescription drugs? What happened to Luke that caused his sudden turn from drug addict to a follower of Christ? The image of the Shroud came back to mind. "You're not going to leave me alone, are you?" she whispered. Shay needed to find out what changed in Luke and why. Tomorrow, she would visit her father's pastor.

Twenty-eight days until Olympic skate

Radiant sunlight blared through Shay's alcove window. An arctic cold front had moved into Detroit. If you factored in the windchill, minus two degrees was the order of the day. Shay dressed and checked her phone to find three text messages from Curt, and she realized she had forgotten to call or text him last night. She tapped a message into her phone: "SORRY. FELL ASLEEP EARLY. LU."

Bethany called to Shay from the kitchen, "Shay, are you up?"

"Coming!" Shay met her mother in the kitchen. "Morning," Shay said.

"I made your protein shake. We need to get going. There's an army of reporters, satellite trucks and all, in the road out by the gate. I'm sure our neighbors are thrilled."

"I'll follow you," Shay said. "I'm meeting Curt for lunch after practice, and then I might go for a massage."

Bethany sighed. "I wish the Games were closer. The next three weeks will be crazy, thanks to your father. I have to give him credit. He's single-handedly created an international incident and involves his only child in the process. I'm not in favor of you driving yourself, but if that's what you want, follow me to the arena."

Shay hated misleading her mom about lunch and the massage, but Bethany would go into full meltdown mode if she knew Shay was involving herself with Luke or his situation.

Shay followed Bethany out of the neighborhood and past an army of news vans and satellite trucks. Shay's heart rate sped up as reporters thrust their microphones at her car as if they thought the BMW could speak. Did they really believe Shay would stop, get out of her car, and hold a press conference? Shay had a sudden appreciation for celebrities and their love-hate relationship with the press. Relief washed over her the moment her BMW made its way past the reporters and entered the freeway. Shay and Bethany were scheduled to meet with the media representative from the Olympic Committee at the arena. Shay's private practice would follow. She had three hours and intended to make the best of it.

When they arrived, Shay and Bethany navigated the press gauntlet with several terse "no comments" and made their way into the arena and then, inside, to Remy's office where the media rep for the Olympic Committee was waiting.

Carla Brunetti, sharply dressed in a red-and-black designer pants suit, extended her hand with a practiced smile. Bethany was taken aback by how young the woman looked, but her demeanor gave a confident and skilled first impression.

"Hi, you must be Shay," Carla said, shaking Shay's hand before shifting her attention to Bethany.

"And you must be—"

"Bethany Dawsey," Bethany replied.

"You two look like twins," Carla said.

A smile bloomed on Bethany's face. "Thank you."

"I've already met Remy, so I think it best we get started so Shay can get back to what's most important, her practice and preparation for the Games," Carla said. "I know this situation was unexpected, but—"

"It's not a situation. It's a sideshow," Bethany said. "If this keeps up, we'll be competing with the Harding-Kerrigan fiasco."

"Not our best moment," Carla said. "But if we manage this properly, we can avoid the circus atmosphere that transpired in 1994."

"How?" Shay asked.

"We can use the fact that this has international implications to our advantage. It is accurate to state that commenting would be inappropriate when one considers the ongoing negotiations between our government and the government of China. That being said, the personal aspects of this story are compelling, so it may benefit you to set up a time each week for Shay to make herself accessible to answer questions unrelated to Mr. Gerrard. If they ask questions related to his imprisonment, Shay can restate that she cannot comment, as per the State Department."

Bethany's facial muscles tightened. "With all due respect, Ms. Brunetti, the 'no comment' strategy has been a dismal failure. Is this the best you can do?"

Carla's eyes narrowed. Like a boxer hit with a moderate jab, she absorbed the blow and then responded, "I have also spoken to the State Department. Their media relations arm will hold a weekly press conference, at a separate time and location, to update the press on the situation." Carla addressed Shay directly, "Once you're in the Olympic Village, we can control press access, so when you arrive in Beijing, we advise you to remain in the Village at all times."

"I want to do what all the other athletes do," Shay said.

Carla's brows lifted. "Well, ultimately, it will be up to you." Carla looked at Bethany. "Given the fact Shay is a strong contender for a medal, you might hire a publicist. It's not uncommon for athletes with possible endorsements and other financial opportunities to have their public image controlled and protected by a professional."

"I'm not in favor of that," Bethany said.

"It's your choice. I'm just making suggestions." Carla turned her attention back to Shay. "During press conferences, it would be in everyone's interest to keep discussions about religion and faith to a minimum. Beijing's the host country, and we want to be respectful of that."

Shay's response was terse. "Respectful? They jailed my father for practicing his faith. Did you know that they forced women to have abortions and slaughtered their own citizens in Tiananmen Square?"

The force of her response surprised everyone in the office, including Shay.

Carla took a moment before answering. "I appreciate your feelings, Shay, but consider the consequences of getting yourself embroiled in religion and politics at the Games. The Olympics are there to bring countries and athletes together, not rip them apart. You can be an agent of unity or conflict. We would prefer the former. Is there anything else I can answer for you?"

"No," Bethany said. "Rest assured, we won't engage in conduct that could harm endorsements or the spirit of the Games, right, Shay?"

Shay hesitated before responding. Being a pawn in a chess game didn't appeal to her. "I'll do my best to honor everyone involved," she said, avoiding eye contact as she brushed her hair back behind her ears.

"Very well," Carla said. "Have a fine rest of your day."

Bethany confronted Shay the moment they left the room. "What's going on with you? All this stuff about the Chinese government. Goodness, mercy, it's that boy, isn't it? He's putting these things in your head."

Shay's back muscles tightened. "I have a mind of my own. No one's putting ideas in my head. I read about Pastor Chen, and that's how I found out about the abortions. Forced on women by the government. It's sickening."

"It's a distraction. You're letting your father's arrest get in the way of what you need to be focused on. If you want to worry about the Chinese, worry about Ling Yue."

"I do worry about her. And I wonder what it must feel like to represent a country that would do such horrible things to its people? Does she support these things? Will she feel pride if she wins and the Chinese anthem is played and its flag is raised? Because if I beat her—and I fully intend to beat her—I will be proud of the country I represent. I will put my hand over my heart and thank God I am here and not there."

"Thank God?" Bethany said.

Shay shook her head. "It's an expression, okay? I have to get on the ice."

CHAPTER 16

When Shay said she wanted to meet Luke's pastor, Jack volunteered to drive. Shay was happy to have the company. Unlike the camaraderie in the rink before nationals, her pursuit of Olympic gold proved to be an isolating experience. The other competitive skaters in the club had failed to make the team. For those who do not make the Olympics, post-nationals is a time to heal physically and mentally decompress.

Shay sat in the backseat, allowing Adley to sit next to Jack. "Never call my podcast again, Jack. And I mean never ever. I spent half the night fending off attacks from my listeners."

"Why?"

"Because we're a podcast, not a Godcast. My callers don't want to hear about—"

"The one supernatural being who actually came back from the dead?"

"That's a point," Shay said, tweaking Adley.

Adley's head swerved to Shay. "Don't encourage him!"

Jack continued, "Your listeners believe in an internet myth like Slender Man but don't want to hear about true supernatural occurrences like the power to raise Lazarus from the grave."

"Which sounds very *Walking Dead* to me," Shay said, knowing Adley was a fan of the popular TV show.

"He walked on water," Jack said.

Shay's voice bristled with mock excitement. "Right above the Loch Ness Monster."

"And he exorcised demons!" Jack added.

"Right up the old paranormal alley," Shay chided.

Adley crossed her arms and glared at Shay. "Fine. A tag team. I get it. You're both banned for life."

Jack suppressed a smile.

"What's so funny?" Adley asked.

Jack mimicked the gravelly voice of the man who called Adley's show the night before. "Just cruising along jammin' to some oldies when it came out of nowhere, just appeared before me like it had been there all along. But the thing is, missy, it *wasn't*!"

Adley punched him in the shoulder. "Cut it."

"Looks like we're headed toward Hill Park again," Shay said. "Is the church close to Luke's apartment?"

"Two blocks away. The church meets in an old theater on Main Street," Jack said.

Jack pulled alongside the curb in front of a brick building. Adley leaped out of the car and looked at Jack's parking job and then at Jack.

Jack rolled down his window. "Not good?"

"I don't get it. You drive the Zamboni? On ice?" Adley said.

"Different machine." Jack stepped out of the car and checked the distance. "Yeah. I need to get closer."

Shay stood beside Adley. Both stepped on one foot and then the other, arms hugging their bodies to ward off the cold, as Jack navigated the VW closer to the curb.

"I can't believe we let him drive us on public roadways," Adley said.

Jack got too close and scraped the sidewall of his front tire against the curb. Shay and Adley cringed. Jack stepped out of the car as if nothing happened.

"You are the worst parker on the planet," Adley said.

Shay read the words displayed on the theatre's antique marquee in bold, scripted letters: LIVING WATERS CHURCH. "Definitely a cult."

Jack opened the door for Adley and Shay. "After you."

They stepped inside the old theater. Shay and Adley paused in the lobby and absorbed the nostalgic feel of the building.

"Pretty cool place, huh?" Jack said.

"Pretty creepy," Shay said.

Adley's smile told a different story. "This is epic! It's like we got transported here in a time machine."

"It was built in 1939."

"Looks it," Shay said.

"It's an old vaudeville theater. It was once thought to be haunted by ghosts of old actors who didn't know they were dead and continued to perform on the stage."

Adley's eyes glittered with excitement. "This is so over-the-top cool!"

"I'm sure the pastor's here somewhere," Jack said.

Shay scoffed. "Sure. Probably in the back trying to convince *The Phantom of the Opera* to be choir director."

"This way," Jack said and directed Adley and Shay through the entrance doors toward the room where services were held. Shay waved her hand in front of her nostrils. "Musty."

"The ventilation system isn't state of the art, but the acoustics are amazing," Jack said.

"You've been here before?" Adley asked.

"Sure. I'm in the band. I play here every Sunday."

"Get...out!" Adley said, punching him in the shoulder for the second time. "What instrument?"

"Keyboards mostly."

"I'm a drummer!"

"That is so cool. I would have never guessed," Jack said.

"So you know the pastor, then," Shay said in a flat no-nonsense tone.

Jack turned to Shay and grinned. "Sure."

"And you never thought to let me know this?"

"I didn't think you'd be interested in where I meet with other Kool-Aid-drinking cult members to have our brains washed."

"That's a point," Adley said.

Shay turned to Adley. "You're sticking up for him now?"

Jack smiled. "Well, this has gone full circle."

"I'm in an all-girl band called the X Chromosomes," Adley said.

"Punk?" Jack asked.

"Pop and rock. We thought of calling ourselves the Pop Rocks, but there's the whole copyright thing if we get famous, which is unlikely, because we only do cover tunes."

They entered the theater. The sanctuary had a gray cement floor, scone lighting along the walls, and a stage protruding in front of an enormous red velvet curtain. Shay noted the lumpy condition of the seats, their coiled springs pressed against the worn upholstery threatening to rip through the fabric.

"I'm getting strong spiritual vibes," Adley said.

"Of course, you're in a church," Shay said.

"I'm talking ghostly, mostly."

"The only ghost in here is holy," Jack said.

A voice rang out from above them. "Jack! Up here!"

When they looked up, a hipster-looking guy with a sculpted beard and Buddy Holly glasses poked his head through the curtain so high up it appeared he was forty feet tall.

"Hey, Pastor!" Jack said.

"Be right down," the man said.

Shay's brows drew together. "That's the pastor?"

The man swiped at the curtain, stepped through it, and bowed as if he had just finished a performance. Dressed in a plaid shirt, blue suspenders, and jeans, Shay thought he looked more like someone she'd meet at a trendy coffee shop sipping a latte than a church. His eyes beamed with natural vibrancy. "I'm Pastor Guff. Welcome to the Church of Living Waters."

"You don't look like a pastor," Adley said.

The pastor smiled. "I get that a lot. My wife likes to tell people I'm a man of the cloth but not cut from it."

"I'm Luke's daughter," Shay said.

Pastor Guff's eyes morphed to a focused gaze. "Yes, I see the resemblance. He spoke of you often. He's very proud of you."

Shay swallowed and looked away from him. "I'm sure."

Pastor Guff continued, "Being arrested for practicing his faith, it's hard to imagine such things happen in the world. We pray for his safe return."

Shay glanced at Adley and Jack and then settled her eyes back on Pastor Guff. "I have questions."

"Of course, you do," Pastor Guff said. He looked to Adley dressed in her everyday hobo-chic attire. "Love your style."

"Thanks. I'm Adley."

It occurred to Shay that she was the odd one out when it came to quirky fashion. Jack, Adley, and the pastor looked like the Three Musketeers, and she was plain Jane.

"Jack, why don't you show Adley around while I spend a few minutes with Shay?"

Jack pointed to the stage. "Wanna try the drums?"

"Duh!" Adley said, and both Jack and Adley ran up the steps and onto the stage.

Pastor Guff turned to Shay. "Let's go to my office. It's this way."

Shay followed Pastor Guff to his office. The room was dimly lit with outdated furniture in a tiny triangle-shaped room. Pastor Guff sat behind his desk and invited her to sit.

"So how can I help?" the pastor asked.

"Actually, part of me wants you to help me, and the other part wants me to get back to practice."

"Ah, the Olympics. Quite a heady experience. I should get your autograph before you leave and avoid the rush."

"How old are you, exactly?" Shay asked.

"I'm thirty-seven."

"You don't look thirty-seven."

"At the risk of being vain, I'm happy to hear that."

"Not that it's really my business. You're just not what I expected."

"My parents say that all the time. They're artists, bohemians of a sort. I think they were hoping for a concert pianist with beatnik sensibilities. The idea their only son would become a pastor was not a career path they imagined. Not that they mind it, they're loving and supportive but remain in a constant state of wonder."

"Oh. Well, it's good they're supportive."

"I can talk to you about your father because he was open about his past. In Bible study, he shared his struggles with addiction, losing his job, and his family, including you, of course."

Shay's lips tightened. "He had a wonderful way of showing it," she said and pushed the conversation forward. "I'm trying to understand how Luke, who wanted nothing to do with religion, suddenly becomes obsessed with the whole God thing."

"I see." Pastor Guff leaned back in his chair and ran a hand over his sculpted beard.

"I don't believe in God," Shay added in a challenging tone. "You should know that. Full disclosure." Shay waited for a moment, expecting the pastor to try to convince her she was wrong, but he said nothing. She prodded. "The moment people get in trouble, they find God or booze or drugs."

"Many do, but—"

"It's a scam."

"You feel strongly about this," Pastor Guff said.

Shay thought for a moment. "I guess I do," she said as if the weight of her feelings surprised her.

"It's good to be passionate in your thinking. It means something is stirring. Still waters in the soul are great, in the mind, not so much."

"So he just walked in here one day, and that was it?"

"No. It was a progression. Part of AA is believing in a power higher than yourself. He rejected the idea at first, but seeing positive results with others in his group, he considered the possibility that Jesus was the Son of God. My point being, he didn't come to believe on a whim. He studied. When I met your father, he knew scripture, both the Old and New Testament."

"I went to his apartment. He has a replica of the Shroud of Turin hanging above his bed."

Pastor Guff smiled. "I'm not surprised. He said it was the most haunting image he had ever seen."

"Well, if he studied so much, he'd know they proved it to be a fraud," Shay said, challenging Pastor Guff with a hard stare.

"*Some* believe it to be a fraud."

"A carbon dating test proved it. They created it in the Middle Ages, long after Jesus died. Don't you believe in science?"

"I do. But science requires rigor, and the piece of cloth tested was at the edge of the Shroud and was likely a piece repaired. Also, the latest testing suggests a date between 200 BC and AD 200."

A wild drumbeat and keyboard riff shook the walls. Pastor Guff smiled. "The acoustics are marvelous, but this office—"

"Why did he go to China?"

"To strengthen his faith. Luke thought faith in this country was easy. But to risk your freedom, sometimes your life, to practice your beliefs? He thought he might gain from people with that depth of faith. We send Bibles to China. Missionaries. It's a dangerous place to be a Christian."

"Did you send him there?"

"No. He went on his own."

"Seems like an expensive trip. Do you know what he did for work?"

"Sales of some sort, I believe."

Shay took notice of all the books in the room when she caught sight of a quote painted on a sign made of rustic wood:

GOD IS DEAD, Nietzsche
NIETZSCHE IS DEAD, GOD

Pastor Guff followed Shay's eyes. "It reminds me that he always has the last word."

Shay shifted in her seat. "I guess it brings some people comfort, if you need that sort of thing."

"I believe we all need that sort of thing. Sometimes, we just fear admitting it."

Shay's eyes met his. He smiled at her. It was warm, genuine.

"To each their own, I guess," Shay said. "Did my father know about all the problems there? I read about that pastor being arrested and all the terrible things being done in that country, and being honest, I'm sorry I did. It's unsettling."

"Then you have a soul. Congratulations. I fear that many have lost theirs."

"My mother thinks my father went to China to steal the limelight."

"And you? What do you believe?"

Shay absently rubbed her palms on her thighs. "He hasn't been a part of my life for a long time. Then I find out he lives a half-hour away. The Shroud, do you believe it's real, that it's the face of…" Shay let her voice trail off.

"Jesus?"

"Yes."

"I think it very well could be, but my faith isn't based on images."

"Right. How can it be? It's blind," Shay said.

"Actually, not blind at all. It's the result of years of study. Do you believe Jesus existed as a human being who walked on this planet?"

"I guess so."

"Good. Because the historical evidence is overwhelming. Jesus lived and was crucified. Do you believe that to be true?"

"I think so."

"So we have a great deal of common agreement. That's where I began."

Shay glanced up at a clock on the wall and realized she would be late for practice. "I need to go. I appreciate the time."

"I find it interesting that the Shroud has captivated both you and your father."

Shay shrugged. "I'm an artist. It's an interesting image."

"Indeed, it is. If you ever want to talk more, I'd be happy to tell you how I came to believe. There was a time when I was like you, a person who thought it was all a bunch of hooey."

Shay had to smile. She hadn't heard the word *hooey* in ages. In was one of her grandmother's favorite words. "Thanks. Maybe some other time."

Shay stood and walked toward the door.

"Luke told me he sent you a letter," Pastor Guff said.

Shay froze.

"He said it was returned unopened."

Shay's eyes sharpened, and she turned back to him. "Addicts lie, Pastor. It's what they do. Thanks for speaking with me." Shay turned and walked out of the office.

CHAPTER 17

Shay remained quiet as the trio drove back to the arena. She willed herself to contain thoughts about Luke, the letter, and the image that haunted him as it now haunted her. She created a box in her mind marked "Luke" and did her best to put each thought inside, to cover it with a promise to come back to it after the Olympics. It was a mental strategy that worked for her in the past, but this time, thoughts about the Shroud and Luke's imprisonment were putting up a fight.

Adley, never one to endure more than a moment of silence, turned to Jack. "So you truly believe Jesus came back from the dead?"

"That's right," Jack said.

"Why?" Shay asked.

"First, either Jesus was who he said he was, or he was a madman, and I don't believe he was a madman. Second, the tomb was empty. Over five hundred people saw Jesus after he was crucified. The apostles were all martyred for their belief in Jesus. They were beheaded, stoned to death, crucified upside down. Would you do that for a lie?"

Shay pushed back. "People do crazy things all the time. Look at the cult of people who committed suicide because they thought aliens would pick them up and take them off into heavenly bliss?"

"Killing yourself is far different from being tortured and murdered by the Romans. They knew how to inflict pain like no other, and that doesn't address the historical evidence," Jack said.

Adley continued on about the Heaven's Gate group. "We're assuming they weren't picked up when it's totally possible they were. The government is slowly admitting to the existence of UFOs."

"This proves my point. People will believe in anything," Shay said.

"Except you?" Jack glanced at Shay in the rearview mirror.

"I don't believe anyone is capable of coming back from the dead or that a spaceship full of aliens picked people up and swept them off to a distant planet."

"You don't believe in an afterlife?" Jack asked.

"That's right," Shay shot back, "dust to dust."

"Which, interestingly enough, came from the Bible."

"Can you just drive? And by the way, the gas pedal is on the right."

Jack looked to Adley and smiled. "Touchy."

"Oh, she can be," Adley said.

Jack pulled into the arena parking lot and saw the reporters milling about with their coat collars pulled up to ward off the cold. He parked, and the three of them got out of the car. The moment the reporters saw Shay, they converged and began shouting out questions.

"Shay, will you use your Olympic platform to help secure your father's release?"

"Have you spoken to your father since his arrest?"

"Do you condemn the Chinese for cracking down on freedom of religion?"

Shay stated, "No comment," and moved past the reporters and into the arena. Adley followed Shay, but Jack, who waited until Shay and Adley were out of earshot, turned back to the reporters.

"What they did to Shay's dad is wrong, and it won't work. Nothing, not even the gates of hell, can stop the spread of the Gospel."

The reporters fed on Jack's comment like a school of piranhas.

"Are you her boyfriend?"

"What is your relationship with Ms. Gerrard?"

Jack turned his back to the reporters and walked inside.

Shay tugged at the laces of her skates.

"What happened to Jack?" Adley asked, taking a seat on the bench beside Shay.

"Who knows? He can be so annoying."

"He annoys me, too, but I can't stop looking at him. He's like an accident on the side of the road. You don't wanna look, but you just can't help yourself."

"He's unique. That's the best I can say for him. You two are like two peas in a pod."

Adley shrugged. "Not really. He's interesting, but he doesn't believe in Bigfoot. That's a hurdle."

"You'll clear it."

"Maybe. But it would be a struggle."

"I need to get on the ice. Talk later?"

"Sure. I'll go look for Captain Jack and make sure he isn't up to no good."

Shay stood, stretched, and glided out onto the ice. As she moved across the rink, she thought about what Pastor Guff said to her about the letter. *It was returned unopened.* Why would Luke lie like that? A letter? Shay didn't think so. She never even got a birthday card.

Shay was early for practice, and one of the other instructors at the rink was finishing up a beginner's class, having the newbies see which of them could hold their shoot-the-duck move the longest. Shay missed the days when she first started skating and participated in the same contest. She still loved to skate, but now it sometimes seemed more like a job than a passion. Not that she disliked skating, but there were times when it consumed her life, especially after her parents' divorce. It was as if her mother had decided the best way for the two of them to move forward was to forget about Luke by putting all their collective energy into skating. And maybe it was? After all, she was going to the Olympics, but the events of the past week had thrown her into a tailspin. *Focus, Shay,* she commanded and began to warm up on her required elements.

Her spins were fine, but her jumps were off, causing wide swings of her free leg on several landings. Remy came out of her office to watch Shay's warm-up and noticed her timing wasn't right. Shay finished her warm-up and joined Remy by the rail.

"You're overthinking everything. Get your mind out of the way, and let your body do what you've trained it to do."

Like all great athletes, Shay knew when it was time to stop tinkering with the mechanics, and aside from the quad Lutz, her time had come weeks ago. Overthinking upsets the delicate balance between mind and body, generally resulting in disaster.

"It's Luke," Shay confessed. "I can't stop thinking about him being in jail, believing in God all of a sudden. I've tried everything to put it out of my mind, but nothing's working. The timing of this couldn't be worse."

"Then maybe it's time to stop fighting it? He's your dad, Shay. What's causing all this turmoil is how much effort you're putting into a lie."

"What are you talking about? What lie?"

"That you stopped loving your dad just because he left. Hating that he left you doesn't mean you don't love him. It means you're hurt and disappointed. It's okay to love him," Remy said.

Shay hugged her coach and felt the reassuring embrace as Remy whispered, "You're strong. You can do this, okay? A little difference…"

"Makes a lot of difference," Shay said.

Bethany watched the embrace from across the arena. Neither Shay nor Remy knew she had come to watch Shay's practice. The longer the embrace continued, the more Bethany fumed. Remy's eyes lifted and met Bethany's. It was a cold exchange.

CHAPTER 18

Shay's stomach twisted into a knot as she watched a video replay of Jack's comments on her phone. How dare he insert himself into her life? Into her father's? She heard footsteps pounding up the stairs and knew her mother had seen Jack's encounter with the press. Once again, Jack had surprised her, but this surprise would have consequences. Bethany pushed the door open, and it banged against the wall.

"What did I tell you about hanging out with Adley and that boy! Now look what he's done!" Bethany's shoulders shook, and she lashed out. "What are you doing behind my back, Shay!"

"Nothing."

"Don't lie to me! I saw you crying in Remy's arms this morning, and now this! That boy just opened the floodgates because you didn't listen to my instructions! I'm not stupid, so tell me this minute what's going on!"

"Fine! I went to see dad's pastor, okay? And I went to dad's apartment!" Shay said, the words coming out of her mouth like a cannon shot.

Bethany flinched. "You what?"

"I'm sorry, but he's my father, and I can't make-believe he's not."

Bethany didn't breathe for a moment. The corners of her mouth turned downward. She began to nod but said nothing. She looked broken.

"Mom—" Shay whispered, but Bethany held up her hand to stop her.

"So you've found a surrogate mother to go along with your surrogate father. How wonderful for you. I did the best I could, but it appears you've decided I'm the enemy."

"That's not true," Shay said.

106

"You're on your own. I will no longer interfere in your skating or your life. So, moving forward, let's be civil, shall we? I'm tired. I'm going to bed." Bethany turned and left the room, closing the door behind her.

Before Shay could begin to process what just happened, her phone rang. It was Curt.

"Hey," she said.

"What's going on with you and that Jesus Freak?" Curt asked. "I thought I told you to stay away—"

Shay disconnected, not only from the call but from any context of who she was or what she was feeling. *This is what it must feel like to have a breakdown*, she thought. Untethered from feeling anything at all, Shay fixed a blank stare at the wall. Curt tried to call several more times, but Shay didn't answer.

It was after midnight when her thoughts returned to the Shroud. Emerging from her mental fog, she lifted the blank sheet that covered her sketch and gazed at the amorphous specter that had captivated millions of believers around the world. She gazed at it until her eyes grew weary, and she fell asleep.

Twenty-seven days to Olympic skate

Shay woke to the buzzing of her phone. Her Twitter and Instagram feeds were running wild. Both accounts now had followers that exceeded a hundred thousand, most of whom were praying for her father's safe return. She looked to the Shroud. "If nothing else, you certainly have a lot of followers."

Curt called five times, and Adley three, plus a series of texts asking if Shay was okay. Shay texted back she was fine but was furious at Jack for sticking his nose in her business. A moment later, Adley called.

"I had no idea he did that. Are you doing okay?"

"I hung up on Curt last night."

"Why?"

"He started ragging on me about Jack, about how he told me to stay away from him. I hate when he does that. He talks to me as if I should follow his commands."

"Truth, girlfriend, guys come in three basic modes: prisoners, guards, or wardens. Honestly, Shay, there's not a lot in between."

Even in her sullen mood, Shay had to smile. "Seriously? That's your thesis?"

"Take it from a future valedictorian. I know of which I speak."

"Oh, and did I mention my mother disowned me last night?"

"Rite of passage. All parents threaten to disown their children. It's a defense mechanism against feeling abandoned when they sense their coveted offspring are about to stand on their own two feet. And don't worry. Things will look better in the morning."

"It is the morning."

"Oh. Right. Tomorrow morning, then. Maybe you should sleep in today?"

"Sleep in? I'm on Team USA. Sleeping in is not an option. There's practice, a press conference, and I need to tell Captain Jack to keep his nose out of my life."

"Don't be too mean. I'm sure he meant well."

"You're sticking up for him now?"

"I'm just saying those reporters were jerks. I almost wanted to scream at them myself."

"He used my life as a reason to push his obsession with God," Shay said. Her eyes moved to her sketch of the Shroud. "It muddied the waters, and that's the last thing I need right now. I need to go, or I'm going to be late. Disconnect?"

In unison, they said, "Three, two, one…," and disconnected.

Shay called Curt and apologized for hanging up on him. "I need to able to make my own decisions," Shay said.

Curt begrudgingly agreed.

"I need your help," Shay said. "Can you pick me up after practice?"

Shay dressed while listening to the news. Jasmine Thomas was on KVOZ TV reporting on Luke's imprisonment and Jack's comments to the media the day before. Jasmine looked into the camera with a steely expression and spoke as if the news she had was on a par with the spread of a deadly plague.

"As you know, Luke Gerrard, father of Detroit's very own Olympian Shay Gerrard, was arrested by the Chinese government for attending an illegal church. It has been widely reported that the State Department is doing all it can to have Mr. Gerrard released. Still, Mr. Gerrard has made it known he would prefer to stay in prison unless the Chinese agree to also release Pastor Chen, militant leader of the controversial church."

Shay rolled her eyes. "Militant leader. How can a church be illegal in the first place?"

Jasmine continued, "Yesterday, Shay was asked to comment on the situation and refused, but one of her companions had a forceful response to questions posed by this and other reporters on the scene."

Shay watched the video of Jack's comments and noted the passion in his voice. "Nothing, not even the gates of hell, can stop the spread of the Gospel."

Shay looked to the Shroud. "Count Jack as a true believer."

The video finished, and Jasmine's face filled the screen. "The question remains, will Shay Gerrard use her platform as an Olympic skater to help gain her father's release? The politics are delicate. Luke Gerrard is being held in the host city of Beijing. This is Jasmine Thomas reporting for KVOZ TV." Shay shut off the TV, grabbed her car keys, and headed downstairs.

Shay found her mother making breakfast in the kitchen. It was awkward, but Shay realized her press conference would begin in less than an hour and knew her mother wanted to be there to control the situation. Shay extended an olive branch to short-circuit the silence. "Mom, I know you no longer want to be a part of my skating career, but I'd appreciate it if you could be there to help me with the press conference. I'm nervous about it, and you're good at handling these types of things."

Bethany set Shay's protein shake on the counter and looked up at Shay. "Your first order of business is to drink up. And yes, I'll go to the press conference, if that's what you want."

"It is. And thanks."

"Remember that Luke's situation is off-limits. If questions are posed regarding your father, you let them know you've been advised by the State Department not to comment."

"I thought they were told those questions weren't allowed?"

"They were, but don't be surprised if one of the reporters ignores that direction and attempts to step over the line, especially after what happened yesterday. They will say they are just following up, but you will firmly refuse to engage."

Despite their many differences, Shay knew her mother had the skill and courage to take charge when needed, traits Shay envied. "Okay, but if I look your way—"

"I'll intervene," Bethany said.

Shay smiled. "I really appreciate it."

The vibe was still tense, but Shay felt this was a first step toward mending fences.

"I'll meet you there," Shay said and walked out to her car.

Shay pulled into the lot and spotted Jack's VW in its usual parking space. When she saw Jack step out of his car, she pulled in beside him, slammed on her brakes, and leaped out.

"Before you say a word, I'm sorry," Jack said. "Adley told me you were upset, and I was going to call you, but—"

"What were you thinking?"

"I wasn't. I just reacted."

"Well, don't. Keep your opinions to yourself. My father's situation doesn't concern you."

"Of course it does. If it didn't concern me, I couldn't call myself a Christian."

"What you call yourself doesn't give you the right to talk to the press about my family or me. I thought I could trust you."

"What you need to do is trust what God is telling you."

"Really? Because I don't hear God telling me anything."

"You hear him. You're just not listening."

Shay held his gaze. "I need to go inside. There's a press conference. Keep your nose out of my business, Jack."

Before Jack could respond, Shay turned her back to him and marched into the arena.

CHAPTER 19

Bethany and Shay waited in Remy's office while reporters gathered in the lobby. Shay paced. Dressed in her blue warm-up suit and clutching her water bottle, she shook out her arms and moved her head from side to side to calm her nerves. In contrast, Bethany checked her makeup in a pocket mirror, touched up her lipstick, and placed the mirror back in her handbag with the focused look of a soldier readying herself for war. Remy looked to Shay.

"You okay?"

"Public speaking isn't exactly my strong suit."

"You'll do fine," Remy said. "How's the ankle?"

"Definitely better."

Remy tapped her fingers on her desk. "Do you think your ankle's well enough to work the quad Lutz on a limited basis?"

Bethany's eyes lit up. "Coming around, are we?"

Remy ignored Bethany.

"I thought our strategy was to skate clean?" Shay asked.

"I'm not talking about putting it in your program. I'm suggesting we let Ling and Dasha know you're capable of it in practice sessions. They saw the reports of your bad ankle. I want to keep the pressure on them all the way up to the final skate."

Ling and Dasha Lukov, from Russia, were one and two in the world. Before Shay's breakout performance at nationals, they were considered the odds-on favorites to win gold and silver at the Olympics.

"We could work it with the pole harness. That would keep landing pressure off your ankle," Remy said.

"We love the idea," Bethany said. "But I think attempting it in the program is worth the risk. Clean programs worked before they changed the scoring system, but—"

Remy was happy to have Bethany interrupted by a knock on her office door. She opened it to find a production assistant standing there with an iPad in hand.

"We're ready," she said to Remy.

Shay wiped the sweat on her palms on her warm-up suit. Remy smiled and put her hand on Shay's shoulder. "Stick to the script, and you'll be fine."

"If the need arises, I'll step in, give them some of the Cruella de Ville they've been asking for," Bethany said.

Her mother's ability to adapt to any situation amazed Shay. Bethany was hurt by the media's portrayal of her earlier in the week, but now she embraced the image of the fierce, unrelenting attack dog they had made her out to be. When a reporter contacted her by phone for comment, Bethany put the phone on speaker so Shay could hear the exchange. Shay watched and listened as Bethany provided the reporter with more than he bargained for and accused the media of being sexist. "If I were a man, I'd be seen as strong, but because I'm a woman, you portray my actions as unhinged. You're outdated and irrelevant," she said and disconnected. She looked to Shay and said, "Let that be a lesson on how to handle people who try to control you. Bullies need to be put in their place."

Shay did her best to channel her mother's strength and headed toward the gathering of reporters.

The press conference was hectic, but Shay stayed on point, deflecting questions about Luke and answering those focused on her skating.

"How are you feeling about the Games?"

"Fantastic. Remy's an excellent coach, and my mom helps me stay on track."

"You had a perfect skate at nationals. How much pressure are you feeling to repeat that performance?"

"Pressure's good. If you're not feeling it, something's wrong. What matters is how you channel it."

Jasmine Thomas was the first to breach the agreement. "When will you speak about your father's imprisonment? Do you know he has now refused to be released unless—"

"As you know, Ms. Thomas, I cannot comment on that under the advisement of the State Department."

"I'm asking if you will ever speak—"

Shay reacted forcefully, looking right into the camera as she interrupted Jasmine's question with a statement. "Ms. Thomas has agreed not to ask questions about my father during the press conference. Her grandstanding reflects her belief that she is more important than her peers who have been respectful of the process. Thank you." Shay turned and walked back toward Remy's office.

Bethany smiled at Jasmine Thomas. "Boundaries, Ms. Thomas. We draw them, and you will respect them."

As Bethany walked away, Jasmine Thomas fumed.

Remy met Shay by her office. "That was amazing!"

"I channeled my mother."

"And it was perfect," Remy said.

Bethany joined them and hugged Shay. "I couldn't have done it better. Ms. Thomas is still lifting her jaw off the floor."

A surge of energy powered through Shay. For the first time in a week, she felt more in control and less like a candle in a whirlwind doing its best to stay lit. It was an empowering moment that helped Shay realize how far down the woe-is-me road she had allowed herself to travel. She removed her sweats. It was time to work on the quad Lutz.

Remy put on her skates and retrieved the pole harness from her office. Skaters had mixed feelings about using the harness. Some loved it, while others, like Shay, felt it was restrictive and could interfere with the development of proper technique. Remy shared Shay's feelings but felt it could be beneficial in limited circumstances.

Shay had watched other coaches use the pole harness. It was like watching a fisherman fight to hold up a huge fish spinning in the air, leaning back and fighting to make sure their catch lands just right. On the ice, Shay went through her long program warm-up and then fitted herself into the harness.

"Let's try a few triples to get the feel and timing down first," Remy said.

Shay agreed. After attempting and landing several triple Lutz jumps, it was time to attempt the quad. As Remy matched Shay's crossovers, Shay jabbed her toe pick into ice, vaulted into the air, and rotated four times before landing softly on the ice as Remy assisted with the harness.

A smile broke on Shay's face. "That felt fantastic!"

"Not bad," Remy said. "You completed the rotation without help, and the landing was clean."

"Try a few more?" Shay asked.

"Let's do it."

Shay felt lighter. It was as if she had shed the anxiety that had been weighing her down. She thought of the thousands of people who were praying for her via her social media platforms and, for a moment, wondered if they were having an effect. *Whatever*, she thought, admonishing herself for allowing the absurd thought to enter her mind.

Shay landed several more quads before removing the harness and proceeding to run through her Olympic warm-up for the long program. Everything was clicking. Her spins were perfectly centered, and she landed the triple-triple with just a slight pitch on the exit edge. She finished with a spectacular Biellman, spinning into a blur before jamming her pick into the ice and striking her final pose. Shay's eyes lit up. She looked to Remy, who clapped as soon Shay's Biellman accelerated. This was it. They were back on track. Shay turned to Bethany, who provided a reserved nod. Usually, such a response would annoy Shay, but this time she enjoyed the moment and skated to Remy to receive a much-deserved high-five.

"Put that in a bottle and cap it," Remy said.

Bethany walked to them and handed Shay her water bottle. Shay took it and drank.

"That's the best we've done since nationals," Bethany said. "A bobble on the triple-triple, but more speed on the entry will fix that."

Remy and Shay shared a knowing smile. Despite the dig, Shay was happy Bethany was still being Bethany. After last night's blowup, it appeared her mother had calmed down and stayed involved after all.

Shay finished practice and was donning her sweats when she heard the Zamboni move out onto the ice. When she looked up, she saw a hand-drawn banner draped over the side of the machine that read, "To Forgive is Divine." Shay smiled, zipped up her warm-up jacket, and grabbed her skates. She had four hours before her next practice session, plenty of time to drive to Luke's apartment and get back to the rink with no one knowing where she went. There was something important she had to look for, the letter Luke claimed he sent to her.

CHAPTER 20

S hay left the arena through a maintenance exit and climbed into Curt's Dodge Charger.

"Go!" she said. Curt took off before any of the reporters knew Shay was gone.

"Where to?" Curt asked.

"Hill Park."

Unlike Jack, Curt had no issues exceeding the speed limit. In twenty minutes, Curt parked his car in front of the pawnshop. Light snow fell as Curt followed Shay inside. A bell announced their entrance into the store, and Iosif, who was down on one knee doing inventory, stood and saw Shay.

"Hello, again to you," he said to Shay and then looked to Curt. "To you, hello is first time."

The size and girth of Iosif surprised Curt. "Hey," Curt said.

"You look like man who likes to arm wrestle. Come, we will see how you do against Iosif." Iosif walked to the counter and propped his elbow down. "I give you quarter head start. This good deal for Big Boy, yes?"

Curt's eyes flashed to Shay, who sported a sly smile. "Go ahead, Big Boy, arm-wrestle the man."

Curt's expression pleaded with Shay to get him out of this.

Shay turned to Iosif. "Can he take a rain check? I only have a few minutes, and I have to get back in my father's apartment. And Curt is about to try out for the Detroit Red Wings, so he needs to avoid injuring his arm. Can I have the key?"

"Red Wings, eh?" Iosif said, turning his attention to Curt.

"Yessir," Curt said.

Iosif retrieved the key and handed it to Shay.

"Thanks. I'll bring it right back."

Curt followed Shay up the snow-caked stairs and into Luke's apartment. Shay flipped on the light.

"What are you looking for?" Curt asked.

"Luke's pastor told me Luke wrote me a letter. I think he was trying to make himself look good, but I need to know." Shay went straight to the bedroom, and once again, the image of the Shroud loomed large when Shay turned on the light.

"That's weird," Curt said.

"It's purported to be the burial shroud of Christ," Shay said. "Some say it's a forgery, but even with modern technology, no one can explain how the image was embedded in the cloth."

"Why would anyone want a dead guy's burial cloth hanging above their bed?" Curt asked.

"To remind them of their faith and the miracle of the resurrection."

"Uh-huh," Curt muttered in the tone of a psychiatrist considering the statement of a deranged patient.

Shay's eyes pinned Curt's. "What?"

"Nothing, it's just…you talk like that's normal," Curt said, pointing at the picture. "I'd hate to see you get sucked in."

"'Sucked in'?"

"Yeah."

"You think there might be a vortex in here? Maybe a rip in the space-time continuum?"

"You know what I mean."

"Stay right there. I'm going into the closet. If I don't come out in two minutes, call Adley and let her know I've fallen into an uncovered manhole on the highway to hell. She'll know what to do."

"You're hilarious."

"But first, I'm looking under the bed, so brace yourself."

"Are you done?" Curt asked.

"Nope. Just getting started." Shay got down on all fours to check under the bed.

"Anything?"

"No." She stood up and noted the CD player resting on the nightstand. Curious, she pressed Play. A haunting ballad played.

The lyrics spoke of being a living sanctuary to God.

Shay gazed at the Shroud as the music continued.

"Shay?" Curt said.

Shay waited for the song to end and kept her eyes on the Shroud. "No one knows how the image could have been forged, and every scientific attempt to copy it has failed." Shay turned to Curt. "What do you think?"

"I think the only biblical thing in the area is the guy downstairs who makes me think David didn't kill Goliath. I think hanging a shroud over your bed is weird, and I think if you don't get your head back into skating, you will trash the opportunity of a lifetime."

Shay considered this for a moment and then brushed it aside. "I need to check the closet."

Shay flipped on the light. The closet was threadbare. Just a few shirts, a pair of worn sneakers, and some marked boxes. A wave of sadness swept through her. There was a time when Luke had a walk-in closet; and Shay, as a little girl, would sit on her parents' bed and help Luke select his outfit for the day. Luke would point at shirts and ties and jackets, and Shay would shake her head or nod her approval until Luke had the day's ensemble laid out on the bed beside her. Then he'd say, "I think we've got it, Princess," and kiss Shay on the forehead. Then he'd dress and meet her downstairs for breakfast. Sometimes, Bethany would mount a protest when Luke's tie clashed with a shirt or jacket, but Luke would insist it was fine.

"I trust Shay's discriminating taste," he'd say. "She has the eye." Then he'd wink at Shay and smile.

Shay discovered when she was older that Luke had a variety of ties in his car and would exchange ties when he left the house. Before coming home, he'd put the tie Shay had selected back on so she'd believe he'd worn it all day. Luke was meticulous about his appearance. Now everything he owned could be put in the trunk of a car. Shay glanced up and saw a shoebox marked "Misc." on the shelf. She grabbed it, opened the lid, scanned the contents, but found nothing. Disappointed, she said, "I knew it. There never was a letter. Let's go."

Curt pulled Shay close and kissed her head. "It doesn't mean he didn't send it."

"Maybe," Shay said, but her tone spoke of her skepticism.

"Can you grab the CD and the CD player?" Shay asked. "I want to take it with me."

"Sure."

Shay stood up, and a moment later, they were back in the pawnshop.

Iosif's thunderous laughter echoed off the walls. "Looou-seee!" he said. "What have you done?" he added, doing his best imitation of Ricky Ricardo's voice.

Curt looked to Shay. "He watches old TV shows," she said and walked up to the counter. Iosif looked up.

"Lucy again?" Shay asked as she handed the apartment key back to Iosif.

"She is always in crazy trouble. You should watch this, yes? For funny bone."

"I'm not a big TV person," Shay said. "I'm taking a CD and a CD player. I promise to bring them back."

"I'm sure father would be glad for you to have this," Iosif said. "I pray for him, for you, every night. To God for his safety and return, for you to know he is…good man. Not perfect, yes? But changed now that is in him Spirit of God."

"I have to get back to the rink," Shay said, brushing Iosif's comment aside. "Thanks." Then a thought came to her. "What happens to my father's mail? I didn't see any in his apartment."

"He asked me to collect for him," Iosif said and pulled a box full of mail from under the counter.

"Can I see?" Shay asked.

Iosif shrugged. "Sure."

He handed Shay the box; and she began rifling through the flyers, junk mail, and credit card offers. Then she saw it—the letter addressed to Shay Gerrard with the notation "RETURN TO SENDER" stamped in red on the envelope.

"You okay?" Curt asked.

"She hid it from me," Shay said, her voice void of emotion as she struggled to process what it all meant.

"Maybe she never saw it? It's just one letter."

Shay lifted the envelope and stared at the words: "RETURN TO SENDER." She wanted to feel something, anything at all; but, at least for the moment, she felt nothing. Shay kept the letter and handed the rest of the mail back to Iosif. "Thanks," she said. She held up the letter. "This was for me."

Iosif held up a piece of paper he had by the TV. "I have times written down for when you skate this Olympic Games. I will not miss you…one minute. You will do good skating, yes?"

"Yes. Well, I hope so."

"They will raise America's great flag, and the national anthem will play for whole world to hear, you will see."

Iosif's comment reminded Shay that in twenty-seven days when she took to the ice, the world would be watching.

CHAPTER 21

Curt glanced at Shay as he drove her back to the arena, but she was fixated on the letter and didn't notice. He expected her to open it as soon as she got in the car, but Shay just held the envelope and moved her fingers across the letters, as if by touch she might reveal its contents.

"When did he send it?" Curt asked.

"What?" Shay moved from her reverie back into the moment.

"The letter. How long ago did he send it?"

She checked the postmark. "January 4. Local postmark."

"Just before he left, then."

"Seems so."

"Must be strange, after all these years."

"Yeah, it is," Shay said, still distant and trying to regain her emotional equilibrium.

"If you want my advice, I'd open it, deal with it, and move on. I know it sounds harsh, but you've got so little time to—"

"I know," Shay said, her voice stern.

"Okay, just trying to help."

"Sorry. I'm just so... I don't know, going in all directions."

Curt smiled. "It's all right. You're strong. You'll get through it. When you get on the ice, it's a clean slate. That's how you need to think about it."

When Curt pulled into the arena parking lot, news trucks, vans, and reporters were gathered at the entrance. The *Twilight Zone* chimed on her phone, startling her. It was Adley.

"Hey, what's up?" Shay asked.

"Check the video I sent you. Your father's been moved to an internment camp for his refusal to denounce Pastor Chen."

Shay's breath caught in her chest. "No, they can't do that!"

"What's going on?" Curt asked.

Shay's phone buzzed again. It was Shay's mother. "My mom's calling."

"Okay, connect later," Adley said and disconnected.

Shay tapped her phone and took the call from Bethany. "Mom?"

"Where are you?" Bethany asked.

"Just pulled into the arena parking lot. I'm with Curt. I heard the news."

"I'm coming out. Don't get out of the car until I'm there. Tell Curt to park as close to the entrance as he can. The vultures are swarming."

Curt parked the car. Reporters were fighting one another for position. "This is crazy!" Curt said.

Bethany shoved her way through the crowd of reporters. Curt jumped out and helped Bethany lead Shay through the gauntlet of mics being thrust in Shay's face. Once again, it was Jasmine Thomas who led the parade. "Any reaction to your father being sent to an internment camp?"

"No comment!" Bethany yelled, pushing through the throng of faces, cameras, and microphones. "Give us space!"

When they finally managed to get inside, a wave of panic swept through Shay. *The letter? Where was it? She had it in her hand, and now it was gone!* Shay tugged at Curt's arm and whispered, "My letter?"

Seeing the panic in Shay's eyes, Curt mouthed the words "I'll look" and turned back toward the door to go look for the letter.

Shay, Remy, and Bethany stood in the snack bar and watched a media report concerning Luke on ESPN. The commentator spoke in a grave tone. A small banner in the corner of the screen identified her as Livy Banks.

"According to sources inside China, Luke Gerrard, the estranged father of US Olympic Team member Shay Gerrard, has been moved to an internment camp in an undisclosed location. He was originally arrested for attending an illegal house church in Beijing. The State Department has condemned the move and continues to engage the Chinese government in talks to negotiate Mr. Gerrard's release."

"This is surreal," Bethany said.

Livy Banks continued, "Human Rights Watch has noted a crackdown on religious freedom, citing the arrest of religious leaders and forcing both Christians and Muslims into 'indoctrination programs.' We turn to Professor Peng Wen of Christian University, a recognized expert on Chinese affairs. Professor Wen, welcome."

A sober-looking man with a round face and black-rimmed oval glasses filled the screen. "Thank you."

"Can you give us some insight into what's happening in China regarding religious freedom, Professor?" Livy asked.

"Yes. Over the past year, the government has shut down hundreds of unofficial house churches. They've removed crosses from buildings, forced churches to hang the Chinese flag, and sing pro-government songs. Religious leaders have been arrested, interrogated, and tortured. Many have been charged with subversion resulting in prison terms. This activity is escalating."

"Specific to Mr. Gerrard, why would they do this now, with the Olympics just weeks away?"

"The government believes Christianity promotes Western values that conflict with China's authoritarian government. I can only speculate that Mr. Gerrard's support of Pastor Chen is something they feel they cannot tolerate. Pastor Chen is a powerful force, and the government has, to this point, been unable to stop the spread of Christianity, especially underground church activity."

"Thanks for your insight, Professor. I'm sure we'll be reaching out to you if the situation isn't resolved quickly," Livy said.

"You're very welcome."

The camera refocused on Livy. "Shay Gerrard has refused to comment on the situation citing a request from the State Department to refrain from doing so. The question is, in the face of what's happening to the Olympian's father, how long will she be able to remain silent?"

The situation was spiraling out of control. Shay looked for Curt but surmised he was still outside looking for Luke's letter. As she thought about Luke, the image of the Shroud came to mind. It was as if the two were entangled.

"We need to practice," Remy said, having turned her attention to Shay. "I know this is a distraction, but we have to believe it will be solved. It's critical to keep our attention and focus on your training."

"I agree," Bethany said. "If the world is testing us, it will find we are up to the challenge."

Shay spotted Curt. His expression made it clear he had not been able to locate the letter.

"Shay?" Remy asked.

Shay turned her attention to Remy. "I'll get my skates."

Bethany checked her watch. "I have to show a house. See you at home?" she asked.

"Okay," Shay said. "I may stay after to watch Curt's practice."

Shay did her best to concentrate but found it impossible to get the letter out of her mind. She chastised herself for losing it. *What was I thinking? Why didn't I read it when I had the chance?* This was the thought at the forefront of her mind when she missed the timing on the triple-triple takeoff and crashed down on the ice. A jolt of pain exploded in her hip as she slid into the boards.

"Shay!" Remy cried and ran to her star skater, now struggling to stand. "Are you okay? Are you hurt?"

Shay stood. "I don't think so."

Shay was losing the concentration battle. She had missed take-offs before but not this badly. This was the type of fall that often resulted in severe injury.

"That's enough for today," Remy said. "You're distracted. It's dangerous to skate at this level without being focused."

"I don't know how to manage it all," Shay said.

Remy put her arm around Shay's shoulder. "You need to give yourself permission to feel what you're feeling."

"Sometimes, I'm not even sure what that is."

"You need a distraction. Go see a movie. Go bowling. Something different."

"Maybe," Shay said.

"Don't be discouraged. You won nationals, right?" Remy smiled. "Skated brilliantly as I recall. You need only repeat what you've already accomplished. With some minor tweaks."

"Because a little difference makes a lot of difference."

"Exactly," Remy said. "See you tomorrow."

When Shay got home, she ran up to her room with the boom box and CD she had taken from Luke's apartment. Bethany wouldn't be back for an hour, so Shay could play the music without interruption. She felt guilty about the sudden divide between her and her mother. She knew Bethany was trying to avoid having Shay being hurt again. The road back from the pain and despair that enveloped Shay after her father abandoned her had been devastating. How can a ten-year-old girl understand the monstrous power of addiction? If a parent dies, you can say that they're with the angels, and they would be with you if they could, but when they've descended into the living hell of addiction, what can you say then? For a little girl who idolized her father, Bethany gave the only explanation she felt she could. Luke had simply decided he didn't want to be her daddy anymore. Shay had cried until the well of her tears ran dry. Then she put her heart into skating and into her art. Now she felt as if she was betraying her mom and dishonoring the sacrifice Bethany had endured for her. Without warning, feelings buried long ago were rising to the surface. Suddenly, Shay and her dad had something in common—a fascination, one might even say an obsession, with the image in the Shroud of Turin. Shay set up the boom box and pressed play. As she gazed at her drawing of the Shroud, the haunting ballad with its powerful lyrics filled the room.

Shay realized this was Luke's ballad. She played the song again, then a third time. With her eyes fixed on her sketch of the Shroud, Shay felt connected with her father for the first time in years.

CHAPTER 22

Twenty-six days until Olympic skate

Shay and Adley met at Sacred Grounds. Shay had called Adley in a panic. The letter was out there, words her father had written especially for her, and it was lost. Shay shifted in her chair. Her hip was still sore from yesterday's fall.

Adley sipped her latte. "Are you sure it didn't get stuck under the seat or something?"

"Curt checked everywhere. He knows how badly I wanted him to find it. He even checked around the arena, thinking the wind may have taken it. Then I went out after he did and checked again. Nothing. The letter's gone."

"Gee, Shay, I'm really sorry."

"I could have read it. Now I'll never know what it said."

"That's not true. Your dad will get released. Then he can tell you exactly what he wrote. Have a little faith, right?"

Shay's eyes bore into Adley's. "'Faith'? You've been hanging around Jack too much."

"I wasn't talking about God faith. Not necessarily," Adley said.

"'Not necessarily'?"

"I'm not joining the God squad yet, but Jack has some good points. And speaking of Jack…"

"One of your favorite topics lately."

"Fine. I find him interesting. Unlike most guys I know, he's unpredictable in a good way."

"And he's cute."

"There's that."

"And?"

"And I'm playing with his band tonight," Adley said.

Shay's chin dropped. "At the church?"

"Yes, at the church," Adley said defensively.

"Holy rollers in your hair, Adley Finch. Do your parents know?"

"They know I'm playing, just not in church. They might get wigged out if they discover I'm playing a gig in a house of worship."

"But they'd be fine if you said you'd be headlining the Sasquatch convention, right?"

"Now you're starting to sound like Jack. He said the same thing."

"Did you tell the X-Chromosomes you're defecting?"

"I'm not defecting. It's a guest gig. Don't overblow it."

"Since when are you interested in religion?"

"I'm not. I'm interested in music."

"And Jack. Not that I'm surprised."

"You should come to the concert tonight!" Adley said with a burst of excitement in her voice.

"Why would I do that?"

"You'll be done with practice, and all you ever do is draw in your room or watch Curt fend off pucks. It's just music. What could it hurt?"

Shay thought of the advice Remy had given her earlier and considered the idea. Before Luke's imprisonment, Shay would have fervently dismissed the notion of attending a Christian youth group. Still, her recent fascination with the Shroud and Luke's conversion to Christianity ignited her curiosity. She thought of the story of Dr. Jekyll and Mr. Hyde. That's how she felt, as if her mind was divided between wanting to believe God was real one moment and chastising herself for thinking such a thing the next.

Adley slid from her chair, got down on one knee, and clasped her hands together. "I'm begging now. Look at me. The little beggar girl just—"

"I'll go, I'll go. Just get up already. Such a drama queen."

"You won't regret it. Promise me you'll come. Cross your heart and hope to die a horrible death if you don't."

Shay crossed her heart. "Satisfied?"

"You can ride with us," Adley said.

"No, thanks. If things get wanky, I want my own car."

"Okay, then. We're leaving at five. You can follow."

"I'll meet you there. What time does it start?"

"Seven, but we're setting up and then going for pizza at Anthony's. It's right there on the main drag and—"

Adley noticed Shay's attention was riveted on something behind them. Adley turned and saw Jasmine Thomas, the reporter from KVOZ TV, standing outside.

"What's she doing here?" Adley asked.

"Who knows? She's persistent. I'll give her that."

Jasmine walked inside and went to the table where Shay and Adley sat.

"Can we help you?" Adley asked.

Jasmine reached into her inside jacket pocket, retrieved Luke's letter, and set it down on the table. "This was left on the windshield of my car. I believe it belongs to you."

Shay stared at the letter.

"I didn't read it," Jasmine said. "Can't say I wasn't tempted, but despite what you think of me, I'm not a bad person." Jasmine turned and walked out of the coffee shop.

"Whoa," Adley said.

"Yeah. Whoa."

"Why would somebody leave your dad's letter on the windshield of her car?" Adley asked.

"Who knows? Nothing about the past two weeks has made any sense." Shay picked up the letter and stood. "I'm going home. See you later?"

"Yeah. I'll be looking for you, so if something changes..."

"I'll text."

Shay left for home. She wouldn't make the same mistake twice. She would read the letter as soon as she got to her room.

Bethany was showing a property, so Shay had the house to herself. She ran upstairs, closed her bedroom door, and removed the letter from her coat pocket. She opened it and began to read.

Dear Shay,

I don't know where to begin. If there are words to express my shame for being such a profound disappointment as a husband and father, I have not found them. Writing has never been my strong suit, but I'll do my best. Let me say at the outset I don't expect forgiveness or reconciliation, nor do I blame you or your mother for moving on with your lives. It gives me a sense of peace knowing you've done so. I'm the sole proprietor of the destruction of my life, and I know how much pain and disappointment my addiction has caused. If you had asked me before the abuse of "my product" that I thought I'd become an addict, I would've called you crazy, just as I called people who believed in God crazy. Now I find myself a believer in the risen Christ, and through his grace and mercy, I have found my way out of the hell of addiction. That is not to say I'm no longer an addict—that battle is a lifelong struggle—but I have been clean for almost seven months now, something else I would've never envisioned. I know what you're thinking: Sure, you "found God," how convenient. Now you expect everyone to act as if all is well. But I assure you I expect nothing of the sort. I write this letter for one reason, to tell you I love you and always will.

I did not find God. He found me. I was the lost one. I did everything possible to mock him, to ignore him, but he persisted. It was little things at first, breadcrumbs, like the people he put in my life that had faith, people who refused to back down in the face of my condescending taunts. Shameful. In AA, you put your life in the hands of a higher power. I rejected the idea at first, but others seemed to find strength in this belief. I studied. Then I met a pastor in a coffee shop, quite an odd fellow, and he intrigued me in a way few people have. I challenged him, told him people who believed in God were weak and they should grow up. His response? He put his hand on my shoulder and asked me if there was anything he could do for me. I wanted to spit in his face, and to my everlasting shame, I almost did. But in his eyes, I saw genuine kindness, and it shook me to the core. Despite my taunts, he showed love, mercy, and caring. Then he said, "My church is down the street. If you ever need anything or want some fellowship, drop in. I'd love to see you there."

My reply? "When pigs fly."

He smiled and said, "Miracles happen every day." Then he paid for my coffee and walked out.

I didn't go the first few weeks. Then one Sunday morning, I went to the odd pastor's church and went in. His sermon was about the Shroud of Turin. Throughout the sermon, they projected a picture of the Shroud on the screen. I couldn't take my eyes off it. The image captivated me in a way no image ever has. Could it possibly be the burial cloth of Jesus? I began researching it, reading everything I could get my hands on about it. I discovered it to be one of the most revered artifacts in the world. That led me to the Bible. Suddenly, I found myself immersed in the scriptures. I bought a reproduction of the Shroud and—check the sky for flying pigs—started to pray. It felt foolish. I mocked myself. Laughed at my stupidity. Grow up, Luke. Fool! Idiot! But the Shroud kept bringing me back to a single question: "Was it possible Jesus Christ rose from the dead?"

God is real, Shay. In my studies, I found out about Christians around the world being persecuted for their faith. I couldn't wrap my mind around it. My faith felt weak compared to theirs. I felt compelled to go and meet these people of amazing faith. When I watched with swelling pride (undeserved, I know) when you made Team USA, I knew it was another breadcrumb. I didn't want to interfere with your dream, but I could go to China and kill two birds with one stone, visit the city where you would soon be, visit the place you would skate, and pray for your safety and success. When you get this letter, I will be in Beijing, but you needn't worry. I will be back before you leave for the Olympics. This moment is not mine; it is for you and your mother. You both deserve it.

That's all. Just that I love you and hope you will feel the power of my prayers when you are there. My friend Iosif and I will watch you skate on TV. He has been a good friend and supporter of my spiritual quest. We will cheer you on every moment.

All my love forever,
Dad

Shay set the letter down and did her best to hold back the tears. "Dad," she whispered. Her lips quivered. She lifted her eyes, and her gaze fell upon her sketch of the Shroud. Her chest heaved. "God, I'm not a believer, so I don't know if you'll hear me or not, but my dad's in prison because he believes in you, so he needs you now more than ever." Her voice broke between her tears.

Shay settled back on her bed and considered the events of the past several days. Was Adley right? Was the universe trying to tell Shay something? Or, as Jack claimed, was God? Did Luke plan on being arrested, or was it a coincidence he went to the one house church the government of China most despised? And the fact it was all happening now when her dream of Olympic gold was within her reach. Was it Murphy's Law? Just things randomly lining up? Just her luck? She looked back at her sketch of the Shroud. "If you're trying to tell me something, it'd be a lot easier if you'd talk to me." Shay lay on her bed and considered something else. "Maybe I'm just losing my mind."

CHAPTER 23

Shay headed back to the arena. She had an hour before her afternoon practice but decided to spend extra time to stretch and focus. After reading Luke's letter, her emotions ran the gamut from an overwhelming sense of joy to feelings of both her betrayal and of being betrayed. Bethany had returned Luke's letter, and now Shay was keeping her discovery of the letter a secret. She knew Bethany was only trying to protect her by returning the letter, but it still made Shay angry. Shay decided to stay focused on skating and deal with her family issues after the Games. Bethany was the one who worked her tail off to pay for Shay's skating, and Shay knew she would've never made the team without her mother's support. If nothing else, Bethany showed Shay it was possible to overcome whatever barriers life put in your way. The more Shay thought about it, the more she respected her mother's single-minded pursuit of success. She decided it was time to return the favor. *Like mother, like daughter*, she thought and entered the arena with newfound determination.

Shay walked into the rink and spotted Jack on his hands and knees on the ice in the corner of the arena. *What is he up to now?* She walked around the barrier and saw him scratching something in the ice with an ice pick. "I'm afraid to ask," she said. Shay looked down at the patch of ice. "If you're keeping score of how many strange things you do a day, you're going to need a bigger patch of ice."

"Funny. Actually, you inspired me. It's a reproduction. Admittedly not exact, but it's close."

"To what?"

Jack handed his iPhone to Shay. "That."

Shay looked at the picture of what appeared to be scratches on a wall. "Okay, so what exactly am I looking at, chicken scratch?"

"Fingernails dug into the walls at Auschwitz."

Shay's stomach lurched. "Oh god," she whispered.

"Yeah. Hard to imagine, but that's the point. Like I said, one image can change the world. People need to be reminded that evil exists."

Shay was reminded of the article she read about the Chinese government forcing women to have abortions. She diverted her eyes from the photograph and looked down at the ice. "That's not a great reproduction."

Jack looked at his etching and back at the photograph. "Guess I'm a better photographer than an artist." Jack's eyes drifted back to Shay. "Have you ever been haunted by an image?"

The comment unnerved Shay. There was no doubt her experience with the Shroud of Turin was one she would describe as haunting. "I think we all have been at one time or another, seen an image that stays with us."

Jack kept his eyes on the scratches on the ice. "This is the one that haunts me. A world that can let that happen needs a savior, don't you think?"

Shay didn't respond. Jack smiled. It was wistful and lightened the mood. "I have a really good feeling about you."

"Is that so?"

"It is."

"A feeling. Isn't that sort of like soothsaying?"

"Now there's a word."

"Sorcery of sorts, isn't it? I didn't think Christians dabbled in that, predicting the future?"

"Have you never heard of prophecy?"

Now it was Shay who smiled. "Oh, so you're a prophet now, is that it?"

"Actually, I don't think having a good feeling about someone rises to the level of prophecy, but I'll check on it to be sure I'm not assaulting the threshold."

Shay looked back down at Jack's etching in the ice. "You're missing eleven scratches."

Jack's brows knit. "You're joking, right?"

"Check it. Eleven." Shay turned and walked toward the barrier. "Clean the ice, Jack. I'm on in twenty minutes."

"Count on it," Jack said. He counted his scratches in the ice and matched them to the picture in his hand. Shay was right. He was missing eleven.

Shay tied her skates, tugging hard at the laces to ensure a snug fit. Determined to rebound from yesterday's disastrous practice, she took to the ice and began skating a series of crossovers. It felt right today. The ice was perfect, and as she accelerated, she got that effortless feeling skater's experience when flow and continuity take over. Some athletes refer to it as being in the zone. Shay described it as Zen, a time when, even in the heat of intense physicality, everything moves in harmony. Her hip loosened up, and after a few minutes of skating and stretching, Shay began her Olympic warm-up. Moving gracefully from her crossovers into an Ina Bauer, she vaulted into the air and completed a perfectly executed double Axel. The landing was impressive. Maintaining speed when exiting jumps was crucial. If you two-footed a landing or failed to complete the required rotation, your exit speed was compromised. With total focus, Shay moved through all the elements of her long program. Everything was clicking. Her signature arabesque into a traveling camel spin spotted perfectly, and the exit speed on her triple Lutz could not have been better. With her warm-up complete, Shay skated to Remy and smiled.

"That felt good," Shay said.

Remy spoke as she moved her coffee cup to her lips. "It was good."

Shay heard clapping coming from the other side of the rink and saw that Bethany had arrived. "That's my girl!" Bethany said, raising her hands above her head as she continued to clap.

Shay turned to Remy. "I think I'm ready to try the quad Lutz."

"You sure?"

"Yes. Just one or two. I haven't landed one without the harness since nationals. If we're going to use it during a practice session at the Games, I need to be ready for it."

"Okay. But we wait until Bethany leaves the arena. I don't want her forcing the issue of including it as a competition element. We'll see where we end up after the short program. Then we can decide if we need to risk it to win."

Shay ran through her long program, and aside from a bobble on a flying sit spin, her performance was flawless. For the first time in more than a week, Shay felt good. The flow of her skating made her realize how much she had been forcing everything during her recent practice sessions.

"Whatever you did to get your mind back in the game, keep doing it," Remy said.

"I will." *If you only knew,* Shay thought, realizing the only thing she had done differently was pray the night before. Not that she put much faith in it, but regardless, she felt better today; there was no arguing with that. And she was about to attend a Christian youth group concert. She thought it might be a good idea to look up when she got outside to see if she could spot any flying pigs.

Bethany left for her office. It was time for Shay to attempt the quad Lutz.

"Feel the edge going in," Remy said. "Don't hesitate."

"Got it," Shay said.

Butterflies flew in her stomach. The quad Lutz was one of the most challenging jumps in figure skating. It was Shay's nemesis, the one jump she never felt comfortable visualizing. Shay built up speed and cut a sharp outer back edge before vaulting into the air. It was a solid takeoff, but she under rotated the jump, crashed down on the ice, and slammed into the boards. Fortunately, the fall hurt but didn't cause an injury. Shay got up and skated back to Remy.

"You okay?" Remy asked.

Shay blew out some air and rubbed at her hip. "Yeah. The take-off felt right, but once I got in the air…"

"Your free leg was too high," Remy said. "Let it go for today. We don't need it."

"Maybe. But I wouldn't be shocked if both Ling and Dasha tried it in the long."

"I'm counting on it," Remy said. "We skate clean. That's the plan."

Shay left the ice and was removing her skates when Curt showed up and sat down next to her. "Hey, future Olympic star, how'd practice go?"

"Not great, not terrible. But what are you doing here already? Your practice doesn't start for an hour."

"It got canceled. I thought we could go see a movie or something, a night just for us."

Definitely Murphy's Law, Shay thought. The one night she and Curt could spend together and she had already promised Adley she'd go to youth group.

"I'd love that, but I can't. I promised Adley I'd watch her play tonight."

"Great. I'll go too. Where's she playing? Sacred Grounds?"

"Hill Park. She's playing with Jack's band, at his church," Shay said and looked away from Curt to pull off her skate.

"Jesus fish Jack?" Curt asked incredulously.

"Yes, Curt, Jesus fish, Jack," Shay responded, clearly annoyed by Curt's attitude.

"I thought I told you to stay away from that guy?"

Shay's head snapped toward Curt. "You told me? Maybe I haven't been clear enough. You don't get to tell me what to do, where to go, or who to associate with. Be a boyfriend, not a warden."

Curt recoiled. "What's going on with you? Ever since you found out about your dad—"

"This has nothing to do with my dad. It has to do with you and me, period, end of story," Shay said.

"Fine. Since it's the end of the story, I'm closing the book. We're done," Curt said.

"Whatever," Shay said dismissively.

"You gonna pray now? Put a Jesus fish on your car and start blessing everybody you see?"

"I can think of worse things."

"You need to get a grip," Curt said and walked away.

Remy walked up to Shay. "What was that about?"

Shay grabbed her skates and stood up. "I was hoping for parole and got freedom instead."

"Oh. Well, that's good, then, right?" Remy said.

"Yeah, it's good."

CHAPTER 24

Shay's phone rang as she walked to her car. She answered. It was Bethany. "Where are you?"

"Just about to get in my car. I'm coming home to change. Why?"

"Ms. Lopez and Mr. Pond will be here in ten minutes. They'd like to update us on the situation and thought it best if you were here. I told them it would've been helpful to give more notice, but you know how that goes."

"On my way," Shay said.

On the drive home, Shay's heart pounded. "If you're out there, God, let this be good news."

Shay pulled into her development and noted the news trucks parked outside the gate. The guard let her through. She drove up the drive and parked her BMW alongside a sedan with government plates. She went inside. She found Bethany, Maya Lopez, and Ray Pond seated in the living room, enjoying the warmth of a fire blazing in the fireplace.

"Hey," Ms. Lopez said, "good to see you again. You remember my partner, Ray Pond?"

"Yes, of course," Shay said. "What's going on?"

"Unfortunately, the situation has worsened. Negotiations are significantly more difficult given your father's refusal to be released unless the government agrees to release Pastor Chen."

"I'm sure," Bethany said. "Anything to muck up the works. That's Luke."

"Is he safe?" Shay asked.

"For now," Ms. Lopez said. "But it's precarious."

"Because he's making it so," Bethany said.

"They made it so," Shay said. "He practiced his faith, and somehow that's a crime?"

Lopez continued, "We have a press conference tomorrow. We will state we have made limited progress but continue to work diligently to have Mr. Gerrard released. We remain optimistic."

"But you're not, right? Not really," Shay said.

"As I said, the situation is tenuous. The Chinese have a lot to lose if they back down."

"And Luke's ultimatum raised the stakes," Bethany said.

"Yes," Maya said.

"If he wanted to be home, he could be. Let's remember that," Bethany said, a statement clearly directed at Shay.

"Do you think they'd let him talk with me?" Shay asked.

Bethany's jaw dropped. "What?"

"To convince him to come home," Shay said.

Bethany was incredulous. "Out of the question. That will escalate this even more."

Shay looked at Maya. "Do you think it's possible?"

"I wouldn't get my hopes up. The Chinese don't like to exhibit weakness, but I'll make the suggestion. The politics here are delicate."

"Thank you," Shay said.

"We'll be in touch," Lopez said, and she and Pond left.

Bethany spoke through gritted teeth. "I cannot believe you'd turn on me this way. After all I've done."

"I'm not turning on you. He's my dad, and you loved him once too. I know you did," Shay said.

"That was a lifetime ago. He's a grown man. If he doesn't realize the damage he's doing, he's not going to change because you talk to him. Luke can end this whenever he wants to, but it's clear that he's more concerned about Pastor Chen than he is about his own daughter."

"Maybe he's concerned about more than Pastor Chen. They put people in prison for practicing their faith. They've forced women to have abortions and murdered their own people. Maybe he's standing up for something. Maybe he really has found something to believe in."

"Right, the Saint of Detroit. I'm asking you not to let him ruin our lives again. I've picked up the pieces once, and I don't think I should have to pick them up again. If you want to involve yourself after the Olympics, I'll support you but not before. I don't think that's too much to ask." Bethany looked at her watch. "I have a house to show."

"I know what he did to you, to us, but maybe he really has changed."

Bethany closed her eyes for a moment to compose herself. "I've tried to do my best for you. I guess it's time for you to do what you think is best for yourself." Bethany left the house, slamming the door behind her.

Shay went to her room and thought about the possibility of speaking with Luke. It had been seven years since she'd heard his voice, and after reading his letter, she felt she had a better sense of who he was. She now believed Luke when he claimed to be a Christian. Nothing else explained the level of sacrifice he was willing to make for his faith. The more she thought about it, the more she felt it was a better path than the one he had been on. *Who cares why he changed?* she thought. *The only thing that matters is he has a purpose now, a reason to stay off drugs and make a difference in his life.*

Shay looked at her sketch of the Shroud. She had prayed the night before. It was quick. She prayed to cover a base, to see if she felt some sudden revelation or to hear God actually speak to her. Jack said she wasn't listening, but no voice came. Nonetheless, she felt compelled to try it again and found herself on her knees by her bedside. With hands folded and fingers laced, she whispered a prayer. She waited to hear the voice of God, but no voice came. It was all so confusing. Her emotions swung between feeling foolish one minute and feeling a path had been set before her with an invitation to follow it the next. This time, praying felt less uncomfortable, and knowing Luke also prayed made her feel closer to him, just as it would if she knew both of them were wishing on a star at exactly the same moment. It made her wonder what the difference was between wishing and praying or if there was really any difference at all. As her mind shifted through this myriad of thoughts and feelings, one thing remained, the haunting image of the man embedded in the Shroud. Shay lifted her eyes to her sketch. "I'll say this—you are certainly relentless."

Shay went to her closet, selected her clothes for the evening, and dressed for the concert. She decided on casual, just jeans and a blue button-down shirt. She was deciding now, taking charge.

While she picked out her clothes, ESPN played in the background. When she heard the name Ling Yue, she stopped getting dressed and ran to watch. Ling was the reigning world champion, a tiny powerhouse with explosive jumps, exquisite form, and steel nerves. Ling didn't falter. Other skaters quipped that "Yue was Yuan," as in Yue was money—you could count on her to come through with a stellar performance, especially when the stakes were high.

Yue sat next to an interpreter who helped translate Yue's responses to the ESPN commentator's questions. Yue appeared shy and reserved, a persona that changed the moment her blades touched the ice. The commentator began with several questions about her training and hopes for the upcoming Olympics. Yue's interpreter smiled as he provided Yue's responses: "Yes, she felt ready for competition," and "Yes, she thought she had a good chance to win gold."

"What about the current US champion Shay Gerrard?" the commentator asked. "She skated brilliantly at the US championships?"

Shay's ears perked up. Yue smiled politely and spoke. Her interpreter answered. "She is good, but it will be difficult for her to not falter in her first Olympics. So much pressure. I wish her the best."

Shay appreciated the gamesmanship. Yue was a competitor.

The commentator quickly pivoted to a question that was, by the look on the interpreter's face, clearly unexpected. "As I'm sure you know, Shay Gerrard's father, Luke Gerrard, is now in prison in Beijing—"

Before the commentator could finish his question, the interpreter ripped the microphone from his lapel jacket and threw it at the commentator.

Stunned, the commentator tried to recover. "Sir, it's a simple—"

The interpreter grabbed Yue by the arm, and they stormed off the set.

Shay was as surprised as the ESPN guy was. "Wow. Touchy, aren't we?" Shay said and then went to her car and drove to Hill Park.

CHAPTER 25

Shay parked in front of the theater and stepped out of her car. Adley was waiting for her in the lobby.

"There you are! I was hoping you wouldn't back out."

"I need the diversion," Shay said. "Besides, seeing the girl who has her own paranormal podcast playing in a church alongside Captain Jack has a certain allure. Can I consider you two an item yet?"

"We're cohorts, not an item."

"'Cohorts,'" Shay repeated flatly.

"We're not ready for the Hallmark Channel, if that's what you're asking."

The number of young people at the event surprised Shay. They were a diverse group but unified in their enthusiasm. The vibe in the theatre was electric. As the attendees grabbed drinks and popcorn from a snack table, Christian music reverberated off the walls. Strobes flashed, and laser lights pulsed to the beat of the music. *This is church?* Shay thought. This was not what she expected. The youth group attendees sang along with the music and performed impromptu dance moves as they laughed and moved toward their seats. Shay felt a tap on the shoulder and turned to see Tahnee Spire, a skater she knew, standing behind her.

"Hi, Shay!" Tahnee said.

"Oh, hey, Tahnee," Shay replied, feeling as if she had been caught where she didn't belong.

Tahnee was fourteen, a midlevel skater with a lot of talent. She had recently moved into the area and had been a member of the Figure Skating Club for the past four months.

"It's great to see you here!" Tahnee said.

"Thanks," Shay said. "I'm just here because my friend's playing in the band." After she said it, Shay wondered why she felt compelled to explain her presence at the concert.

"That's cool. We're all praying for your dad, not to mention the thousands of others praying for him. You've got an amazing following on social media."

"Yes, I'm shocked every time I look and see how many people there are on my feed. And I'm grateful for the prayers."

Pastor Guff walked on stage signaling the start of the event.

"Where are you sitting?" Tahnee asked.

"Near the front. My friend saved me a seat."

"Awesome. Enjoy the concert!"

Shay loved Tahnee's enthusiasm. "Thanks. I'm sure I will."

Shay made her way down the main aisle and took her seat. A moment later, the music ended, and Pastor Guff ran up on stage. He wore brown velvet pants, roman sandals, and a white cotton shirt topped off with a colorful bowtie. "Welcome, everyone! What a great turnout!"

The group hooped and hollered their approval.

"I have a joke."

The audience groaned.

"You'll love this one, promise," Pastor Guff said. "A woman has a heart attack and is taken to the hospital. On the operating table, she has a near-death experience. She sees God and asks if this is it. God says no, she has another thirty years to live. Upon her recovery, she stays in the hospital and has a facelift and tummy tuck. She figures since she's got another thirty years she might as well make the most of it. Then she walks out of the hospital and is killed by an ambulance speeding by. She arrives in front of God and complains, 'I thought you said I had another thirty years.' And God replies, 'I didn't recognize you.'"

A collective groan reverberates in the theater.

"No?" Pastor Guff said. He looked up. "It's a tough crowd tonight, Lord."

The hipster pastor charmed Shay. There was something disarming about him, a sense she could trust him, and his fun side—if not funny—was endearing.

"Let's pray," Pastor Guff said.

Shay lowered her head.

"Father God, we welcome you into this place. Help us feel your Spirit as we rejoice in song and praise. And for our brother in Christ Luke Gerrard and for those oppressed around the world for recognizing the one eternal truth, that you are God, may you be their strength. Bring him home to us, Lord. And I hear a great big loud and enthusiastic…"

"Amen!" the group said.

"Tonight, we have two special guests. First, Adley Finch of the all-girl band the X-Chromosomes is joining our very own Mustard Seeds as a guest drummer." Pastor Guff joined the others in applause and then looked at Shay seated in the front row. "And it thrills us to have Luke's daughter and Olympian, Shay Gerrard, with us tonight." Pastor Guff pointed at Shay, and more applause followed. Shay smiled sheepishly and waved back at Pastor Guff. What she wanted was to disappear. Adley and Jack must have told Pastor Guff she was coming.

When the band played, the theater erupted with the attendees bouncing, dancing, and singing along with each new praise song. Jack was rocking out on keyboards, and Adley was keeping the beat on drums. Shay couldn't help but get caught up in the experience. To see so many young people praising God with such reckless abandon carried with it a wave of emotion, and Shay, to her surprise, was swept up in it. It felt so right to be there and to become a part of one voice praising Jesus, but it also felt strange. How could she suddenly entertain the notion of a man coming back from the dead? Stranger still that God came into the world to be fully human as a baby born of a virgin. Maybe Curt was right. Maybe she needed to get a grip. An internal tug-of-war had begun the moment she discovered the reproduction of the Shroud. The image seeped inside her and caused her to challenge everything she believed or, more accurately, didn't believe. Now here she was singing praise songs! As the band played an upbeat rendition of "Amazing Grace," a picture of Christ beaten and bleeding as he carried his cross was projected on two big screens on either side of the stage. Shay's eyes teared up. When the concert was over, Shay met Adley and Jack in the lobby.

"How did you like it?" Adley asked.

"It was good," Shay said. "People really get caught up, don't they?"

"That's what happens when the Spirit moves you," Jack said. "He was moving here tonight. Did you feel it?"

"The music was great. I'll admit that. How much did you guys practice together?" Shay asked, deflecting Jack's question.

"Once," Adley said.

"Then I'll admit I witnessed a miracle here tonight," Shay said.

"You should grab a tattoo," Jack suggested, pointing to a table set up on the other side of the lobby.

"What?" Shay said.

"NOTW. Not of this world," Jack said. "They're henna." Jack displayed the NOTW tattoo on his inner forearm.

"Let's do it!" Adley said, grabbing Shay by the shoulder and moving her toward the table. "It'll be fun!"

Shay followed Adley to the table where henna tattoos and rope bracelets with the same lettering were being given out by members of the youth group.

"Two tattoos, two bracelets," Adley said.

"I'm not wearing a tattoo," Shay said.

"You never know when you might need one," Adley replied and handed Shay a bracelet and a tattoo.

When they walked outside, it surprised Shay to see Curt standing by her car with a dozen roses in hand.

"Speaking of the Hallmark Channel," Adley said.

Shay walked over to Curt. "Well, this is a surprise."

Curt handed the roses to Shay. "I've been a jerk, and since Jesus said to forgive is divine, I thought this was a good place to beg for it."

Shay smelled the roses. "They're beautiful. Thanks."

"So am I forgiven?"

"If you do one thing for me for an hour," Shay said.

"Name it."

An hour later, Curt sat with Shay, Adley, and Jack in Anthony's Pizzeria.

"Is my hour up yet?" Curt asked.

Shay checked her phone. "Nope. Nine minutes to go."

Between bites of pizza, Jack said, "I think it looks great."

"Me too," Adley said.

"I think it suits you," Shay said, staring at the NOTW tattoo on Curt's forehead.

"Minutes?"

"Eight," Shay said.

Curt sighed and took another bite of his pizza.

Adley sipped her soda and set the cup down on the table. "Any news about your dad?"

"I might be able to speak to him," Shay said.

Adley's eyes widened. "Really?"

"I asked the people from the State Department to try to arrange it."

"What are you going to say?" Adley asked.

"That's just it. I'm not sure. Come home, I guess. Stop demanding Pastor Chen's release, and just come home. He's not safe there, and it's not his fight."

"It's every Christian's fight," Jack said.

"Easy for you to say, Jack. Your father's not in prison," Shay said.

"Not anymore," Jack said.

Shay's eyes shot up and met Jack's. "What are you talking about?"

"Your father was in prison?" Adley asked.

"In India. He was charged with trying to convert aboriginals and sentenced to six months in prison."

"But he's okay now?" Adley asked.

Jack shrugged. "He seemed fine tonight."

Adley's eyes widened. "He was there?"

"Sure. He's the pastor," Jack said.

"Get…out!" Adley said, punching Jack's shoulder. "Wait, there's no way he's old enough to be your father."

Shay held up her hands. "Don't punch me, Adley, but the hipster pastor's thirty-seven."

Adley's jaw fell open.

"I know, hard to believe," Shay said and looked to Jack. "There is a slight resemblance. You're both incredibly odd."

Curt, who felt like the odd man out in the conversation, interjected, "Is my time up yet?"

Shay checked her watch. "Yes, time's up."

"Excellent. I'll be right back." Curt headed to the bathroom to remove the tattoo from his forehead.

Shay turned her attention back to Jack. "So you think I shouldn't ask him to come home, is that it?"

"That's not up to me. I'm just saying some people are willing to risk everything for something greater than themselves. Look at this." Jack found a picture on his phone and showed it to Shay. It was a photograph of Pastor Guff, standing in the rubble of a demolished church with several other men, holding up the large cross that had once been mounted on the outside of the building. It reminded Shay of a different iconic photograph.

"It's like those Marines raising the flag," Shay said.

"Iwo Jima. That's why I want to be a photojournalist, because…"

"One image can change the world," Shay said, finishing Jack's thought.

"Exactly."

Curt returned from the bathroom with a clean forehead. Shay stared at him for a moment.

"What?" Curt asked. "It's all off, right?"

"Yeah. But now your forehead looks kinda bare," Shay said.

"It's a forehead, not a billboard," Curt replied.

Shay glanced at the clock on the wall. "I need to get going. I've got practice in the morning. Can you take me, Curt?"

Curt wrote "YES" on a napkin and held it up to his forehead.

"Cute," Shay said.

Curt wrote "LOVE YOU" on the flip side and put it up to his forehead.

"Okay, that's…just…stop," Shay said.

Curt grabbed another napkin, but Shay ripped it out of his hand before he could write on it. "Your forehead's perfect. I love your bare forehead."

"You shouldn't talk dirty in front of Jack, being as he's a pastor's kid," Adley said.

"My apologies, Jack," Shay said, and the group left the pizzeria.

Shay returned home feeling better than she had since the news broke that Luke had been imprisoned. Her reconciliation with Curt was an unexpected surprise, and her night with the youth group went far better than she could have imagined. She felt something spiritual in that place, a connection, and she wondered if her father's faith in God might not be so foolish after all. Shay gazed at her sketch of the Shroud and whispered, "Okay, God, what is it you want me to do?"

CHAPTER 26

Twenty-five days until Olympic skate

Sunshine radiated through Shay's alcove window. She forestalled getting out of bed in favor of basking in the warmth beneath her covers. She had been up late thinking about Luke's situation and waiting to see if God would speak to her heart. She didn't know what to do yet, but she felt herself drawn closer to agreeing with Jack. She was being nudged. Forces beyond her understanding were in play. Now, for the first time, she opened her mind to the possibility there was a God. She would follow his lead to save her father. She had to do something, but what?

Shay got out of bed, tucked her feet in her slippers, and went downstairs. Bethany was in the kitchen, and it was clear she was still angry with Shay. Shay hoped word would come from the State Department regarding her call with Luke. As much as she knew her mother wasn't happy with the suggestion, Shay believed it was the right thing to do.

"Good morning," Bethany said in a monotone voice.

"Morning," Shay said.

Bethany and Shay moved around the kitchen as if each had no idea the other was there. It was tense and awkward, and when Bethany finally left for work, Shay was relieved. She dressed for practice and headed to the rink. It was in the car, listening to music, that the idea came to her. A revelation of sorts. It had been there all along, one way to help her father's cause. It would require help from Adley and Jack, but Shay was confident they would help. She decided it was best not to share her intentions with anyone. For her idea to work, so many things would have to go Shay's way. *Or God's way,* Shay thought.

Shay pulled to the side of the road and called Adley.

"I need you to do something for me," Shay said, "but it has to be our secret. You can't tell anybody, and that includes Jack."

"Sure, what is it?" Adley asked.

Shay described what she needed, and Adley could hardly contain her excitement. "Wowza! Are you sure you want me to do it?"

"Yes, absolutely. You don't have much time. What do you think?"

"I think I should disconnect and get at it," Adley said. "And Shay?"

"Yeah?"

"I won't let you down."

"Never entered my mind."

They disconnected, and Shay continued on to the arena.

Practice today would include several runs of both her short and long program, concentrating on flow, transitions, and musical interpretation. Remy insisted on shifting focus from the athletic elements to the artistic components to be sure Shay maintained an appropriate balance between both aspects of her skating. Shay loved the integration of art and athleticism figure skating provided but agreed with Remy that the new scoring system encouraged taking risks in athleticism at the expense of skating a clean program. If you attempted a quad Lutz and fell, it could reward the attempt beyond the deduction for the fall.

"I'd rather see more flawless performances," Remy said. "The unique aspect of our sport is the art, the musical interpretation, the emotionality. I'm against any rule that marginalizes art and encourages attempts over proper completion. But the scoring system is what it is, and we need to consider the implications in our decision-making."

Shay spotted Jack. Having just finished resurfacing the ice, he navigated the Zamboni off ice and parked it. If her idea had any chance of playing out the way she envisioned it, she would need Jack's help. She had a few minutes before her ice time began, so she caught him as he was climbing down from the machine.

"Hey, Jack," Shay said.

Jack had his back to her and was listening to music through his earbuds, so he didn't hear Shay. Shay tapped him on the shoulder. He turned and removed the earbuds. "Talk to Remy," he said defensively. "She insisted I clean the ice."

"It's fine," Shay said. "I'm practicing first skater in the group today. Forget the whole thing about resurfacing the ice. I'm over it."

"Oh. Okay."

"Listen, how late do you stay after hockey to clean the ice?"

"A few hours. I clean the ice, then empty the trash around the perimeter of the arena, mop the floors. Why?"

"Because I want to work on some changes to my choreography without my mother and Remy knowing about it. I need to have it worked out before I show it to them. Is there anybody else in the arena that late?"

"Just the security guards, one inside and one in the parking lot."

"How does the building get locked up at night?"

"Ozzie, the supervisor of the guards, locks up after I leave."

"Do you resurface the ice first?"

"No. Last. I like to finish on a high note."

"Well, I need you to switch notes while I work this out. I want clean ice. Can you do that?"

"Yeah, sure."

"Good. We start tonight. I'll spend an hour in the rink after hockey is over and work on my choreography after you've resurfaced the ice. No taking pictures. I can't work with anyone watching."

"Okay. It takes an hour for me to finish the trash and the bathrooms. I can't promise Ozzie won't take a moment to watch, but I doubt he'll look for long. He has to make his rounds. Ozzie's cool, but he takes his job seriously."

"Do you think he'll say anything about me being on the ice that late?"

"If you were just anybody, then maybe. But you're our very own Olympic hopeful. He'll think you're putting in extra time before you leave for Beijing."

"Great," Shay said. "Then I'll see you later."

Dealing with her mother wouldn't be an issue. Bethany went to bed early. If she let her mother know she was watching Curt's hockey game and would have Curt follow her home after the game was over, Bethany wouldn't question it.

Shay changed into her practice outfit and stretched. She spotted Bethany standing in her usual spot, ready to oversee Shay's practice just as she had so many times over the past seven years. Shay was relieved to see her there. Her mom could be stubborn, but Shay knew Bethany was the reason she was an Olympian, and her mom deserved to share fully in the Olympic experience. Shay understood Bethany's resentment toward Luke. From Bethany's perspective, she had helped turn Lukewarm Luke into one of the best salesmen in the country. She left her career in real estate, which was just beginning to flourish, to raise Shay and care for things on the home front so Luke could concentrate on his work, and he had thrown it all away just to get high. Now Shay was attempting to contact him, and Shay knew her mother was concerned it would break the mother-daughter bond forged by a shared dream—to win Olympic gold. Now, at the moment the dream might be realized, Luke appeared on the scene and threatened Shay's chance to stand on the top of the podium as the top female figure skater in the world. After their last argument, Shay feared that Bethany might follow through and boycott her practices, so seeing Bethany in the rink was a blessing.

Remy walked up to Shay with coffee cup in hand. "Ready to take on the short?"

"First to skate, right?"

"Yes. Follow the scripted warm-up, and be off the ice twenty seconds before the warm-up period is complete."

"Got it."

Shay moved through her short program warm-up. Her spins were fine, but Shay's takeoff on the triple flip was flawed, causing her to under rotate the jump and two-foot the landing.

"Shoulders square and pace your timing," Remy said. "You're rushing the takeoff."

Shay nodded and attempted another triple flip, this time landing with only a slight bobble. Her timing was wrong. She skated to Remy with her head down.

"What's the matter?" Remy asked.

"I don't know. I feel a little off today."

"Perfect," Remy said. "We need a few days like this, so we can work our way through it. When you get to Beijing, your adrenaline will be in overdrive. We need to be ready for that. Your shoulders are ahead of your hips. What do we do when we're overhyped?"

"Breathe, relax, reset."

"You've got thirty-five seconds. Try another flip?"

Shay shook her head. "No. I'm ready."

Shay was into the first thirty seconds of her program when she attempted another triple flip. This time, she landed on a sure edge but felt a shooting pain in her ankle. Shay winced, stepped off her right foot, and waved at Remy to turn off the music.

Bethany rushed around the boards to get closer to Shay. "Stay off it!" Bethany yelled.

Gingerly, Shay made her way over to Remy, hands on the boards to balance herself as she rolled her ankle in a circular motion.

"How bad?" Remy asked.

Shay put weight on the ankle. "I think it's okay. I just landed funny."

"You landed perfectly," Remy said. "That's enough for today. Go home and ice it. We'll go again tomorrow."

"I have your crutches in the car," Bethany said.

"I don't need crutches."

"Use the crutches, Shay. Better safe than sorry," Remy said.

Shay rolled her eyes. "Fine. Get them. But you're both overreacting."

Shay removed her skates and felt her ankle. She would use the crutches, but she had no intention of staying off it for the day. Her plan required that she be on the ice tonight; and nothing, not even a potential injury, would stop her.

CHAPTER 27

Shay watched the final minutes of Curt's hockey practice in awe of his ability to keep the other team from scoring. He scissored his legs, swatted his hands, and sprawled on the ice using everything at his disposal to stop the puck from entering his goal. Shay loved watching Curt play and thought he looked gallant in his hockey gear.

"How do you like my ensemble?" he asked, skating up to her the first time she stayed to watch a game.

"Not exactly shining armor, but you look quite regal," Shay said.

It was an innocent flirt. It suggested he might have a chance of becoming *her* knight. Curt lifted his hockey stick in the air and said, "And within it, dear lady, I shall defend your honor and my goal to the death."

"Please do," Shay said.

Two months had passed since they first started dating. Now Shay was proud of him not only for his prowess on the ice but for his understanding and apology. After the game, he skated to the boards, and Shay handed him a cold bottle of water.

"Nice job!" Shay said. "If I manage to get anything past you, I'll feel quite proud of myself."

Curt removed his goalie mask and guzzled some water. "Let's hope the scout for the Red Wings agrees." Curt noticed the crutches resting on the seat next to Shay. "What happened?"

"Precautionary. I'm fine. In fact, I need to work on some choreography tonight. No jumps or spins, just footwork, nothing too strenuous on it."

"Can I stay with you? It can get creepy if you're alone in here after everyone's gone."

"It'll be boring. I'm just working out some steps, mapping it out the next few nights. Jack will clean the ice for me, and then I'll get started."

"I want to follow you home. Is that overly protective?"

Shay smiled. "No, it's perfect. I'll be about an hour."

"Good. I videotaped the game. I can review it while I wait."

Shay stretched and tested her ankle. It felt okay. She watched as Jack stood atop the Zamboni in the same pose he displayed the first day she met him. She had misjudged him. Jack was strange, but he was so sure of who he was and what he believed. Shay was envious of that. She had always thought she was confident in who she was, but Luke's imprisonment and Jack's unfailing belief in God made her realize she had never thought much about anything but skating and her art. It amazed her it was possible to live life in such a secluded way yet fool yourself into believing you were worldly and thoughtful.

Shay stood by the boards and put earbuds in her ears. It was time to work through the choreography she had visualized over the past several days. The ice glistened in the overhead lights. The cold air invigorated her. Shay had read about actors who worked to become the character they were about to portray. The image in the Shroud captivated her, but in the past week, it was the agony Jesus endured on the cross that gripped her. She thought about Mary and how painful it must have been for her to watch the spikes being driven through Jesus's wrists and feet, to see him suffer the excruciating pain as they raised the cross, leaving his body to hang in one of the most torturous ways to die ever devised.

Shay pressed Play on her iPhone, and "Sanctuary" played. This was the song that had inspired Luke, along with "The Shroud," to be all in for his faith. As the haunting melody played, Shay glided onto the ice and began the painstaking work of recreating Mary's plight as Jesus, the Son she adored, sacrificed himself to save a broken world. Shay's goal was to draw people in and make them feel what Mary felt. With blades beneath her feet and the music infused in her soul, Shay went to work. Less than thirty-minutes later, she had completed her first attempt and found Jack sweeping in the snack bar.

"That was quick," Jack said.

"I'm not finished. I need you to resurface the ice."

"I just did."

"Well, you missed a spot."

"I did?"

"Jack, just—I need it resurfaced, okay? It's important."

"But—"

"I think God's trying to talk to you. All you need to do is listen. Sound familiar?"

"Vaguely."

Shay crossed her arms and glared at him.

"On my way," Jack said.

Jack was resurfacing the ice when Shay skated out in front of the Zamboni. Jack turned off the engine and looked down at her. "Something wrong?"

"No. I just wanted to thank you for being your authentic self. I admire that because I'm not sure I ever am, you know, my authentic self." Shay looked down and nervously scratched her pick into the ice.

"I just resurfaced that," Jack said.

Shay ignored the comment. "It's ironic. You believe in something with all your heart, and I thought you were a freak. I believed in nothing and thought I was the keeper of the truth. I'm sorry for that. I'm sorry for all of it."

Jack was about to respond when Shay pointed down to where her toe pick had dug into the ice. "You missed a spot," she said, and before he could say a word, she turned and skated away from him.

Jack smiled and called out to her "You amaze me, Frank!"

"I learned from the best!" Shay said, never turning as she skated back to grab a drink before returning to the ice.

As the music played through her earbuds, Shay worked her new exhibition choreography, cutting edges in meticulous detail, absorbing the words and music until their meaning moved through her—body, mind, and soul. She transcended time and felt Mary's crushing despair as she watched Jesus drag the cross, the instrument of his coming torture and death, toward Golgotha. Shay's movements felt technically effortless but emotionally devastating. When the music ended, she dropped to her knees and wept.

Curt's voice seemed distant. It was his touch that brought her back as he lifted Shay up off the ice. "What happened?"

Shay wiped the tears from her eyes and forced a smile. "Just thinking about my dad…what he's going through."

Curt cradled Shay in his arms and guided her off the ice. Shay felt a painful throbbing in her ankle.

"Can you get me an ice pack?" Shay asked.

"Sure. Just give me a minute. You want your crutches?"

"That would be great," Shay said. "And find Jack. Tell him I need him to clean the ice before he leaves."

Shay unlaced her right skate and massaged her ankle. The pain didn't concern her, but it was her landing foot, and she could ill-afford to have issues with it. She leaned back and rested her ankle on the chair in front of her. Despite the pain, she felt good about what she had accomplished. If it went as planned, it would all be worth it. Curt returned moments later with crutches in hand.

"Thanks," Shay said, setting the crutches beside her.

"I found Jack. He wanted me to remind you it's an ice rink, not…"

"An Etch-a-Sketch, I know. Don't let him fool you. He loves riding that Zamboni. It's like his personal yacht."

Curt laughed. "I don't mind him too much. Besides the whole Jesus freak thing, he's okay. Perfect for Adley. They're both a little odd."

When Curt and Shay left the arena, the weather had changed. It had been a calm night; but now a slashing wind, icy and harsh, shifted and swirled, causing sheets of white powder to levitate and spin beneath the overhead lights. Curt held Shay's arm as she attempted to navigate on crutches but decided it was best to carry her. Before she could mount a protest, Curt swept her up in his arms and carried her to her car. Shay cuddled her head into his shoulder, thankful that he was there to help. When he set her down, she huddled close to him.

"So I guess chivalry is not dead," she said.

"Not on my watch. It's freezing out here, so drive slow. I'll be right behind you."

Curt put her crutches in the backseat, went to his car, and followed Shay's BMW out of the parking lot and followed her home. He parked, got her crutches out of the car, and walked her to her front door.

"I hope it works out for your dad," Curt said.

"Thanks."

Shay looked out at the snowfall. "It's strange, but the world seems so much bigger to me now, as if I'm seeing it for the first time. Does that sound weird?"

"No."

"I better get inside," Shay said. "Be careful driving home. Text me when you get there."

"I will."

They embraced, and Shay went inside.

Shay gazed at the Shroud. She was as mesmerized by the image as the first day she saw it hanging above Luke's bed. She had never been interested in religion, but the Shroud and Luke's commitment to his faith had changed that. "I believe in you because of my dad, so I'm counting on us to get him out of that prison. That's my prayer, that the Chinese will let me speak with him. Answer this one prayer. That's all I ask."

It was a prayer that wouldn't be answered.

CHAPTER 28

Twenty-four days until Olympic skate

Shay was at the rink about to put on her skates when she got the call from Maya Lopez. The Chinese had refused Shay's request to speak with Luke.

"It's a complicated situation," Lopez said.

Bethany, who was standing beside Shay, overheard Lopez and, to Shay's surprise, grabbed the phone from Shay. Bethany hit the speakerphone button so Shay could hear. "With all due respect, Ms. Lopez, it's not complicated at all. They're refusing to let his daughter speak with him. It's inhumane, unconscionable, and I demand to know what the State Department plans to do about it."

It stunned Shay. Was her mother sticking up for Luke now?

Lopez did her best to explain the State Department's position, but Bethany refused to stand down. "If you want Shay and me to stay neutral in this situation, we expect you to solve it. Luke is a US citizen being held captive in a foreign country. And for what? Praying to a God the Chinese government doesn't even believe in? If they believe God doesn't exist, why are they so afraid?"

Maya struggled to respond. "I understand your frustration, but—"

"No more excuses. Have you seen or spoken to Luke? Are you even sure he's okay?"

"We have not spoken to him, but they have assured us—"

"Assured? By the Chinese?" Bethany said. "It concerns me they won't let us see him or speak to him, and it should trouble you and the State Department as well."

Lopez tried to convince Bethany it would not be in Luke's best interest to antagonize the Chinese. "I would advise you not poke the bear. Bad things could happen."

"I am the bear, Ms. Lopez, and the problem is that bad things could happen right now, so I suggest you and your colleagues get to work. Call when you have this resolved."

Bethany disconnected and turned to Shay. "This is why I didn't want him back in our lives. Nothing but disappointment and heartache."

"It's not him," Shay said. "I let myself believe something that was never true. Joke's on me. Tell Remy I changed my mind about practice this morning. My ankle's really sore."

"Shay—"

"I need time. I'll be at this afternoon's practice. Promise."

Shay removed her skates, grabbed her skate bag, and walked out of the arena.

Jack arrived and spotted Shay walking to her car. He pulled into the space beside her BMW and greeted her.

"Everything okay?" he asked.

"Go away, Jack."

"I'll take that as a no."

"Take it however you want."

"Did I do something I'm not aware of?"

"No. You did something you're totally aware of. You sold me on a god that doesn't exist."

"That's not true."

"You told me I wasn't listening. Turns out, he's the one who doesn't listen. I get on my social media accounts and ask people to pray with me for a chance to speak with my dad. For the first time in my life, I got down on my knees and prayed with thousands of others, and guess what. Your Almighty God couldn't even make a phone call happen."

"He's God, not a genie in a bottle. He doesn't grant wishes."

"Then what's the point? Do me a favor—leave Adley alone. She's better off believing in zombies."

"God is at work in your life, Shay. It may not be what you want and how you want it, because our plans are not his plans. God's perspective is eternity, not the here and now."

"How convenient."

"And what's your father's will? What do you believe he's praying for?"

Shay's eyes burned into Jack's. "I'm sure it's not to remain in a Chinese prison, Jack. Not that it's any of your business."

Before Jack could respond, Shay got in her car and sped away, spinning her tires in the process.

As the snow continued to fall, Jack grabbed his phone from his pocket and called Adley.

Shay's hands gripped the steering wheel until her knuckles turned white. How could she be so stupid? And Luke? What had his faith done other than move him from the prison of addiction to a prison in China? Conflicting thoughts pummeled her mind. Was God nothing but a cosmic joke? "Show yourself!" Shay screamed, pounding her fist on the steering wheel. Her phone played the theme music from the *Twilight Zone*. It was Adley. Shay didn't respond. Fifteen minutes later, Shay arrived at Bebchuk's Pawn & Trade. She got out of her car and marched inside.

Iosif was watching *The Price Is Right* on his tiny television. He looked up and spotted Shay. He could tell she had been crying.

"You look like cat dragged something in. What is wrong?"

Shay extended her hand. "Keys to his apartment, please."

"Did you hear bad news for father?" Iosif said. "I have prayed for you...and for him...every night."

Shay let out a condescending laugh. "You and thousands of others. A lot of good it did. He's still in prison, and the Chinese won't let me speak to him. Ask and you shall receive? More like ask and be ignored."

"This is not true. God is there...always...listening."

Shay rolled her eyes. "Fine. He listened, then did nothing."

"Maybe nothing is better."

"I prayed for them to release my father. How could it be better that he stays in prison?"

"We are just people. He is God."

Shay was incredulous. "You believe this."

"When I was younger, I hated this God. What fools were people to believe this nonsense? I was atheist. My father, big atheist. But Mother, she believed in this God. She would pray…each night. And it was this that so many of her prayers were never answered that made my father mock her. But she did not stop. For much time, I hated this. Then one day, I asked her, 'Why do you believe this God who never does what you ask?' She turned to me with a fire in her eyes I had never seen before and said, 'Jesus died on the cross to save me from my sins, so what does he owe me that I should make demands?' You think I should say, 'Jesus, your blood and suffering were not enough. Give me more, or I will turn from you'? Who is foolish, Iosif? You believe none of my prayers are answered when you stand before me, the son I prayed for after doctors told me I could not conceive. You, the miracle of my life? What prayers are not answered I leave in his hands, because he is God and I am not. That is my answer.'"

Shay closed her eyes and pushed her hand through her hair. "Can I have the key now?"

Iosif handed Shay the key.

"Thank you."

"You are welcome."

Shay turned and walked toward the front door.

Iosif called to her. "In this place, people pawn their things, trade away what is precious to them for things the world makes them think they need. Then realizing what they've done, they come back and pray to get back what they so foolishly traded away."

Shay turned back to him. "You were a good friend to my dad. Thank you for that." Shay left the pawnshop, letting the door close behind her.

Shay walked to the back alley through a pristine blanket of snow. She was drawn to this place to feel closer to her father. She had so many questions. *Was he okay? What drew him to God? Why was he willing to sacrifice himself for something he once thought a fairy tale?*

She was angry at God. But as her mother had said about the Chinese government, why be mad at a God that didn't exist?

The snow had drifted in the alley, and the bottom steps leading to Luke's apartment were buried in white powder. Shay kicked the snow away with her boot and trudged up the stairs. With every step, her boots crunched into the snow. On the landing, she fumbled with the key and pushed it into the lock. Once inside, Shay closed the door behind her and lifted the shade on the front window. Sunlight flooded the room. As she stood there, she thought of Odette from Swan Lake and felt as if she were standing on her own lake of tears frozen over by a heart hardened by time and circumstance.

Shay gazed at Luke's recliner, its busted springs straining against the tattered fabric, its arms worn through where elbows had rested for so many years. Shay walked to the recliner and sat down. She picked up the devotional resting on the tray table and noted the ear-marked pages. Shay closed her eyes and tried to feel Luke's hands on hers. Feeling nothing, she set the book back down. *Get a grip, Shay Gerrard.* She gazed back at the book.

Don't be stupid…

Open it…

Stop it, Shay…

Just open it to a page and see what it says…

Shay grabbed the book, opened it, and started moving through pages until she saw a sentence Luke had underlined in red: *I believe; help my unbelief.*

Shay stared at the note and realized Luke shared her struggle. He understood what it felt like to want desperately to believe while struggling with doubt. She set the book down and walked into Luke's bedroom. She flipped on the black light and gazed at the image that had ignited her curiosity about faith. She sat on the floor and let her eyes settle on the ethereal face of a man many believed was the Christ and prayed. An hour passed, and then another. The words her father wrote resonated in her mind. *I did not find God. He found me. I was the one who was lost.*

Tears rained down Shay's face before she even knew she was crying. "Help me," she said. The relentless torrent of emotions she experienced over the last few weeks had taken a toll. She knew she had been drawn here, to the room where her father slept beneath a reproduction of the Shroud. "I want to believe. Help me with my unbelief." Another hour passed. She continued to gaze at the image in the Shroud and realized how many "coincidences" had happened over the last several weeks. *Breadcrumbs, that's what her father had said in his letter.* She thought about meeting Jack and his showing her the picture of Tiananmen Square, the Olympics being in Beijing, the same place her father visited to test his faith, and the Shroud of Turin, how both she and her father had been moved by the image. Had God guided her to this place and time for a purpose? Or was it all a coincidence? In that moment, it was as if pieces of a puzzle were floating in the air; she could see them, each one connecting to the other until the picture became so clear it couldn't be ignored. She wiped the tears from her eyes and, emotionally exhausted, leaned her back against the wall and fell asleep. Several hours passed until she woke to the sound of Iosif's voice.

"You are in here, yes?" he asked, his baritone voice echoing off the walls.

Shay scrambled to her feet. "Yes, I'm"—Shay opened the bedroom door and peered out from behind it—"just thinking. That's all."

"It's getting dark out. You should be on drive home, yes?"

"Dark? What time is it?" Shay ran to the bedroom window and drew back the shade. The sun was setting. "The rink!" She patted her pockets. "My phone?"

"On coffee table," Iosif said.

Shay ran to her phone and checked it. She had received multiple calls from Adley, her mother, and Remy. Shay tapped a number and put the phone to her ear. Bethany answered on the first ring.

"Where are you...? Are you okay?" Bethany asked, clearly shaken.

"I'm fine. I fell asleep, and my phone was in a different room."

"You're at the house?"

"No, I'll explain later, okay? I need to call Remy and get to the rink."

"I'm at the rink with Remy now. Jack and Adley left ten minutes ago to look for you. Jack said you might be in Hill Park."

Shay rubbed her hand across her face. "Yes. I'm here...in dad's apartment."

There was a brief silence. "You're safe. That's all that matters. You scared the life out of us. You never miss practice."

"I'm coming. I'll be there in thirty minutes."

Shay disconnected and was about to call Adley when Pastor Guff showed up at the door bundled like an Eskimo. He fought to catch his breath. "Whew. Those stairs. I think I just froze the inside of my lungs." He leaned forward and put his hands on his knees. "People are looking for you. Jack called and told me to...to... Whew, I'm out of shape. I need to call him."

"Tell him to turn around. I'm heading back to the rink," Shay said. "Sorry for the trouble, Pastor." Shay grabbed her things and headed for the door.

The pastor had his phone in hand. "It's fine. Drive safe. We're all praying for you."

Shay smiled. "I know. Call Jack." Shay headed to her car.

Shay arrived at the arena, and the usual gaggle of reporters and TV trucks were parked outside. As the start of the Games edged closer, the story of Shay and her father gathered momentum. At first, she was intimidated by the attention, but Shay's emotional skin had grown thick, and reporters would find the once-reserved Shay Gerrard to be defiant and self-assured. She marched through the line of reporters with a terse "No comment" and entered the arena.

Bethany embraced Shay and pulled her close. "We're in this together, okay? Please don't shut me out."

"I won't," Shay said.

Shay yanked the laces of her skate until they bit into the leather boot. Remy stood over her and gave her the latest news about the Olympic venue. "You'll be rooming with Ella Clayton."

Ella was an ice dancer and current US silver medalist with her older brother, Michael. Shay liked Ella, but their relationship was casual, and Shay wondered how they would get along in closed quarters. Stories about the Olympic Village were legend, and many spoke of roommates who cracked under the pressure inherent at the Games, ending up at each other's throats.

"Ridiculous rules," Bethany muttered as she fumed over the policy that prohibited parents from staying in the Olympic Village. "Like I'm a leper."

Remy and Shay ignored the comment. Bethany loved to be in the middle of things, and the rule regarding parents in the Olympic Village put a cramp in her style. Shay was excited about staying in the Village without constant oversight. Still, several former Olympians had warned Shay that the Village was like a college campus, and if you weren't prepared, it could cause you to lose your focus. Unlike college, there was no time to adjust to campus life, but Shay was confident her coach would have a strategy to keep her on task.

Shay was ready for today's practice. She had one path now and was determined to follow it. The Chinese government's refusal to allow her to speak with Luke made one thing clear. Taking part in the Olympics would not be enough. For her plan to work, she had to win.

"We'll run the long program skating in the third slot," Remy said.

The ladies' long program was four minutes, plus or minus ten seconds. Accounting for scoring, and time in the kiss-and-cry area, Remy timed Shay's entry onto the ice to be between fifteen and eighteen minutes. It wasn't an exact science, but it was close. Remy followed with instructions. "When the music starts, you're Odette, the swan princess. You flow. You let your body do exactly what you've trained it to do. I want you to really see it today, feel it, the atmosphere, the crowd, the television cameras. Put yourself in the arena two skaters before it's your turn to take the ice."

This was the process Remy had walked Shay through before nationals. The goal was to minimize the awe factor and keep Shay focused on her performance. Ling Yue was counting on the spectacle of the Olympics to unnerve Shay, and Remy was determined to neutralize the glitz of the Games and keep her star skater from being overwhelmed.

Twenty minutes later, Shay was on the ice, accelerating toward the triple-triple. She felt a sense of clarity that had been missing until this moment. The incidents over the past several weeks had left her in a fog. But now that she had a plan and a mission, she had her eye on one thing, forcing the Chinese government to its knees.

Remy watched as Shay nailed the triple-triple, then...

Speeding up...

Effortless speed across the ice...

Hard left outer back edge, stab the pick into the ice, catapult into the air...

Three revolutions, land the triple Lutz...

A smile broke out on Remy's face. Her star skater was in the zone!

Shay cut another hard edge and centered the Biellman, grabbed the blade of her right skate with both hands, and extended her free leg high above her head into a perfect teardrop position.

Spins into a blur...

Fantastic!

Shay finished, stopped on a dime, and threw her arms into the air, hitting her final pose.

Remy and Bethany clapped wildly. This was what they were waiting for.

Shay finished and skated to Remy.

"Beautiful," Remy said.

"Thanks."

"I heard about the Chinese refusal to let you talk to your father. I'm really sorry, Shay," Remy said.

"Don't be. They made a mistake, and I will make them pay for it."

Remy's brows lifted. "On a mission?"

"Totally," Shay said.

CHAPTER 29

Fifteen days to Olympic skate

As the commencement of the Games grew closer, the media and political firestorm escalated. The story was now international news that had taken on the scope of the infamous scandal between Tonya Harding and Nancy Kerrigan in 1994. The media did everything they could to get Shay to engage but had failed to bait her into fueling the fire. Even Bethany had held her tongue, an impressive feat for a woman who was all about taking charge. The only media conversation Shay had was with Jasmine Thomas; and it was, for the time being, off the record. Despite their previous negative encounters, Shay felt she owed Jasmine for returning her father's letter unopened. There was no doubt it would have helped Jasmine's career had she read the letter and reported its contents, but she did the right thing instead. Shay felt she could trust the reporter to follow the plan and hold their interview until after Shay's Olympic skate.

The foundation of Shay's plan was in place. After spending two weeks on the ice working through her new exhibition choreography, Shay was confident her performance would have an impact. Since her plan required secrecy, she continued to run the exhibition program Remy had choreographed. It was a three-minute "moving through the decades" number that included dance moves from the '50s, '60s, and '70s. Shay loved performing the routine, but running through it in practice was awkward. Shay hated keeping things from Remy but knew her decision to skate to a religious theme would be discouraged. If Shay got on the Olympic podium, the sky was the limit in terms of lucrative promotional deals and other opportunities to secure Shay's future. But with a robust economy like China's in play, sponsors would avoid signing Shay if they perceived it offended the Chinese government, and if all went as planned, Shay would do that in spades.

The days leading up to Shay's trip to Beijing went by in fits and starts. In a single day, time flew, stood still, and lumbered along in ways Shay had never experienced. It unsettled her, but Shay leaned in on her newfound faith to help her stay grounded. She continued to enjoy going to youth group, and tonight, just one week before she would leave for Beijing was no exception. With Curt by her side, Shay sat in the front row as Pastor Guff took the stage with the gusto of a Vegas performer. "Welcome, welcome! Another full house, Lord! It warms your pastor's heart to see you all. I have a joke."

There was the expected collective groan, then laughter as several kids in the audience shouted out comments, "Save us!" "Lord, help us," "Make it quick!"

"Okay, okay…quick it is," Pastor Guff said. "So a guy named Pete buys a lottery ticket and prays, 'God, if I don't get money, I could lose my house. Please help me win the lotto.' Lotto night comes, and nobody wins. The next night, Pete says the same prayer, and somebody wins but not Pete. The next night, Pete prays again, 'God, I'm about to lose everything. Please let me win tonight's lotto so I can get back on my feet.' Suddenly, a flash of light appears, and Pete is confronted by the voice of God who says, 'Pete, meet me halfway on this. Buy a ticket.'"

The audience groaned, and a voice rang out from the back of the room. "Don't quit your day job!"

Pastor Guff looked around the auditorium and replied, "And leave all this? Not a chance."

Then another voice called out from the audience. "We love you, Pastor!"

"I love you too," Pastor Guff replied. The sincerity in his voice touched Shay. As strange as she found the pastor to be, his genuine nature captivated her. Like so many of the preconceived notions she had about people of faith, he defied her expectations. He wasn't pushy or judgmental. He was caring. Shay recalled the words her father had written in his letter: "I wanted to spit in his face, and to my everlasting shame, I almost did."

"Before we begin the festivities, I'd like to take a moment to pray again for our brother in Christ, Luke Gerrard. As you know, he remains imprisoned in Beijing. I'm thrilled to see his daughter, Shay, is with us tonight." Pastor Guff smiled at Shay and winked. "Let us pray," Pastor Guff said. And something amazing happened. Without a word from Pastor Guff, the young people in the auditorium gathered around Shay, clasped hands, and bowed their heads. Pastor Guff stepped down off the stage, put a hand on Shay's shoulder, and prayed, "Dear Lord, we ask that you move in amazing ways in Beijing, that Shay will arrive safely, and that you will bring her home to us, victorious in your eyes, with your servant Luke by her side. And everyone said...?"

A hearty "Amen" came from the congregation, after which Tahnee stepped forward and presented Shay with a gift box. "This is from all of us."

Shay took the gift box, opened it, and saw that it held a small gold cross on a gold chain. Shay's eyes filled with tears as she looked at all the young people around her. "I'm...wow...it's beautiful." Shay swallowed hard, doing her best to blink back the tears. "I never expected this and..." Shay lifted the cross from the box and admired it. She extended the chain to Tahnee. "Can you?"

"Sure," Tahnee said. Shay turned, and Tahnee placed the chain around Shay's neck and secured the clasp. "All good."

Shay placed her palm on the cross. "Thank you. I'll cherish it."

When the festivities were over, Shay told her friends to wait for her in the lobby. She wanted to speak with Pastor Guff. She knocked on his office door, and he welcomed her in.

"Shay, come in!"

Shay took a seat across from his desk. "I only need a minute."

"Take all the time you want. I've been praying for God to give you strength and courage. I can only imagine how hard this must be for you."

"Actually, I'm okay. It was confusing at first, overwhelming, but I feel like I'm in a good place, at least for now." Shay absently touched the cross resting at the base of her neck. "I came here to tell you I was wrong about the letter. My father didn't lie. I found it in his apartment stamped 'RETURN TO SENDER.'"

"Good, but I'm not surprised. The Luke I know impressed me as a man interested in both living and discovering the truth."

"Thank you for showing him such kindness and compassion. You're the reason he came to church, and his fascination with the Shroud started with your sermon. Now I feel like I'm on the same journey. It's hard to put into words, this feeling I have."

"Connected," Pastor Guff said.

Shay nodded. "Yes. And now I'm going to be where he is. A month ago, Jack said God was nudging me, and I thought he was crazy. Now I'm not so sure."

Pastor Guff rested his elbows on the desk. "If you're asking a pastor if he believes God is at work here, I'm sure you know the answer."

Shay ran her hand through her hair. "Why doesn't he just say something?"

Pastor Guff smiled. "Maybe he is. Maybe he's asking, 'Why doesn't she just listen?'"

"Now I know where Jack gets it from."

"I often hear people say God moves in mysterious ways, but more often than not, I think he moves in obvious ways people ignore. Miracles happen every day. We walk by them, dismiss them. At times, I imagine Jesus sitting across from me in that very chair venting his frustration."

Shay laughed. "Really?"

"Yes. And he says, 'Guff, what do I need to do? I put stars in the sky, the sun, the moon. I put the entire human race on a planet that spins a thousand miles an hour. Not a single person falls off, and what do they say? Gravity. And how did gravity get there? Accident. You see my point here, Guff? I come back from the dead, and five hundred witnesses see me, not one or ten, *five hundred*, Guff, and still…'"

Shay laughed more than she had in weeks. Much like Jack, the pastor continued to surprise her. "That's some imagination you've got there, Pastor."

"Set your doubt aside. I've seen you jump...all those triples. Take a leap of faith. He won't let you down."

"Thanks. I need to go meet Adley, Jack, and Curt."

Shay stood up and walked toward the door.

Pastor Guff called to her. "Shay?"

Shay turned.

"Your father wanted you to be proud of him."

Shay smiled. "And I am."

CHAPTER 30

Seven days to Olympic skate

Today was it, the last day of practice before leaving for Beijing. Shay and Bethany pulled into the arena parking lot and pushed their way through a crowd of reporters. News that the Chinese government had cut off talks with the State Department rocketed around the world, and commentators were doing their best to hype the already volatile situation. They framed the conflict as "David versus Goliath," with Shay portrayed as a young woman standing alone to face China in a global confrontation on the ice.

Adley and Jack were on the Zamboni, resurfacing the ice when Shay walked into the arena. Shay knew they were boyfriend-girlfriend, but they were doing their best to keep it on the lowdown. Adley had a habit of keeping her relationship status in a state of flux. Jack pulled the Zamboni up to the barrier near Shay and cut the motor.

"I made a decision," Jack said, standing atop the Zamboni looking down at Shay.

"About what?"

"You're the artist, and accidental art can be art if the one who views it appreciates it."

"I helped him get there," Adley said.

"Well, Jack, I can only say I wasn't losing any sleep over it."

"Last practice?" Adley asked.

"Yup. This is it."

Adley turned to Jack. "Then let's get this finished so the next Olympic gold medalist can take to the ice."

Shay ran her short and long programs twice, each skating in the last position. This left plenty of time to stretch, listen to her playlists, and get herself ready in case she drew the final slot during the competition. Her ankle felt good, just a little stiff before her warm-up, but otherwise, it was not posing a problem. She had tested her competitive costumes, so there was no need to test them again, and Shay convinced Remy to allow her to skip running the exhibition program.

"I feel like it's counting chickens," Shay said.

Remy agreed, having chalked it up to Shay's tendency to get superstitious before major competitions.

When practice was over, Remy, Shay, and Bethany confirmed their plan to skip practice tomorrow morning and use the travel day to stay off the ice. This gave Shay's ankle an extra day of rest.

"I think we've done everything we can to get you ready," Remy said. "How do you feel?"

"Good. I'm glad it's time. It's been crazy here."

"Skates, costumes, passport."

"Already packed."

Shay spent the afternoon with Curt, Jack, and Adley at Sacred Grounds. With the fire blazing, they played board games, enjoyed hot cocoa, and the music. Curt had become more accepting of Jack, and although Shay knew they would never be best friends, it made her happy to see them able to find common ground. Patrons in the shop stopped by the table to wish Shay luck. Shay's only regret was she wouldn't be able to watch Curt's tryout with the Red Wings. They scheduled it while she would be in Beijing.

"No worries," Adley said. "Jack and I will show up to cheer him on."

"That's unnecessary," Curt said.

Jack chimed in. "I'll put a big banner on the Zamboni, 'Go, Curt!'"

Curt glared at Jack.

"Or maybe not."

Later that night, Curt dropped Shay off at her house and presented her with a card. "Open it on the plane," he said.

"Is it mushy?" Shay asked.

Curt wasn't sure how to respond. Shay kissed him. "I'll miss you."

"Same here," Curt said.

"Text me the minute the Red Wings make the best decision ever and sign you."

"As Jack would say, from your mouth to God's ear."

"The roads are icy. Drive carefully."

"You sound like my mother."

"Because she loves you, and so do I," Shay said. She was surprised the *L* word came from her lips, but it was true—she really did love him.

"Love you too," Curt said. "When you get back, we'll celebrate everything, okay?"

"Sounds awesome."

Curt left, and Shay went to her room. Tomorrow would be a long day. She needed to sleep.

Six days to the Olympic skate

Shay, Bethany, and Remy left for the Detroit Metro Airport at 2:00 p.m. Their flight didn't leave until 6:30 p.m., but Remy planned for them to arrive at the airport three hours and forty-five minutes before their nonstop flight to Beijing. The flight was thirteen hours and forty-five minutes. They would arrive in Beijing six days before the commencement of the Games to give Shay adequate time to deal with jet lag. If all went well on the plane and Shay slept eight hours as planned, the impact of the time change would be minimal. Remy left nothing to chance.

They arrived as planned and headed into the airport. Remy's hope that no reporters would get word of their itinerary vanished the moment she and Shay entered the automatic doors. Shay was unfazed. She expected the intrusion and powered her way through the reporters and television cameras, ignoring their questions until she heard Jasmine Thomas. "Have a safe trip, Shay. We're praying for you and your father."

Shay stopped, turned, and met Jasmine's gaze. "Thank you."

"Anything to say before you leave?" Jasmine asked.

"Just that I hope to make my country proud and pray for my father's safe release."

"Good luck, Shay," Jasmine said.

The trio continued to move toward security when Shay spotted Adley, Curt, and Jack. Adley was clinging to so many balloons Shay worried she might float away. Jack, dressed in his usual black shirt, pants, and duster jacket, stood beside Adley, holding up a handmade sign that read, "Godspeed, Shay Gerrard!" It was covered with signatures from Living Waters Church members. Curt held a single white rose.

Shay's heart soared. Shay let go of her luggage and ran to them. She hugged Curt first and then Adley before taking Jack's hand and placing it in Adley's. "Hang onto her, will you? I'm afraid she might end up in the rafters."

Jack held Adley's hand. Shay kissed Jack on the cheek. "Thanks. Don't let go."

"Count on it," Jack said.

Shay turned to Curt, and he handed her the rose. "Go get 'em, beautiful," he said.

"I love you," Shay said.

"Love you too."

Remy and Bethany waited, allowing Shay a moment to enjoy her friend's farewell, and then interjected, "We need to get through security," Remy said.

Shay smiled at the trio. "You guys are the best."

They moved through security without incident. Bethany checked on their flight. "On time," she said, "miracles never cease."

An hour later, they boarded the plane. Several passengers recognized Shay and wished her luck. Bethany paid for the upgrade to first class for the three of them. Shay opened the card Curt gave her. It was mushy, and Shay loved every word.

Shay slept the full eight hours. When they landed, she felt refreshed and excited to see the Olympic Village firsthand. Bethany had booked a hotel room in the city. The idea that she was not allowed in the Village still annoyed her. By the time they got their bags, it was after nine. Shay hugged Bethany, who took a cab to her hotel.

Shay arrived at the Olympic Village with wonder in her eyes. She heard from former Olympic participants it was a fairytale place, and as snowflakes touched Shay's face, she took in the majestic atmosphere. Security was tight, so it took over an hour to gain entry to their new temporary home. After having their passports scrutinized, they issued Shay and Remy large photo IDs. They were warned they would not be allowed into the Village without them. They walked toward their assigned apartment building and immersed themselves in the moment. The various venues, including the infamous Bird's Nest, the national stadium, were lit in colored lights, creating a winter wonderland where only the most accomplished athletes in the world gathered with their trainers and coaches.

"It's so beautiful," Shay said.

Remy had also taken a moment to take in the landscape. "You imagine what it might be like. But this? Wow."

As they strolled along, taking it all in, Shay looked at the map they received when their badges were issued. It surprised her to see that the Village had a mayor, a post office, a hair salon, laundromats, shops, an interfaith worship center, entertainment venues, and a twenty-four-hour cafeteria with every variety of healthy food you could imagine. And, to the delight of many, there was even a McDonald's! Shay saw the iconic, oversized Olympic rings and ran to pose in front of them. Remy used Shay's camera to take a picture, and Shay sent it out on Instagram.

I'm here in Beijing! she posted. *Stay tuned!*

They assigned Shay and Remy to different apartment buildings in the Village. Remy arrived at her apartment first.

"So it begins," Remy said and turned to her star skater. "Whatever happens, let's promise one another we'll live in the moment, just fully experience it all."

Shay hugged her coach. "Promise."

Shay's apartment was only minutes from Remy's. She wondered if Ella would be there. She presented her credentials to security and took the elevator up to the sixth floor. Her apartment was 6A, and she knocked before opening the door with a keycard. The room was barren, just a pair of twin beds, a desk, TV, and two small dressers.

The walls were bare, but Shay knew once Ella arrived, that would change quickly. This would be Ella's second trip to the Games, and they had already discussed room decorations. Shay was exhausted from the trip but too excited to sleep. She decided to take a walk around the Village and acclimate herself to the surroundings. It felt surreal to be in Beijing. Just as Shay was about to leave the room, she heard the door lock engage, and Ella walked in.

"You're here!" Ella said and embraced Shay. "You're going to have a blast. Have you walked around the Village yet?"

"Just about to," Shay said.

"Great! Let's go!"

As they walked around the Olympic Village, Shay and Ella took selfies at the different venues and sent them out on social media.

"I know it's been crazy for you," Ella said. "Any news about your dad?"

"No. Just the Chinese continuing to refuse our request to see or speak to him."

"I'm sure he'd want you to stay focused on you," Ella said.

"That's the plan."

"The trick is not to let the experience overwhelm you. I should help you with some yoga and meditation," Ella said. "I teach classes back home."

"That would be great."

When they got back to their room, Shay and Ella were asleep the moment their heads hit the pillow.

CHAPTER 31

Four days until Olympic skate

Shay had breakfast with Remy. The cafeteria was enormous. The clatter of silverware, clanking dishes, and the chatter of athletes from around the world getting ready for the most significant event in their lives made eating an adventure. Eating in the Olympic cafeteria was like walking through an international food court that offered a dish for every conceivable palate.

"This is incredible," Shay said, looking around the room.

Remy was just finishing her fruit cup. "I must admit, being wowed by a cafeteria was the last thing I expected, but I fully intend to take a video of dinner tonight."

Shay saw athletes from France, South Africa, and the UK before her eyes landed on Ling Yue, who entered the cafeteria with several other members of the Chinese contingent. Shay remembered what others said about the current world champion: *Yue was yuan*. Ling glanced toward Shay, and their eyes locked. Ling glared. One of the male athletes saw Shay, and his smile vanished in favor of a sneer. Shay pulled her eyes from his and went back to eating her breakfast. Remy noticed the exchange.

"The first salvo," Remy said. "Remember what we talked about. No interaction here is random, and even if it is, it quickly morphs into an opportunity to chip away at a competitor's confidence. Real friendships can happen, but the idea is to gain the upper hand. All's fair in love and war. Think of what Ling said during her interview. It wasn't directed to the world. She directed it at you. It was her first attempt to keep you off-balance. She said you were good, but it would be difficult for you not to falter because it's your first

Olympics. When you know what to look for, you can see it coming and neutralize it. Her coaches will let her interact with you for one reason—to get in your head. If you were sitting across from Ling during that interview, how would you have responded?"

"I thrive under pressure. My best performances happen when the stakes are high. I can't wait to get on the ice in Beijing."

"That's my girl. The more confident you are, the better chance you have to win the other competition at the Olympics known as the mind games, and that includes all the athletes, especially from the Chinese team. In their eyes, your father's an outsider who entered their country to stir up trouble."

"That's ridiculous."

"They only hear what the Chinese media wants them to hear. You need to be strong."

Shay reflexively touched the cross resting on her chest. "I will."

"It's like chess," Remy said. "The more you anticipate the other skater's moves, the better prepared you are to react."

Remy's references to chess weren't incidental. Her brother was one of the top chess players in the US, and Remy spent her teenage years listening to his thoughts on strategy and gamesmanship. She used the information she gleaned to her advantage both as a skater and as a coach. Remy was relentless in her effort to know everything she could about Shay's competitors.

"This morning's our first practice. Ling will finish her warm-up and then try to intimidate you."

By researching their media appearances, social media platforms, and networking with other coaches, Remy gathered information on the strengths of Shay's competition on and off the ice. "Ling counts on her competition to react to her taunts. She'll stare you down, do little things to unnerve you," Remy said.

"Like what?"

"Skate close to you on purpose and try to make you move. Stand your ground. If you miss a jump during practice, she'll repeat the exact jump a moment later to prove her superiority. Off ice, she will follow competitors just to intimidate them."

"Seems childish," Shay said.

"Maybe so, but she's won worlds twice, and on both occasions, her competition underperformed. Dasha's a different story. She's pretty poison, all sugar and spice but a viper on ice. She'll play the diva. She moves, skates, and speaks as if her winning should be a foregone conclusion. Unlike Ling, she won't engage directly. She won't treat you like competition. She'll treat you like you're a member of the Dasha Lukov fan club."

"Got it," Shay said.

Remy and Shay finished their breakfast and headed to the arena for their first practice session.

Shay removed her US Team Olympic jacket and handed it to Remy. She looked around the rink at the banners and flags of the various countries attending the Games.

"You ready?" Remy asked.

"Ready," Shay said.

Shay took to the ice with eight other skaters, including Ling and Dasha. Being on the ice for the first time in Beijing was both thrilling and intimidating. Shay was practicing with the top-ranked skaters in the world. *Did she belong here? Was her performance at nationals a fluke?* Ling flashed by Shay and performed a flawless triple Lutz. *Let the mind games begin,* Shay thought, and a moment later, Dasha skated by Shay and smirked. It was almost imperceptible, as if Dasha suddenly realized Shay wasn't worth the effort. Once again, Remy was right on target. Shay was ready to counter the efforts of Dasha and Ling. Her practice session was work-like in its precision, strategically choreographed to build confidence and put Shay's best elements on display.

"We'll be in no hurry to get to spins and jumps," Remy said. "We let Ling and Dasha outpace us during the first three to four minutes. Stretch. Perform your crossovers. Get used to the ice. Don't be surprised if it's hard. I wouldn't put it past the Chinese to create hard ice for the first practice. Their athletes will be ready for it, but it will catch visiting athletes off guard."

"Unless you skate for a great coach," Shay said.

"Open with your Ina Bauer, let the photographers take pictures of your smile, lean back, and take in the moment. You're here. You earned it. Then move to the arabesque."

Shay performed the Ina Bauer and arabesque as instructed. Shay knew Remy's plan would counter Dasha and Ling's expectations and give Shay a chance to settle in before performing her more challenging elements. As Remy guessed, the ice was hard. Again, Remy had thought of everything. Now it was up to Shay to execute. Once Ling and Dasha started jumping and spinning, Shay shifted from pose moves to her spins and jumps. Given the texture of the ice, Shay worked her way to the triple-triple combo. With the ice this hard, they would wait until the second practice session to show the quad Lutz. Shay considered the fast ice and did her best to adjust her timing, especially on pick jumps, where hard ice gave Shay the most trouble. She stepped out of a triple Salchow, but everything felt okay, considering it was her first practice.

Ling made several blatant attempts to land her most difficult items right in front of Shay. Knowing it was purposeful made it almost comical, but Shay had to admit Ling was a fantastic tactician. Shay saw Ling land a triple Axel but wouldn't give Ling the satisfaction of knowing.

Shay skated to the barrier to get a sip of water.

"You're doing amazing. You're frustrating Ling. Keep at it," Remy said.

"You were right about the ice. It was fast. And Ling? Wow. If gaslighting was an Olympic sport, she's a champion of that too."

"I saw the look Dasha gave you—the 'why are you even here' look."

"I know. The princess and the peasant."

Remy checked the time. "We have ten minutes. Hit a few more triple-triples, and we finish five minutes early with big smiles on our faces, as planned."

Shay skated back out onto the ice, and Ling skated toward her. *Here it comes*, Shay thought. Shay stood her ground, and a moment later, Shay and Ling both sprawled across the ice! Ling expected Shay to move, and when she didn't, Ling slammed into Shay's shoulder. A collective gasp erupted in the arena. Remy ran toward Shay; but both skaters got up and, like boxers who refused to acknowledge a blow, stared each other down for a moment before skating back to their respective corners.

"You okay?" Remy asked.

"Fine," Shay said. "You called it. She expected me to move."

"Maybe we should have. I didn't expect *that*," Remy said.

Shay looked across the ice at Ling and whispered, "Round one goes to me."

"Ankle okay?"

"Yes. If I keep it wrapped and ice it, it should be fine. I'll get with the trainer and let her wrap it. Then I'm meeting Ella at the coffee shop."

"Okay. Meet for dinner?"

"I'll be there."

After having her ankle wrapped, Shay walked toward the coffee shop and checked her phone. Her social media accounts were going wild. TV cameras had picked up the collision on the ice between Ling and Shay. The narrative was straightforward. It wasn't just two skaters facing off in a bitter battle for superiority—it was two countries. Shay got a text from Adley: "THAT WAS EPIC! UR OK RIGHT?"

Shay texted back to Adley: "PEACHY. XXOO."

Bethany left two messages. Shay called her back and assured her mother she was fine. "That was on purpose. Anyone could see that!" Bethany said.

"And I stood my ground. Don't worry. I can handle it. Are you doing okay?"

"Other than feeling like I've been booted from the island?"

"Yes, other than that."

"Well, the accommodations couldn't be nicer. First rate in every way. And I've met parents of other skaters, so it's tolerable. Ella's mother, Danelle, is a gem. Sweet as pie, tough as nails."

Shay smiled. It was a much better response than Shay expected. "Excellent."

They spoke for a few more minutes, and to Shay's surprise, it was Bethany who wanted to end the conversation.

"I'm meeting Danelle for lunch. Talk later?"

"Perfect," Shay said and disconnected the call.

When Shay got to the coffee shop, it was clear everyone knew what had happened between Ling and Shay. As Shay walked toward Ella, she could feel the eyes of the athletes in the shop tracking her.

"Sit, sit!" Ella said. "Your smackdown with Ling has already gone viral. Over half a million views, and it just got out there. I knew it would get real between you two, but wow."

Shay brushed it off. "She thought I'd move. She didn't intend to hurt me."

"I know. Get a load of the shocked look on her face."

Ella showed Shay the video. Shay shrugged. "Ling's a fierce competitor. I appreciate that. It'll make for a fascinating event."

Shay didn't realize the depth of the Chinese government's anger. They saw Shay refusing to move as an act of disrespect. The video of the incident was being viewed millions of times around the world, and the American skater's insolence would not be tolerated. There would be consequences. Timing would be considered. Like searching the body for the most painful impact of a strike, the government would make sure their actions would have the desired result.

CHAPTER 32

Three days to Olympic skate

Shay glanced around the arena and immersed herself in the moment. As she marched side by side with other members of Team USA, the glamour of the opening ceremonies, culminating in the lighting of the Olympic flame, was a mind-blowing experience. The sights and sounds, the excitement, and the fellowship of athletes from around the world were awe-inspiring. It was an event to experience and to remember. When it was over, Shay went to the entertainment room with Ella and other members of Team USA to mingle and do their best to throttle down before the Games began. Shay left early. They scheduled the short program for the day after tomorrow; and Shay, who rarely slept well the night before a performance, wanted to get to bed so she wouldn't have consecutive nights of little sleep.

As Shay walked to her apartment, a light snow fell, and she reminded herself of how blessed she was to be an Olympian. She slowed her walk and thought of her dad. She didn't notice her tears at first, but as their warmth mixed with the chilled wet flakes melting on her face, Shay wiped them away and realized she was just a little girl missing her father. As much as it hurt her heart, she was glad for it. She recalled something the artist and poet Kahlil Gibran once said, that it was better to laugh all of your laughter and cry all of your tears. Despite the pain, it was freeing to feel what she had suppressed the last seven years, that she loved and missed her father. She sent an update text to Adley, hugs and kisses text to Curt, and a thank-you to all on her social media accounts who wished her and her father well. She called Bethany to say good night. Bethany gushed about the opening ceremonies.

"I've never felt so proud," Bethany said. "You did it, Shay. You made it."

"*We* did it, Mom. Now we need to take the next step and gain a good position after the short program."

"Get some sleep, and we'll talk tomorrow," Bethany said.

"Will do."

Shay disconnected the call and headed into her apartment. The next forty-eight hours would be crucial. She needed to be ready.

One day to Olympic skate

Today's practice session was a highly anticipated event. News stories about the collision between Ling and Shay dominated the media. As always, Remy had specific instructions for Shay to manage the tension of the moment.

"Ling thrives under pressure. She expects you to be rattled, so we remain focused and methodical. This is exactly why I choreographed your practice and your program."

Ling and Shay came close to one another several times, but despite the high-wire tension, practice continued without incident. Shay drew the first slot to run through her program and hit every element, skating clean and delivering a strong performance both technically and artistically. She hit the quad Lutz, and she knew both Dasha and Ling knew it. Remy made the decision that they needed nothing more. Shay left the ice after her run-through. It was gamesmanship at its best. No need to watch Ling or Dasha. Shay was confident and ready to compete.

Later that night, Shay and Remy met Bethany for dinner in Beijing. To avoid the media, Bethany had a private limousine pick up Remy and Shay just outside of the Olympic Village and planned for their escort through a service entrance at the hotel. They ordered room service and dined in Bethany's hotel room, which had an incredible view of the city.

Shay stood by the window and looked out at the skyscrapers lit up in colored lights and wondered about her father. *Where was he being held? Was he okay? Had they hurt him?* She imagined a dank, cold prison where he was shivering and hungry. How could she eat and enjoy her time when her father was suffering?

"You hardly had anything to eat," Bethany said.

"I'm not hungry."

Bethany turned her attention to Remy.

"Do you think Ling will try the quad in the short?"

"Guessing, I'd say no. It heightens the risk in the short program. You miss a required element, and in a two-minute-and-forty-second program, a fall or miss is more disruptive."

"And in the long?" Bethany asked.

Shay knew where the conversation was headed, but her mind was still on Luke.

"Again, it depends on what she sees happen before she takes the ice. She's hit it once, stepped out of it once, and fell once. It's risky," Remy said.

"And Shay? Have you considered it for her?"

Remy continued to chew her food for a moment before answering. "Shay's stronger artistically than Ling, so a disruption in her program is more costly. I haven't ruled it out, but it would take a lot for me to risk it."

Remy waited for Bethany to challenge her, but Bethany tempered her response.

"You know how I feel about it. I just hope you'll keep an open mind if the situation warrants."

"I will, but the reality is we'd be trying to beat Ling where she's got the advantage. Shay's an artist. I will play to her strength unless it's clear she's too far behind technically to catch up without it."

Bethany glanced over at Shay. Seeing her daughter's forlorn expression reflected in the window, Bethany knew Shay was thinking of Luke. The divorce hardened Bethany, but the stark contrast between Luke's current circumstances and hers gave her pause. There was something grossly unfair about imprisoning a man for believing in God, and Luke's imprisonment was weighing on her.

"Shay?"

Shay turned, her arms crossed as if cold but more to comfort herself as she thought about Luke.

"You should eat. Tomorrow's a big day, and you know you never eat much before you skate," Bethany said.

Shay didn't feel like eating, but Bethany was right. She would need the energy to do what needed to be done. At the very least, Shay needed to be in the top three in the short program to have any chance of winning the gold. Shay sat and sampled bites of food, her mind still drifting to Luke. *Hang in there, Dad*, she thought. *I'm coming.*

After dinner, Shay returned to her apartment but couldn't sleep. She walked to the interfaith center. It was just before midnight, but the Olympic Village still had its share of athletes milling around. Once in the chapel, Shay was happy to discover she was alone. She needed to find solace in the one place she would have never sought it just four weeks ago—in church. In less than twenty-four hours, she would take the ice in the short program. If she faltered, her plan to help free Luke would fail. It was in the chapel that Shay felt closest to Luke. As she sat and prayed, it felt as if he were sitting beside her, his hands clasped close enough to brush hers. The feeling was so powerful Shay opened her eyes for a moment to see if he might really be there. He wasn't, not physically, but the connection Shay felt was palpable. Her dad was with her. Shay looked up at the cross and prayed for his safety and her own miracle on ice.

When Shay left the chapel, she spotted Ling seated on a bench on the opposite side of the street. Their eyes locked. Shay recalled what Remy told her, that Ling followed her competitors off ice to unnerve them. *She's playing head games*, Shay thought. Shay held Ling's gaze until a man's voice rang out and startled them both. Shay saw the man, and the fear in Ling's eyes made it clear the man frightened her. He was densely muscled with a sharp, commanding voice. Ling scampered to his side. He grabbed her arm, and then his eyes locked on Shay's. He barked at her in Chinese. Shay drew back. She didn't need an interpreter. She was sure it was a hostile version of "Mind your business!" The man turned and walked away with Ling obediently by his side. Shay found the encounter bizarre. If Ling was out that late at night to intimidate Shay, wouldn't Ling's coaches know about it and approve? Was it possible Ling needed to escape the watchful eye of her handlers just to gain a moment's peace? *Maybe she needed time alone before the event, just like I did*, Shay mused. But Ling was sitting directly across from the chapel when there were a hundred other places to choose from. Shay decided she needed to let it go. She needed to sleep. Her Olympic debut was at hand.

CHAPTER 33

Day of Olympic skate—short program

Much like the previous day's practice, the lady's session was well-attended.

"It's like NASCAR," Remy said. "People are hoping to see a wreck."

The practice went on with few incidents, just Ling and Shay skating by one another and inadvertently brushing shoulders. Shay was a little off on the triple-triple but not enough to cause a fall. With practice over, there was nothing left to do but wait.

And wait...

And wait...

Shay did the best she could to relax. She spoke to Curt, exchanged texts with Adley, and updated her social media accounts with pictures she had taken of the different venues in the Olympic Village. As the media hyped the battle on the ice between Shay and Ling, it was clear the political pot was being stirred. Shay knew many people within China saw her father as a troublemaker. But she also knew that news being broadcast around the world outside China was not favorable, and the Chinese government could not be pleased. The last thing they wanted was for Luke's daughter to beat their star skater in front of the world. The stakes couldn't be higher, and no one knew that more than Shay.

When the moment finally came, Shay was relieved. Waiting was torturous. Now she was primed and ready to skate. Shay drew the third position in her group. She would've preferred first, but third wasn't a bad draw, especially for the short program. You weren't the first on the ice, but the proximity of your warm-up to your performance was ideal. Dasha would skate fifth; and Ling, who had drawn the eighth position, would be last in the group. Shay's American counterparts, Kimberly and Gemma, would skate in the group following Shay's. Shay stood by the barrier with Remy to receive last-minute instructions.

"You are so ready for this, Shay. Warm-up exactly as we rehearsed. Love the moment. Embrace it. Skating in third position is perfect. How do you feel?"

Shay shook out her hands. "Nervous."

"Exactly as expected. If something's off, we'll correct it. The audience and judges will love you."

They called the group to the ice for their warm-up, and as instructed, Shay followed her warm-up precisely as planned. She felt a stiffening in her left calf but shook it out. Her first attempt at the triple Lutz-triple loop was a disaster. She fell…hard. There was a collective gasp from the audience. Shay responded by getting right back at it, hitting the combination on her second attempt with only a minor bobble on the landing. The warm-up ended, and Shay skated off ice. Remy handed Shay her blade guards and headphones. Shay went to the waiting area and listened to her selected song, "Sanctuary," bowed her head, and silently prayed. *You got me this far, God. Now I need to take the next step. I know my dad is praying for me, as I am now praying for him. May I make you both proud. Amen.*

Remy signaled to Shay. It was time to skate. A skater from Germany had skated before her, and her scores did not reflect a strong performance. Shay removed her guards and handed them to Remy.

"Well, here we go," Shay said.

"Enjoy the moment, Shay. So few get the chance to be where you are now."

"I will," Shay said and embraced her coach before skating out onto the ice. A minute later, she was introduced over the public address system. "Representing the United States of America, Shay Gerrard."

Back in Detroit, Adley absently dug her nails into Jack's wrist. The youth group had gathered at the church with the congregation to watch the event.

"Impaling," Jack said.

"Sorry." Adley loosened her grip.

Shay settled at center ice, touched the cross beneath her outfit, and positioned herself in her opening pose. A second later, Shay's calf muscle tightened. She felt that muscle wrench once before. Her trainer told her it might tighten to compensate for the weakness in her ankle. The seconds between her pose and her music starting seemed like an eternity. The muscle went into spasm. Shay flinched, flexing her leg just as her music began. Shay's mind raced. *Don't panic! Keep it together!* A bolt of pain radiated from her calf. Shay winced but continued into her opening footwork sequence. Next, she would flow into her spiral, a move that would allow her to stretch her leg and hopefully untie the knot in her calf. If this weren't the Olympics, Shay would stop skating for fear of tearing her Achilles, something that often happened if you continued to skate with a wrenched calf. Shay flowed into her spiral, and the movement seemed to help, causing the pain to subside. *You're fine. Just focus. Let it happen.*

Shay regained her composure and moved on, completing her triple Axel, camel-sit-camel, and layback spin flawlessly. *Pick up speed*, Shay told herself. *Tuck tight! Spin rate!* Shay moved into her most challenging item, the triple Lutz-triple loop, vaulted into the air, and nailed the landing! Just one more required element, the triple flip. Shay felt good on the entry. She jammed her pick into the ice and knew instantly she had failed to draw back as far as she should have. She made an adjustment in the air, tightening her wrap to increase her spin rate, helping to avoid the catastrophic result of landing too far back on her heel. She landed perfectly. Shay completed her program, finishing by striking her arms into the air on the final beat of music.

As roses rained down onto the ice, Shay looked up at the appreciative audience and embraced the moment. It wasn't a perfect outing, but she had fought through the muscle spasm and delivered a solid performance. She spotted Bethany seated next to Ella's mom in the audience and waved.

Back in Detroit, the congregation was ecstatic. Jack and Adley hugged and leaped up and down with the rest of the congregation of the Living Waters Church.

In the kiss-and-cry area, Shay sat with Remy and awaited her scores. When they flashed, the 76.54 was a solid score, but Ling and Dasha had yet to skate. When the evening was over, Shay was in second place, just ahead of Dasha and two-tenths of a point behind Ling.

Later that evening, Shay agreed to a sit-down interview with NBC analyst Anna Cohen. Shay's second-place finish in the short program left Shay in a tight battle for gold with Ling. The showdown was set. The fact that Ling represented China, the host country that had her father imprisoned, heightened the drama of an already highly anticipated event. Shay was at war with herself, walking a tightrope between honoring the Games as a vehicle to unify the world and containing her outrage that Luke was still a captive of the host country.

The sound tech adjusted Shay's mic and gave Anna a thumbs-up. They were ready. The director pointed at Anna, a sign they were on.

Anna looked into the camera and introduced Shay. "I'm here in the Olympic Village with Shay Gerrard just hours after her near-flawless performance in the short program." Anna turned to Shay. "Shay, welcome."

"Thanks, Anna. I'm happy to be here."

"You must be pleased with your performance earlier today. Many believe you should have scored higher than Ling."

"Ling skated wonderfully. She's so dynamic, so explosive on the ice. Scoring has a subjective element, and I'm happy with the position I'm in."

"Can you tell me about the collision between you and Ling during that first practice session?"

Shay smiled. "There's a lot of pressure, and things happen. We were both playing mind games, and our bodies got in the way. No big deal."

"You feel good about your chances in the final?" Anna asked.

"Yes. My coach, Remy, is a stickler when it comes to being prepared to skate, and I feel really good about being ready for the long program."

Anna shifted in her seat. "Now I know you've been cautious about discussing your father's imprisonment, but it's the pink elephant in the room, and it's growing by the moment. Can you give us an update on your feeling of when, or if, your father will be released?"

Shay took a sip of her water. Unlike her media interviews before arriving in Beijing, Shay felt in control now and smiled at Anna. "A pink elephant on skates, I suppose. The only thing I will say is that I pray for his release, and I'm grateful for my followers on social media who are praying for him as well. I want to respect the spirit and intent of the Games as an apolitical gathering to unify the world. My intent moving forward is to let my skating speak for me, for my father, and for my God."

"Fair enough," said Anna. "Have you changed your choreography to express yourself and your feelings at this point?"

"Well, when I think about the story of Swan Lake, and specifically the princess swan—"

"Odette—"

"Yes, Odette. In the ballet, she skates on ice created by her parents' tears. I can tell you in my soul and spirit, I will think of that during my performance. The ice has greater meaning to me as the swan princess skating on a lake made by the physical expression of human suffering."

Anna, surprised by the depth in Shay's answer, paused a moment before responding. "Well, all I can say is we wish you all the best and look forward to your performance."

"Thank you, Anna, I appreciate it."

When the interview ended, Shay met Remy at the rink for her next group practice session. She checked her phone on the way over and noticed her social media accounts were going wild. Now she had over 150,000 followers, and the number was growing by the minute. Shay posted a selfie and a thank-you for all their thoughts, prayers, and encouragement. It was overwhelming to have that kind of connection with so many people. The practice session went well. Shay's ankle felt better, and she and Ling had minimal interaction on the ice.

Later that afternoon, Shay met with Remy, Bethany, and Maya Lopez in Bethany's hotel room to discuss the comment's Shay made during her interview with Anna Cohen.

"I understand the position you're in, Shay, but when you consider the dynamics, your comments during the Anna Cohen interview were not helpful," Maya said.

"Not helpful?" Shay retorted. "Let me tell you what's not helpful. I asked the host country to allow me to speak with my father, and they refused. And with all due respect, Ms. Lopez, the State Department's done nothing constructive. Regarding my comments, they've been reserved and sensitive to the spirit of the Games, and I won't allow myself to be silenced or intimidated by anyone."

Maya's eyes widened. "No one is trying to intimidate you."

Shay continued, "I respect what you're trying to do, and I can tell you I'm done speaking publicly about it. As I told Anna Cohen in my interview, I intend to let my skating do the talking. The Chinese government is the issue here, and believe me, when the time is right, I will let the world know what they've done, and they will wish they had never arrested my father. Is there anything else?"

"Yes. I'm afraid there is," Maya said. "They insinuated that if you don't stop insulting their country, they'll consider charging your father with subversion."

The comment sucked the air out of the room.

"'Subversion'? What does that mean?" Shay asked.

"It could mean a fifteen-year prison term."

Shay's lips trembled.

Bethany spoke. "You can't be serious?"

"They're playing hardball, and you need to know what's at stake."

Shay was incredulous. "They can't do that, can they? Just make something up?"

"I think we need to keep in mind that your father"—Maya looked to Bethany—"by your own admission, put himself in this situation for the sole purpose of drawing attention to himself."

Bethany's eyes hardened. "Not to himself, to a cause, something I didn't fully realize or appreciate at the time. But I do now. I wish he wouldn't have done it, but the Chinese government has had every opportunity to release him, yet they refuse. The problem is theirs to solve. We won't be intimidated. Shay will do what she believes to be right, and whatever that is"—Bethany turned to Shay—"she has my full support."

"I understand, but you should consider your father's safety before you escalate the situation."

"I'll consider it," Shay said. "I will base my decision on what my father would want me to do. For now, I'll refrain, but beyond that, I cannot promise anything."

CHAPTER 34

Shay was in the fitness center running hard on the treadmill. Sweat poured down her face, and her thigh muscles burned as she pushed herself to suppress the rage threatening to derail her focus. *That's what they want*, she thought. *That's why they're doing it, to get to me.*

The threat to charge Luke with subversion rattled Shay. If she didn't do as they asked, Luke could spend the next fifteen years in a Chinese prison. Did Luke know what he was risking? Shay felt light-headed. She pushed forward, powered by seething anger that refused to subside.

Shay glanced to her left and noticed Nari Moon, the silver medalist from North Korea, stepping onto the treadmill beside her. Shay tapped the treadmill Stop button and slowed her pace. The machine throttled down.

"I need to speak to you about father," Nari whispered, her voice so low Shay wasn't sure if she heard Nari correctly.

"What did you say?" Shay asked.

Nari glanced back and saw a Korean athlete standing behind Shay's treadmill. Shay looked back and noted the young man's warm-up jacket with the North Korean logo on it. He was waiting for Shay to finish so he could use the treadmill. His appearance unnerved Nari. Shay shut down her treadmill and turned to the male Olympian. "All yours." He gave Shay an icy stare before stepping on the treadmill. Shay looked to Nari, but she was now in a full run. She was done speaking to Shay.

Shay walked out of the fitness center. Confused by the encounter, her mind raced. How could Nari know anything about her father? And it was clear Nari was intimidated by her teammate. Had he shown up by chance, or was he watching Nari's attempt to speak with her?

As Shay walked back to her apartment, she considered another possibility, that they had staged the entire episode to intimidate Shay. China and North Korea were allies. Shay wondered if Ling had engaged Nari in a ploy to get in Shay's head and disrupt Shay's focus. Did Nari wait to take the treadmill next to Shay? *Maybe the male athlete was Mr. Johnny-on-the-Spot because that's the way they had planned it?* Thanks to Remy, Shay was aware of Ling's reputation of playing mind games with her competition. *Ling is a squatter living rent-free in her opponent's heads. Don't let her in.* Was this East versus West? Nari finished sixteenth after the short program and was out of medal contention. She had nothing to gain by upsetting Shay.

When Shay got to her apartment, Ella was in the middle of her afternoon yoga practice.

"Hey," Ella said. "Just finishing up."

Shay was blown away at Ella's ability to perform pretzel-like yoga moves. Ella was in the handstand scorpion, one of the more challenging yoga poses to hold.

"It's fine," Shay said.

Shay sat on her bed, lost in thought.

"You okay?" Ella asked, still holding the impossible pose.

Shay considered telling Ella about her encounter at the fitness center. Ella released her legs from her handstand and, with remarkable control, exited the pose and looked up at Shay. "Is it about a guy?"

Shay laughed, relieving some pent-up tension she'd felt since leaving the fitness center. "If only."

"Is it about your dad?"

"Yes," Shay said. "Look—and please don't take this the wrong way—but can I trust you to keep a confidence? Because I could really use some perspective right now."

Ella scooted over to Shay. "Yes, you can trust me. I know it's hard to trust a fellow competitor in this gossip-laden, back-stabbing, throat-cutting—"

"Whoa, is it really that bad?" Shay asked.

"We're serial killers, metaphorically spreading death with a thousand cuts."

"And here I thought you were into peace, tranquility, and positive vibes."

"I am. But I'm also a realist. My word is my bond, and to show my commitment, I extend my pinky for the time-tested pinky promise never to speak a word of what we share in this room."

Shay smiled, and they engaged pinkies.

"Okay," Shay said. "I need to know if I'm being paranoid. Here's the scenario." Shay explained what happened earlier at the fitness center.

"Wow. Did you tell your coach?"

"No. It just happened. If Nari has information about my father, I'm afraid Remy will tell me to stay away from the North Korean team until I'm finished competing."

Ella lay back on the floor and thought a moment. "I'm leaning toward your conspiracy theory. I wouldn't put it past them to mess with your head."

"That's my thinking too. The fitness center was packed, but it so happens one Korean athlete ends up right next to me with a 'secret' just as another just walks up at the exact moment she's about to speak. Too pat, right?"

"Especially when you put it that way," Ella said.

Shay reflected a moment. "Still, Nari acted terrified when that guy showed up."

"My advice, same as Remy's would be, avoid the North Korean team. Stay focused."

Shay went to the interfaith center to clear her mind. She entered the chapel and gazed up at the cross on the wall. A crown of thorns rested atop the cross; and Shay thought about the agony Jesus suffered as they mocked him, beat him, and hung him on a cross to die. If God could see her heart as Jack said, then he must know her faith was not as deep as Jack's. Shay was about to turn and walk out when the image of the Shroud flashed in her mind. Once again, it seemed God was speaking to her—but was he? How much of this thinking was self-imposed versus God imposed? Shay focused on the cross and whispered, "Why do you put up with me?" She paused a moment, then took a seat, clasped her hands, and prayed.

Shay left the chapel and took a stroll around the Olympic Village. It was twenty-eight degrees, but the lack of wind and the sun high in the sky made it a comfortable walk for a girl who was used to Detroit winters. The Village had a magical atmosphere that reminded Shay of her visit to Disney World when Bethany, Luke, and Shay were still a family. She smiled as she recalled how they all sang "It's a Small World" as they sat in a boat and made their way through the attraction. She was lost in the moment when she spotted Nari across the street. Shay scurried up the road toward the Village shops. Was Nari following her? Shay turned and absently bumped into a male athlete from Australia.

"Oh, sorry," Shay said.

"No worries, mate. Carry on." He winked at Shay.

Shay ducked into a cafe crowded with athletes. Several were from North Korea, including the intimidating guy from the gym. His attention was focused on the girl sitting across from him, an ice dancer wearing a warm-up jacket that had JAPAN stitched across the back. Shay ordered a latte and peered through the window. Nari was there, standing on the opposite side of the street. Shay decided enough was enough. She would grab her latte and confront Nari, but when Shay got outside, Nari was gone. Shay needed to get back to her apartment, change, and get to the arena. The ladies' practice session started in an hour.

The arena was a hotbed of activity. Anticipation for the show-down between Ling and Shay had reached a fever pitch both on tele-vision and social media. Would there be another confrontation on the ice? Shay was scheduled to run through her program last, so it forced her to remain in the arena for the full session. Dasha had sev-eral misses during her run-through and had a tantrum before leaving the arena in a huff. Such behavior at this point in a competition was a strategic mistake. You never wanted to let your competition see you unravel.

Ling lived up to her reputation. She was focused, determined, and skated as if she owned the ice. Several times, Ling and Shay came within inches of one another, but neither moved, and neither flinched. Shay considered this a win. She refused to give in to Ling on the skater's home ice. As Shay was about to begin her run-through, Ling left the building. She was making a statement. Whatever Shay did on the ice didn't matter, Ling was in control.

Shay was happy Ling left. Her run-through was a disaster. She missed the triple-triple and fell on the triple Lutz. Knowing practice was being televised, Shay did her best to hide her concern, but beneath her calm exterior, she was in a panic. She skated to Remy, who sported the smile that said, "No biggie."

"All is good," Remy said. "More speed into the Lutz. Engage the hips earlier in the triple-triple. Easy corrections."

Shay went back on the ice and hit both jumps, but her confidence was shaken. When practice was over, Remy could see the miss and the fall rattled Shay.

"Remember what got you here, Shay. You missed the triple Lutz in the warm-up at nationals. You said you felt off, then skated flawlessly. One event is not connected to the other. Trust me, when you take the ice tomorrow night, it will all fall into place."

Shay left the arena with the one thing skaters hate most just before a big event—doubt.

CHAPTER 35

Shay sat on her bed, knees clasped to her chest, and tried to regain her composure. Ella was at practice leaving Shay alone with her thoughts, and they were bad company. The Chinese threat to charge Luke with subversion was unraveling her ability to stay focused. She felt helpless and wasn't sure how to deal with it. She needed to clear her mind. She touched the cross on her necklace and whispered, "I'm really lost here, God. I'm not sure what to do." Shay put on her coat, hat, and gloves and went out for a walk hoping for a whisper back, anything to settle her mind on a direction.

Snow fell, and millions of colored lights reminded Shay of the tiny village Luke set up beneath their Christmas tree before their lives were torn apart. Athletes milled about, talking and laughing, snapping selfies to send home and post on social media. Shay wondered how it was possible to feel so alone amid all this activity. She noticed a group of athletes milling around the sculpture of the Olympic rings. The guy she bumped into earlier from Australia saw Shay, waved her over, and offered her an Olympic pin, a long-standing tradition at the Games.

"Thanks," Shay said and offered the Australian athlete a Team USA pin.

He took it, examined it, and smiled at Shay. "Bloody ripper, I love it! You're Shay, right?"

"Yes. And you're...?"

"Max. It's actually my middle. My first is Robert—Bob—but being a bobsledder..."

"Right. Bob, the bobsledder."

"Bloody ridiculous. So it's Max. Nice to meet you, Shay."

They embraced, and Max noticed Ling standing behind them. He whispered to Shay, "Your competition…"

Shay turned and came face-to-face with Ling. Ling's eyes radiated a palpable intensity. A coach hovered nearby. Ling was being watched. It seemed there was never a time when she wasn't under the watchful eye of a handler. It reminded Shay of the ESPN interview where Ling was yanked off camera as if she was nothing more than a rag doll. Ling's eyes did not reflect the fierce competitor Shay encountered on the ice. Like a frightened child, Ling appeared more like a captive than a star skater soaking in the joy of the Olympics. Ling offered Shay an Olympic pin, pressing it into Shay's palm, wrapping her hand around Shay's until Shay held the pin in a closed fist. Shay used her other hand to reach into her pocket and offer Ling a pin from the United States. Ling took the pin from Shay and nodded. Ling's overseer barked something in Chinese, causing Ling to flinch before she turned and obediently followed the coach as he walked away. Shay watched as the man reprimanded Ling.

Max commented, "Bloody shame what they're doing to your dad. I'm one of your followers on social media. Bob-sledder."

Shay smiled. It was absent, reflexive. Her thoughts were still on the encounter with Ling.

"Well, good luck to you," Max said. "Got to hit the bed."

"You're welcome. And thanks for the Aussie pin. It's beautiful."

Max paused a moment, thought of saying something more, and then walked off.

Shay turned her attention to the Ling's Olympic pin. She removed the clip and was about to attach it to her warm-up jacket beside the others when she noticed a flaw. The backing was scratched, and when Shay looked more closely, she realized why Ling had closed Shay's fist tightly around the pin. Ling had etched a cross into the backing and, beneath it, had scratched Savior into the enamel. Shay's eyes darted upward to be sure no one was watching. Ling had etched the pin at considerable personal risk, and Shay had no intention of allowing anyone else to see what her rival had done. Shay replaced the backing and kept it tightly in her fist. Her heart raced as she headed back to her apartment. A knot formed in her stomach.

She had another person's life literally in the palm of her hand. She picked up her pace. She wanted to hide the pin—secure it where no one else could find it. As she hurried down the street, she spotted a group from the Chinese ski team walking toward her, their eyes confirming recognition. Shay did her best to avoid eye contact and smiled nervously as she and the ski team members crossed paths. Shay squeezed Ling's pin in her fist just as one of the Chinese athletes purposely bumped into Shay, glaring back at her for a moment before continuing down the street. Shay's chest tightened, and she had trouble taking in air. She panicked. *Don't pass out. You'll drop the pin! Just breathe! Breathe!*

"Shay, are you all right?"

Startled, Shay turned to find Ella beside her. "Yes, I just... I need to sit."

Ella walked Shay to a bench and sat beside her. Shay felt clammy and then shook.

"What is it?" Ella asked.

Ella's presence had a calming effect on Shay. Her heartbeat slowed, and as snow flurries melted on the heat of her reddened face, Shay slowly regained her composure. Ella pulled Shay close to her. "Panic attack?"

"I don't know," Shay muttered.

"You want me to take you to the medical building?"

"No. I just want to get back to the apartment. Can you walk with me?"

Moments later, Ella and Shay were just outside their apartment building when something occurred to Shay. This was the Chinese government's turf. Her apartment was in their building. She grabbed Ella's arm and stopped her. "We need to go somewhere else."

"Why?" Ella asked.

"Because they might be listening."

"What are you talking about?" Ella asked, not getting it.

Shay glared at Ella. "Not...here."

"Where then?"

Shay thought for a moment and then motioned for Ella to follow her. She led Ella to the interfaith center and went inside, guiding

Ella into the Christian chapel. There were only two other athletes in the chapel, both from Finland, seated in the front of the room. Shay sat in the back of the chapel and motioned for Ella to sit beside her.

"What's going on?" Ella asked in a hushed tone.

"I'm worried our apartment might be bugged."

Ella's brows furrowed. "What?"

Shay knew how crazy it sounded, and yet... "Think about it. They have my dad in prison. It's become an international incident with political implications. It's their building, Ella."

Ella thought for a moment. "Do you really think they'd do that?"

"It's possible, and I can't risk it, especially not now." Shay opened her palm so Ella could see the pin.

"What, you think that's a bug?"

"I got it from Ling," Shay said.

"Ling wouldn't just hand you a bug and—"

Shay turned the pin over to display the tiny cross, and the words etched in the enamel. Ella's eyes widened. "Oh god," she whispered. "Ling...?"

Shay nodded. "Now do you see why I need to be careful?"

"What are you going to do?" Ella asked.

"I will make sure no one else ever knows about this pin. Ling risked everything to give it to me."

"Why would she put herself in danger like that?" Ella whispered.

"To show she supports what my father is doing. I think that's why Nari was following me. She wanted to let me know Ling was a Christian. We come by our faith too easily." Shay glanced up at the cross on the wall in front of the chapel. "I never really understood. But I understand now. Listen. We can't talk about this in the apartment, agreed?"

"Agreed. I'm sorry you're so wrapped up in all this while you're trying to skate. I don't know how you're keeping it together. If there's anything I can do."

"I'm fine. I have practice after you, and then I'm meeting my mother for dinner in the city. I'm going to chill out here for a few, and then I'll head back. See you at the rink."

"Okay." Ella hugged Shay and left for practice.

Shay stayed in the chapel clutching the pin between clasped hands as she prayed for the safety of her father and her new friend.

Bethany picked up Shay outside the security entrance to the Olympic Village. They drove to a restaurant in Beijing. Bethany ordered a glass of wine with her meal and sipped at it.

"Has Remy considered the quad Lutz?" Bethany asked.

Shay's stomach tightened. The last thing she needed after having her nerves frayed by Ling's pin was to get in an argument about Remy's coaching. "No. She still believes—"

"You skated clean at nationals. If your ankle wasn't an issue. Skating clean is the best strategy and so on," Bethany said.

"Mom—"

Bethany waved Shay off. "I know you think I've been hard on Remy. She got you here. I give her that. I know it's time for me to take a step back, but as you well know…" Bethany sighed. "When you were young, I was a good soldier, but after your father did what he did, I had to be different. Maybe I overcompensated? The point of my little diatribe is that whatever happens, I'm behind you."

It stunned Shay.

"Look at that," Bethany continued. "I've rendered my daughter speechless. I know what you're thinking. Is another shoe going to drop? Is there something in the wine? Did she stop at an opium den before dinner?"

Shay laughed. "Do they have those here?"

"Yes, down the street. They gave me a hook-up pipe, a pillow, and—"

"Hookah."

"What?"

"It's called a hookah pipe."

"Oh. Well, one of those."

"You're joking."

"Of course. China has some of the toughest drug laws in the world. I read up on the host country before we left the States."

Shay smiled. "You amaze me."

"Do I?"

"I love you, with my whole heart, Mom. You're my hero."

"I thought your father had first position in that category." There was no antipathy in Bethany's voice. "I've gained a small amount of admiration for what he's doing."

Shay's eyes widened.

"Having trouble keeping up?" Bethany asked.

"Sort of."

"Clearing the air in China seems appropriate. The smog here is oppressive. Did you notice?" Bethany smiled again and sipped her wine.

"Okay, I'll play along," Shay said. "I think what dad did was a step in the right direction."

"'The right direction'? Beijing?" Bethany laughed. "Well, your father never was map savvy. Did I ever tell you about the time he got lost at the zoo?"

"What?"

"We were dating, and I was feeding the giraffes. It was hot, and Luke went to get us something to drink. He came back an hour later with the following explanation: 'I turned left at the hyenas, and it went bad from there.' How could you not fall in love with a man like that?"

"I could use some wine," Shay said.

The server came with the food and set it down on the table. Shay welcomed the pause in the conversation.

Bethany continued the moment the server left. "It was good once. That's all I'm saying. Now eat before your food gets cold."

"It's sushi."

"Fine. Before it gets warm, then."

They spent a few minutes sampling each other's food before Bethany set her fork down, tapped the napkin against her lips, and continued. "Don't get the wrong idea. I don't think Luke's the saint the world suddenly thinks he is, but this Chinese government, you know how I despise bullies."

"I do," Shay said.

"I hate the timing, but he's doing something good, and I'm trying to respect that. Now the Chinese are bullying him and bullying you, and I won't have it," Bethany said, throwing her napkin down on the table to emphasize the point. "So the first thing we're going to do is beat them on the ice, and once you're done skating, I'll be done being quiet. Deal?"

"Deal," Shay said. "But in the meantime, there's something else I need you to do for me." Shay removed Ling's pin from her pocket and handed it to Bethany. "Keep that with you at all times. I can't risk anyone else seeing it, but if I get on the podium, I want it with me."

"A Chinese pin?" Bethany asked.

"Turn it over," Shay said.

Bethany turned the pin over and noticed the image and etching. "I don't understand?"

"Ling gave it to me."

Bethany was momentarily confused. "She's a Christian?"

"They watch over her all the time. Handlers, coaches, fellow team members. She's never alone. She gave me that with one of those handlers just ten feet away. She wanted me to know," Shay said. "If it's ever discovered…"

"How could it be?" Bethany asked. "How would they know you didn't etch it yourself after Ling gave it to you?"

Shay wondered why she hadn't thought of that herself. Maybe she was being overly paranoid? Her mother was right. Unless the handler had caught Ling handing Shay the pin, they could never tell it was Ling who had etched the words and image. "You're right. I don't know why I didn't think of it that way."

"Still want me to keep it?"

"For now."

Bethany put the pin in her purse. "Ready to get back?"

"Yes."

"Good. I still haven't adjusted to the time change. I've been going to bed at eight."

Shay needed to get back to the Olympic Village. She needed to find Nari Moon.

CHAPTER 36

Shay met Ella by the shops in the Olympic Village. For Shay's plan to work, she needed to get a message to Ling. But how? Shay decided that using Nari as an intermediary was the best way to communicate with Ling. Earlier in the day, Shay had purchased a teddy bear at one of the shops. In her room, with music blaring, she sat with Ella as they carefully undid the stitching and inserted a note inside the teddy bear before stitching it back up. Teddy bears were frequently exchanged by athletes in the Village, so it wouldn't seem unusual for Ella to give one to Nari. When Shay met Ella, she was disappointed to see Ella still clutching the teddy bear. Shay's heart sank. Something had gone wrong.

"What happened?" Shay asked, flicking her eyes at the teddy bear.

Ella smiled. "Nothing. I got this from a skier from Sweden."

"You got it to her?"

"It took some work, but, yes, she has it. I was so nervous, but I managed to get her alone for a few minutes in the cafeteria. I felt like I was in the middle of a James Bond movie."

Shay hugged Ella. "Thanks. I really appreciate it."

"You're welcome. I just hope you know what you're doing."

"I do," Shay said. "Now I just have to pray things fall in place."

"You should never say 'fall' to a skater about to take the ice."

"You're right. I take it back. You're helping me take a stand. How's that?"

"Perfect."

"Okay, then. There's nothing left to do but wait," Shay said.

"Right. A figure skater's version of eternity. I'm really proud to know you, Shay Gerrard. You're one of a kind."

"Same here," Shay said. They shared another hug and made their way back to their apartment.

In eighteen hours, the battle for gold between Shay Gerrard and Ling Yue would commence—East versus West, and in Shay's eyes, most importantly, her one opportunity to help gain her father's freedom.

CHAPTER 37

The Bird's Nest was a hotbed of anticipation. The arena was packed, and the energy and excitement in the air was palpable. Shay was in the waiting area listening to her playlist as she visualized a perfect skate. She went through a series of breathing exercises to quell her nerves. She was ready.

Remy summoned Shay from the waiting area. It was time. Ling had completed her skate, and from the audience's reaction, it was evident she skated brilliantly.

NBC figure-skating commentator Evan Kay sat beside former US champion, Anna Cohen, and continued their commentary on the long program.

"Wow, just wow," Anna said as Ling Yue pumped her fists in celebration of her near-flawless performance. "Masterful. She brought her best today, Evan."

"I agree, Anna. Ling is such a physically gifted skater. She didn't try a jump until two minutes into her routine. Good strategy?"

"Yes. Under the current scoring system, it makes sense to load the second half of the program to take advantage of the ten percent bonus on top of base value."

"But you're not a fan?"

"I'm not. In my view, it creates an unbalanced feel to the program, but of course, I'm old school," Anna said, smiling into the camera.

"But she left the quad Lutz out?"

"Yes. It was hard to tell if she intended to or not, but Ling has shown the capability to perform it beautifully."

As roses and teddy bears rained down on the ice, Anna and Evan continued.

"Shay Gerrard's up next. She has to be perfect, and even then, given she's slightly behind after the short program..."

"Anything less than perfection won't do it," Anna said. "But given the pressure she's been under, can she deliver?"

Shay paced. The threat by the Chinese government to charge Luke with subversion had ignited her indignation. How dare they? She felt as though the gag they had imposed on her was a wet rag stuffed down her throat. A tempest of emotions swelled in her chest. Shay touched the gold cross beneath the fabric of her costume and adjusted the pattern of her breathing. She engaged in silent prayer. *Please, Lord, be with me.* She had imagined this moment thousands of times. Shay had put herself into this place, anticipating the crowd, the TV lights, even a delay in being able to take the ice if roses were to rain down from the audience after a stellar performance. She tensed and relaxed her muscles, focused on her breathing. Thunderous applause continued as Ling waved to the audience before picking up the flowers and stuffed animals. Shay looked to Remy.

"The quad?"

"She didn't attempt it. There's room. This is exactly where we wanted to be. It's about artistry and grade of execution now. I know how hard it's been for you to restrain from speaking out, to have to bow to their demands. But it's payback time. Winning in their country, in their arena, on their ice would be the best revenge."

"Thanks for getting me here."

"Don't make me cry. We're not in the right area yet," Remy said, indicating the kiss-and-cry area behind them. "Go."

Shay and Remy bumped fists, and Shay took to the ice to loosen up as they announced Ling's scores. The crowd roared as the scoreboard flashed a score of 156.65, solidifying Ling's first-place standing. Shay was the only one capable of stopping Ling, and China, from winning gold.

A moment later, the announcer's voice reverberated in the arena. "Representing the United States of America, please welcome Shay Gerrard to the ice."

Shay skated to center ice and positioned herself in her opening pose. The arena went quiet. Five seconds passed...eight... Then the first beat of *Swan Lake* played. From her still position, Shay performed several fluid moves with her arms, mimicking the swan princess on the lake of tears. Then she turned and skated as if floating above the surface, effortlessly building up speed as she prepared to perform her opening jump—the triple Salchow. For any skater, hitting the opening jump is crucial. Shay had loaded the second half of her program with her most difficult jumps to capitalize on scoring, but nailing the Salchow would set the stage for the performance to come. She turned, cut a deep inner edge, and vaulted into the air, tucking her arms and completing three revolutions before executing a flawless landing. *Yes!* She was elated, and a smile blossomed on her face. The next forty-five seconds of her choreography helped Shay connect with the audience and show her artistry. Shay's ability to draw people into her performance was her strength, a mode of expression designed to move people, to touch their hearts. Shay became an extension of each musical note, connecting the senses to cement an emotional connection with her audience. She performed a series of intricate turns—rockers, brackets, and counters—reversing direction, her body moving in symmetry with each note of music before building up speed transitioning into her camel-sit-camel combination.

Anna commented, "Her speed and extension are exquisite—like a ballerina on ice."

"I agree, Anna. She's the consummate artist. But she needs to hit all her elements to have any chance of overtaking Ling for the gold."

Shay moved from her spin combination to another series of deep edges and turns, every movement perfectly synchronized with beats of the music, flowing effortlessly across the ice. She was in the zone, that state of being where the years of training took over, and the expression of the swan princess swimming on a lake of tears came from deep within her soul.

She picked up speed and dropped into her signature Ina Bauer before shifting position and taking off for the triple Axel. She landed it perfectly but felt a sharp pain flare in her ankle. *Not now, Lord,* she prayed and ignored the pain. She powered across the ice, cut a sharp outer back edge, and leaped into a flawlessly executed triple Lutz-triple loop combination. The crowd roared!

"That was exquisite," Anna said. "She's feeling it now, and so is the audience."

Evan chimed in, "We may be watching a true Olympic moment. Just eighty seconds left to go, Anna."

Shay flowed into her second combination spin, moving from an outer back camel into a scratch spin. She accelerated as she raised her hands above her head, clasped her hands, and became a blur. She moved out of the spin, flashed across the ice, and performed a triple flip / double toe loop / double loop combination, again executing it flawlessly. Her adrenaline surged. She felt her performance building. She hit a triple flip and resisted the urge to pump her fists. *Stay in the performance*, she told herself. She sped across the ice, cut a sharp outer back edge, and nailed her triple Lutz. *Just one more jump combination*, she thought. The pain in her ankle had been washed out by the adrenaline, and she stepped up into her double Axel / triple toe loop. When she landed, the elation she felt was overwhelming. She performed her final spin, the Biellman, extending her leg above her head until her body formed a teardrop—one more for the lake of tears—with a performance so powerful it would melt them away.

The arena was silent for a moment and then erupted into a thunderous ovation. The spectators leaped to their feet. Flowers and stuffed animals rained down onto the ice as the audience displayed their appreciation for Shay's stellar performance. Members of Team USA waved the American flag as the US contingent, including Bethany, joined the collective chorus of "USA, USA!" The cameras panned up to the area where several of China's government leaders sat stone-faced, disturbed by the cheers from the crowd being given to the American skater. Shay stood at center ice and absorbed the adoration before lifting the cross she had received from the Living Waters congregation. It took several minutes for the applause to die down. Shay skated off the ice into Remy's arms.

"That was amazing!" Remy said.

They went to the kiss-and-cry area, took a seat, and awaited the scores. They both knew it could go either way. Ling had a razor-thin lead after the short, but both of their performances had been technically and artistically inspired. It took more time than usual for the scores to post. The audience stamped their feet, rocking the arena as they anticipated the scores of one of the most fiercely fought ladies free-skate competitions in Olympic history. Then it happened. The scores flashed on the screen, 157.1. It took a moment for Shay and Remy to be sure; but when the realization hit, they jumped to their feet and danced, hopping up and down like school kids. Shay had edged past Ling for the gold!

The audience gasped, and then the applause started again, a rousing display of their appreciation for both Ling and Shay. Ling walked over to Shay and hugged her close.

"God bless you," Ling whispered. And then, even more quietly, she said, "It's arranged."

Shay hugged Ling, and they both took the ice and acknowledged the appreciation of the crowd. Shay did her best to soak it all in, knowing she had one more thing to accomplish before leaving Beijing.

CHAPTER 38

When Shay saw Bethany walking toward her, she ran to her mother and hugged her. "This would've never happened without you."

Bethany was never one to show emotion, but she couldn't stop the flood of tears from ruining her mascara. "You did it, Shay. You're an Olympic gold medalist!"

Bethany looked up and saw Remy. She released her embrace with Shay and walked over to the coach that had helped Shay secure an Olympic victory.

"I owe you an apology," Bethany said.

Remy held up her hand. "It's really not—"

"No, it really is because I underestimated your ability to win at this level, and I can only say I'm sorry...and grateful for what you have done."

"You wanted the best for your daughter, I've always understood that."

"I appreciate your letting Cruella off easy. Dinner's on me tonight. Let's celebrate!"

Shay was physically exhausted and emotionally drained. "That sounds great, but I'd just like to go back to my room and crash. How about tomorrow night after the exhibitions?"

Bethany was about to argue with Shay but caught herself. "Know what? That works better. It gives me time to make reservations. Remy?"

"I'm in."

"Tomorrow night it is, then."

Shay changed out of her outfit and strolled back to her room. On her way back, she enjoyed the heartfelt congratulations from athletes who had watched the event. Despite the elation swirling around her, Shay's heart was heavy. She did her best to mask her sadness, but beneath her forced smile, she grieved. Her father was still imprisoned and unable to celebrate with her. It would have been fantastic if he was in the arena when the scores were announced. Shay thought about the prayer Luke told her about in his letter. *I didn't want to interfere with your dream, but I could go to China and kill two birds with one stone—visit the city where you would soon be, visit the place you would skate—and pray for your safety and success.*

Alone in her room, Shay swallowed hard. "We did it, Dad," she whispered. "At least for tonight, we beat them."

Shay called Curt, and his voice was the pick-me-up she needed.

"Is it possible? Am I talking to an Olympic gold medalist?" Curt asked.

"As a matter of fact, good sir, you are."

"Well, then, I feel compelled to say you are speaking to the newest member of the Detroit Red Wings farm team!"

"That's just...wow!" Shay said.

She finished her call with Curt and called Adley.

"You better not suddenly be all full of yourself," Adley said, teasing Shay.

"I won't. Promise."

It felt good to speak with her friends.

"The entire congregation watched from the church. It was epic!" Adley said.

"Don't miss tomorrow tonight. Your costume makes its world premiere."

"Oh, you bet I won't. We're all meeting again at Living Waters."

"Okay. It won't be long before I'm home."

After the call, Shay fell asleep faster than she had in years.

Shay woke the next morning rested and restored. News outlets were eager to speak with her. Still, she refused, stating she would talk to the press after the exhibition programs were complete. She went to the interfaith center and prayed, thanking God for getting her this far and for her dad's continued safety. She was a force now, an Olympic champion, and she intended to do her best to use her new status to help her father. She told Remy and Bethany about her new choreography. They were surprised, but both understood Shay's determination to perform the routine that night. It was clear nothing they said would change her mind. Everything was set. The only thing left to do was skate.

Shay pulled her exhibition costume from her garment bag and saw a note pinned to the sleeve. *Thanks for the honor of selecting me to design your exhibition costume! I'm giving up my podcast and pursuing my dream of becoming a designer! Love U! Adley.* Shay smiled and changed into her costume. It was still difficult to wrap her mind around being the Olympic champion. She felt humbled, blessed, and free. She was about to perform an exhibition program that may do permanent damage to her skating career but was at peace with her decision. Her thoughts drifted to the image of Jesus in the Shroud and to her newfound faith. She realized her journey was just beginning. She still had moments of doubt, yet she fully believed God had a hand in the events that had unfolded in the past few weeks, and she intended to follow his lead and trust in his direction. She kissed the tiny gold cross on her necklace and made her way back into the arena.

"You know what you're risking," Bethany said.

"Yes. Everything you've worked for and dreamed of for me," Shay said.

Bethany looked at Shay and smiled. "You're an Olympic champion. How you carry that torch moving forward is up to you."

Shay embraced her mother. "I can never repay you."

"Thank you. And I hope that whatever you do helps free your dad. I've come to be proud of him. After all, going from Lukewarm Luke to the Saint of Detroit is quite an accomplishment." Bethany examined Shay's costume. "Who made the outfit?"

"This? It's an Adley Finch design."

"Well, it's not jules k. but not bad," Bethany said.

Shay looked out at the ice, where Ling Yue was absorbing the thunderous applause for her exhibition performance. Despite Ling's second-place finish, their star enthralled the audience and roses rained down onto the ice. Shay glanced at Remy, who stood by the boards waiting for Shay.

"I better get going," Shay said.

"Bring down the house," Bethany said.

"That's the plan."

Shay walked to Remy, her guards still covering her blades.

"I will make it clear when this is over that you didn't want me to perform this exhibition," Shay said.

Remy brushed the comment aside. "You're an artist. Who am I to dictate the expression of your art?"

Shay and Remy watched as Ling enjoyed the hometown exuberance for their resident star. As Ling left the ice, Shay's eyes found Ling's, and Shay mouthed the words "Thank you." An almost imperceptible smile lifted on Ling's face. Without Ling, Shay knew her exhibition performance would have limited impact. As Ling stepped off the ice, Shay and Ling embraced. In broken English, Ling whispered, "God be with you," before being rustled off by her coach.

Shay looked to Remy. "You have the lace, right?"

Remy opened her palm and showed Shay the skate lace balled up in her hand. "Am I ever not prepared?"

Shay smiled and walked over to a man with a walkie-talkie and showed him her right skate. "My lace broke," she said. "I need about ten minutes to replace it."

The man glanced down at Shay's skate, then to Shay, and nodded.

Shay added, "Maybe you could resurface the ice to save time?"

The man spoke into his walkie-talkie in Chinese as Shay walked back to Remy. Remy handed Shay the extra lace. "Think it worked?"

"We'll see," Shay said.

Shay walked over to the kiss-and-cry area and began replacing her broken lace. Her heart pounded as she waited to see if they would resurface the ice. A moment later, the Zamboni was on the ice. Remy and Shay shared a knowing glance. Ten minutes later, Shay was introduced as the gold medalist. Costumed as Mary, Shay removed the guards from her blades and glided out onto the ice a few feet from the boards.

The lights went down; and a single spotlight shone down on Shay, posed on one knee, arms extended, hands reaching, her expression a portrait of a mother's pain. As the song "Sanctuary" played, Shay let the haunting music infuse itself into every part of her body. It is the moment the artist becomes the instrument, the fingers on the keys, the brush on canvas, each being moved by an invisible hand. Shay needed to let go and to allow herself to become Mary bearing witness to the beating, torture, and crucifixion of her Son. As the words moved through her, Shay skated.

Tears moved down Shay's face as she recreated the moment Mary watched the nails pierce Jesus's wrists. She convulsed, clutched herself as she glided across the ice, visualizing the cross being raised as a battered and bloodied Jesus endured the agony of crucifixion. Shay swept into a blur spin, her hands outstretched, pleading. The music swelled, and the words struck like anvils. Shay cut a series of edges into the ice. Her movements were tight and meticulous as she etched the surface with her blades and then swept into a layback Ina Bauer, arms draped back, head tilted in a moving portrait of Christ's body as he hung on the cross. She pushed upward, mouth agape, as if gasping for breath, and then allowed her body to once again fall into an extreme layback. She moved with intention, cutting intricate edges into the ice as she expressed Mary's agony. Without jumps and limited spins, the choreography was a display of tightly executed footwork, dramatic forms and poses all culminating in a riveting display of artistry. Shay paused center ice and moved through a series of balletic poses in concert with the song's lyric.

With the pick of her blade, she cut at the ice.

With the audience in the palm of her hand, Shay moved into her final pose, her arms extended, her face contorted in agony as she envisioned the Savior of the world taking his final breath. The music faded; and the spectators, spellbound, sat in stunned silence as the lone spotlight on Shay funneled to a pin. The black lights used in Yue's performance illuminated the ice, and the audience gasped.

"My god," Anna said, her hand moving reflexively to her mouth.

As the TV cameras pulled back from high above the ice, the haunting image of the Shroud of Turin etched in the ice effervesced in the arena's darkness.

"Am I seeing what I think I'm seeing?" Evan asked.

Shay, prone on the ice, felt a surge rush through her, a feeling so intense she felt as if she were being lifted by an unseen hand. She rose to her feet, and the audience erupted in thunderous applause. Roses rained down on the ice, falling on the magnificent work of art Shay etched into the frozen canvass. Moved by the ongoing ovation, tears streamed down Shay's face. In the arena, and around the world, millions viewed her etching in the ice—the Shroud of Turin. Cameras flashed as spectators took pictures of the etching. As she stood, the words Jesus spoke just before he died on the cross flashed in her mind: *It is finished.* Shay looked upward, and for a second, it seemed as if the universe had stilled. She was at peace. She had done it; she had made her statement to the Chinese government and to the world that their attempt to contain the spread of the gospel message would fail. She knew this was what her dad wanted, for her to join him in his stand against religious tyranny. Her voice was his voice; and Luke Gerrard, a man who had fallen from grace, inspired her art and her message.

Shay left the ice and fell into Remy's arms. Remy's eyes were riveted on the image of the Shroud of Turin being televised around the world, to the Chinese people and their government.

"How did you do that!" Remy asked.

Shay pulled back from Remy and looked at her. "Don't you know? Miracles happen every day."

In the announcer's booth, Anna stammered, "This is…unprecedented, and…we've seen unique exhibitions before, but—wow, I'm at a loss."

"You're right, Anna. This is a moment, folks. We were all wondering if Shay Gerrard would make a statement at the Olympics about her father's imprisonment. We need not wonder anymore. She etched the face of God on their ice, in their arena, and into the minds of viewers around the world."

"It's stunning, Evan. The performance alone was breathtaking. And the art? It's miraculous, just…divine."

Adley and Jack were glued to the monitors above the stage at the Living Waters Church with members of the youth group and parishioners who had gathered to witness Shay's performance.

Jack turned to Adley. "Did you know about this?"

"I made the costume, but I had no idea she would do that!" Adley said.

Jack suddenly realized why Shay needed to sneak into the arena all those nights.

Haley Edwards of NBC walked up to Shay with a mic in hand. The commentator looked around the arena, wondering if the applause would ever subside. Realizing it might take some time, she did her best to speak over the noise.

"Shay, it's clear you've stunned the world. What are your thoughts at this moment?"

"First and foremost, I praise God for the opportunity and ask the government of China to release my father and Pastor Chen. They seek only to worship their God without interference."

"I have to ask you about the astonishing image left in the ice. How in the world did you do that?"

Shay smiled. "I just turned my blades into brushes and the ice into canvas."

"Well, you've merged art and sport in a way no one ever imagined. I was prepared to ask you about your performance on the ice, but not...well, what you've done is almost unimaginable."

Shay looked straight into the TV camera. "I have a friend who told me an image can change the world. I'm hoping he's right."

Adley turned to Jack. "That's you she's talking about!"

Haley continued, "The choreography, how you made it all come together—just astonishing. And I love your outfit," Haley said.

"It's an Adley Finch design," Shay said.

Adley's jaw dropped. "Get...out!" she said and punched Jack's shoulder.

A deluge of roses continued to rain down onto the ice. Then the call of her name echoed throughout the arena. "Shay, Shay, Shay!"

Shay skated back out onto the ice and acknowledged the crowd. She had trusted in God, and he had used her to make a statement to the world.

CHAPTER 39

Shay, Bethany, and Remy were having dinner when Shay glanced at her social media accounts. She now had more than a million followers. Shay's etching of the Shroud was a worldwide phenomenon. It was the first time a figure skater had left such an indelible mark not only on the ice but in it. The etching was being called the *Image in the Ice* and had spurred discussion not only in the sports world but in the art world as well. Famed artists in various mediums showered Shay's etching with glowing praise.

"She used everything at her disposal to create something never to be forgotten," one said.

"A breathtaking accomplishment," said another. "This is what art is all about, and it's something that will be spoken about for years to come."

Even the Catholic Church spoke of the profound influence Shay's performance had on bringing awareness of the Shroud of Turin to people who had never known of its existence. The response astonished Shay. Her goal was to free her father and Pastor Chen. It never occurred to her it would impact the collective consciousness of so many.

The next morning, Shay and Remy were waiting for their ride to the airport when Maya Lopez called. "Shay, this is Maya Lopez. I'll get right to it. They have released your father and Pastor Chen."

It took a moment before Shay could respond. "You're sure?"

"Your father's already on a flight back to Detroit. They did this as quietly as they could. They didn't want a media scene with you and your father reuniting in Beijing. They also released Pastor Chen."

"Thank God," Shay said. "My dad, how is he?"

"In good shape and good spirits. Most of all, like the rest of us, he's stunned by what you accomplished. It's truly remarkable."

"Pastor Chen?"

"We don't have a good handle on how he is, at least not for now," Maya said.

"He's remarkable."

"I agree. I'll let you go. I'm sure we'll connect again once you're back in the States. Congratulations on winning the gold. It almost gets lost in all this."

"If it does, I'm fine with that," Shay said.

Shay disconnected and turned to Remy. "They released my dad and Pastor Chen."

"That's wonderful news!" Remy said.

Bethany joined Remy and Shay on the plane ride back to Beijing. In the airport, Shay informed Bethany of Luke's release.

"Well, that's good then. I'm proud of you, and…well, I'm proud of him as well. But don't you dare tell him I said so."

Shay smiled. "Deal."

As they boarded the plane and made their way to their seats, the passengers applauded. Shay blushed. The attention made her uncomfortable. After the flight took off and everyone settled down, Shay relaxed and thought about all that had transpired since she made the Olympic team. The past six weeks had been a whirlwind where two improbable things had occurred—she won Olympic gold and became a believer. Now she was going home an Olympic champion and a well-known artist. As much as she loved the competition, she felt it might be time to retire from competitive skating, go out on top, and create a path that would allow her to pursue skating with an emphasis on its artistic merits. At heart, she was more artist than athlete. She would have time to consider her options. She was going home.

A few hours into the flight, Bethany turned to Shay and said, "I will be cordial with Luke. He was a good person once. Maybe he really has changed. I'll need proof. As you know, I'm no pushover. But I won't stand in the way of you trying to reconnect with him."

Shay hugged her mother. "That's all I could ask for."

When they landed and exited the plane, Shay, Remy, and Bethany were greeted by a huge crowd. Pastor Guff was front and center with a group of Living Waters members behind him, waving signs stating, "Welcome Home, Shay," "God Bless," "Our Miracle Worker!" Curt greeted Shay with a kiss and a dozen roses, and Jack and Adley were there with the Living Waters Youth Group, singing an a cappella version of "Sanctuary." With tears of joy, Shay hugged her friends. It was good to be home. Then the group stood back, and Shay saw her dad, his arms extended to the daughter he hadn't seen or spoken to in seven years. Shay felt like a little girl again and ran into his arms. It was a reunion many, especially Shay and her father, would never forget.

Six months later

After winning the gold and stunning the world with her reproduction of the Shroud, Shay retired from competitive figure skating to pursue a career in art. Not that she didn't love skating, but she felt a calling to further her art and express her faith. It wouldn't mean hanging up her skates, as one commentator had suggested, because her *Image in the Ice* had become one of the most-sought-after etchings in the world. After selling close to a hundred thousand reproductions in crystal, demand for Shay's art in the ice was off the charts. Her exhibition performance at the Olympics had opened the door for Shay to pursue skating as a pure art form—this being the aspect of the sport she enjoyed most. She would trade her canvas for ice and her brushes for blades and create images people would treasure. She would skate in shows and exhibitions where the audience would experience not only the power of her performance on the ice but her signature art etched in it as well.

Jack let Adley steer the Zamboni as it made a last pass over the glassine surface. Tonight, in an empty arena, Shay waited by the boards as her friends resurfaced the ice for the third time. Shay's first two attempts to etch her rendition of Jesus carrying his cross toward Golgotha had minor flaws in symmetry and detail. Just like her performance at the Olympics, anything less than perfection wasn't acceptable.

"Let's hope three's the charm," Adley said.

Shay worked through her choreography a third time and, satisfied with the etching, ran to the top of the arena to look at her finished work. Jack and Adley lagged behind Shay, who took the stairs two at a time. Shay reached the top and looked down at her friends, both struggling to make their way up.

"Hurry!" Shay said. "I think this is it!"

Jack collapsed into a chair with Adley right behind him. Both fought to catch their breath.

"You guys need to get in shape," Shay said.

"We are in shape," Jack replied.

"Yeah, we're in the same shape most people are in. You're the one that's out of shape," Adley said.

"Give the signal, Jack," Shay said, eager to see her etching.

Jack unclipped the walkie-talkie from his belt and radioed Ozzie. "We're ready, Oz. Turn on the black lights, and kill the rest."

"Ten-four," Ozzie replied, and a moment later, the arena went dark aside from the black lights illuminating the ice.

Adley's eyes widened. "Whoa, that's beyond epic."

The image of Christ, bloodied and beaten, carrying his cross toward Golgotha, seemed to effervesce. Shay turned to Jack. "What do you think?"

"It's amazing," Jack said.

"Then it's ready, Jack. Take your shots," Shay said.

Shay had engaged Jack to be the photographer for her work. Now that Shay's etching was complete, Jack would take the picture that would be used as a print to create reproductions in crystal. Shay also hired Adley on as her social media manager to help keep up with Shay's 1.5 million followers. Bethany oversaw the financials, and Luke managed sales and marketing. Her parents had found common ground again, and Shay prayed that one day they would get back together.

Things were falling into place for Shay. Each Sunday, she attended church at Living Waters with Jack, Adley, and Luke, where

Adley had become a permanent member of the Mustard Seeds. Jack's influence had convinced Adley that Jesus was a supernatural being to believe in. Even Curt began attending. Adley still hosted her paranormal podcast, but Shay sensed her friend's passion for Sasquatch was waning as her faith in God grew.

"Frick and Freud are beside themselves," Adley admitted.

Shay laughed. "Well, to their credit, they're letting you find your own way."

"They're hoping it's a phase. But if I suddenly disappear, they kidnapped me and sent me to a cult recovery program where I'll be reprogrammed to believe in the accidental universe, hot yoga, and meatless burgers."

Shay's best day so far was the morning her mother got up on Sunday and announced she intended to attend church with Shay and Luke.

"Really? That's so great, Mom!" Shay said.

"Well, you've been so busy lately I hardly get to see you. I'm not going over the barrel with it. I just think a little church can't hurt."

Shay knew there were times her prayers would not be answered, but she believed what she wanted at the moment was not always best for her in the long-term. As Jack often told her, "We see now. God sees eternity."

Luke spent hours telling Shay about his spiritual journey. "In China, Christians imprisoned for their faith memorize passages of scripture smuggled to them on small pieces of paper, because, as one prisoner told me, 'the government can't confiscate what's hidden in your heart.' The night they arrested me, I gave my Bible to a woman, and you would have thought I was giving her the world. She thanked me and fell to her knees. Tears streamed down her cheeks, and she kissed the book before clutching it to her chest. It's a moment I will never forget. We are blessed to live in a place where we are free to worship."

As Shay looked down at her latest etching, she reflected on all that had happened and believed now more than ever that God's hand had played a role in bringing the *Image in the Ice* to the world. Now she hoped her images would influence others to consider the truth about Christ. Like Luke, she had hung a reproduction of the Shroud of Turin above her bed and just beneath it had written,

> For God so loved the world, that he gave
> his only Son, that whosoever believes in
> him should not perish but have eternal life.
> —John 3:16

CPSIA information can be obtained
at www.ICGtesting.com
Printed in the USA
LVHW111639190821
695554LV00003B/342